continued . . .

FINAL LAP

erin mccarthy

BERKLEY SENSATION, NEW YORK

THE BERKLEY PUBLISHING GROUP
Published by the Penguin Group
Penguin Group (USA) LLC
375 Hudson Street, New York, New York 10014

USA • Canada • UK • Ireland • Australia • New Zealand • India • South Africa • China

penguin.com

A Penguin Random House Company

FINAL LAP

A Berkley Sensation Book / published by arrangement with the author

For information, address: The Berkley Publishing Group,
a division of Penguin Group (USA) LLC,
375 Hudson Street, New York, New York 10014.

ISBN: 978-0-425-26175-0

PUBLISHING HISTORY
Berkley Sensation mass-market edition / October 2014

PRINTED IN THE UNITED STATES OF AMERICA

10 9 8 7 6 5 4 3 2 1

Cover photo of "Couple" © Claudio Marinesco; "Sports car on display"
© citybrabus/Shutterstock.
Cover design by Rita Frangie.
Interior text design by Kristin del Rosario.

Dear Reader,

It's hard to believe it's been six years and eight books since the Fast Track series first sprang to life! When I originally conceived the idea, I didn't have a series in mind, just the idea that I wanted to return to contemporary romance (which I very much did!) after writing paranormals, with a sexy and very loyal hero. So on a road trip with a friend, *Flat-Out Sexy* was born, and Elec Monroe, his siblings, Tammy and her kids, and Ty and Ryder all became reality. In my mind anyway. I fell in love with the world of racing; Charlotte, North Carolina; and these drivers and the strong sense of family they all share. Through racing wins and losses, injuries, pregnancy scares, trips to Vegas, adoption, marriage, and remarriage, I laughed a ton with them and felt satisfaction at each of their subsequent happy endings.

So I have to say it's with a great deal of sadness that I say good-bye to the series, but I hope you'll enjoy this final chapter featuring Harley and Cooper. Everyone from the previous books reappears in *Final Lap* so you can get a sneak peek into their lives and see who is doing what. Hint: Imogen and Ty finally get married, and Elec and Tamara do adopt a baby.

As Suzanne Jefferson might say, it's been fine as frog's hair split four ways writing these books. Much love to all of you who have supported and enjoyed the series, and happy reading!

ERIN

CHAPTER
ONE

HARLEY McLain felt like Cinderella at the ball. Well, without Prince Charming. So far the only man to pay her any mind at this wedding was the groom's stepfather, who was thirty years her senior and blind drunk. But still, standing on the terrace looking down over the gardens of the beautiful Biltmore estate, at the wedding of the illustrious stock car driver Ty McCordle and his PhD bride, Imogen Wilson, Harley definitely thought the night was magic. A million twinkling lights were strung across the enormous heated tents, and red and orange spotlights in a floral pattern lit up the side of the mansion to reflect the autumnal beauty of the mountains.

It was chilly outside in her cocktail dress, the November air brisk, leaves swirling across the stone floor, but Harley had wanted to take a minute to pause alone against the railing and appreciate the majesty of the mountains and the scene spread out before her. When her friend Eve Monroe had invited her to the wedding she had been reluctant to attend initially, knowing she would feel like an outsider in the racing crowd and being an add-on guest, having met the bride and groom only a few times. But Eve had insisted she needed a plus one, since Eve's new husband, Nolan, wasn't able to attend with her, which was actually a plus two because of Harley's identical twin, Charity, being there as well. Now Harley was glad she had come just to experience the beauty of the estate inside the tent and out.

Besides, the groom had teared up when he had seen his bride appear on the stone steps of the mansion and descend toward him. That was worth the two-hour drive from Charlotte, just to see that love wasn't the fictional unicorn Charity was convinced it was, and Harley was starting to waver on herself. She didn't want to be that girl who felt bitter, but she was starting to question why love seemed to come easily for everyone else but her. It felt like the last time she'd been on a date, Christ had been on a potty chair. It had been that long, honest to goodness.

"Do you mind?" a masculine voice asked her, the air shifting as someone stepped in alongside her.

Actually, yes, she did, but that would be rude. Harley turned to give Mr. Whoever a polite smile and instead almost swallowed her tongue when she realized who it was. Cooper Brickman. Playboy driver. Good-looking as sin. The object of many a schoolgirl crush, including her own. And technically it wasn't a schoolgirl crush, since Harley still got a little weak-kneed every Sunday when Cooper climbed out of his car, and she was way past the classroom.

Now he was standing next to her on the terrace under the fairy lights, wearing a tux. She was no longer cold, that was for damn sure, though her nipples were suddenly standing at attention underneath her dress.

He was holding up a cigar and a lighter, asking her permission to fire it up.

Like she would say no to him. For any reason. Whatsoever. "Sure, go for it."

"Thanks. I needed a breather. A break from all my dance moves." He winked at her. "I'm Cooper, by the way."

As if she didn't know that. "Harley. Nice to meet you."

"You, too." He puffed on his cigar, expensive lighter clicking shut.

Harley thought the stogie reeked like yesterday's tire-kissed skunk, but she didn't mind since when the hell was she ever going to get to stand next to Cooper again? Never. That's when. She could have sex with him via osmosis. He didn't even have to touch her. It was just enough that there was only six inches between them. It was like a virtual orgasm.

Sneaking a look over at him, she studied his profile. He was gorgeous, with a strong jaw, a narrow nose, rugged shoulders, and dark blond hair falling in his eyes. Beautiful, almost.

"Damn, beautiful, isn't it?" he asked.

Harley started. "Huh?" Her heart started pounding overtime.

"The estate. I've never been here before. It's amazing."

Right. The gardens. Not him. Not her. Not this moment. "It is. The mountains are just beautiful. Our room has a view, but I guess every room has a view."

"Our? You here with your husband?"

She was going to tell herself he cared whether or not she was single. "No. My twin sister." Eve had gotten her own room because she didn't like to share. At all.

"Y'all identical?" he asked, looking over at her curiously.

People always wanted to know that. They found the twin concept intriguing, for some reason. She nodded, used to the question. "Physically, yes. Otherwise, not so much."

Charity was the sexy sister. Harley was the serious one. Or at least that was the label everyone slapped on them because Charity was outspoken and fond of displaying her cleavage. Harley preferred the natural look, makeup-free for the most part, and she preferred the girls to remain in her sweater, not catching air and creepy stares.

"I have a sister, too," Cooper said. "She's twelve. She just moved in with me and I think she might kill me, honestly. Been driving for twenty years and I have never felt at risk of dying, but it's this kid that's going to be the death of me, I'm telling you. It's stressful as hell to be responsible for another human being."

"I'm a nanny for a couple of preschoolers," Harley told him. "I love kids. But I haven't dealt with any preteens yet. You have my sympathy."

"I'll trade ya."

She laughed. "That only works in reality shows."

"Damn, so you mean this is real life?" He gave her a grin. "Shit. I'm screwed."

"I'm sure your sister will settle down. Twelve is a tough age for a girl." Harley remembered legs that were too long and a sudden painful awareness of boys.

"She's had it really easy and really hard at the same time," he said. "That doesn't sound like it makes sense, but it's the truth. I want to do right by her. But I don't always know what I'm doing. Actually, I don't know what I'm doing at all."

The laughter had left his voice and Harley heard the sincerity, the worry, in his voice, which she respected. It did her heart good to hear that he cared so much about his sister. To her, he'd always just been the cocky grin jumping out of the 78 car, sexy and confident.

But then he shook his head. "And I have no idea why I

am boring you with my troubles. You just have one of those faces. Makes me feel confessional."

She did. Everywhere Harley went people wanted to overshare with her. The bank teller spilled about her divorce, the dental hygienist confessed to an affair, the man behind her in line at the grocery voiced his fears over his upcoming surgery. She was used to it and didn't mind, most of the time.

Though she did wish, on occasion, someone would ask her how *she* was doing. If people would see her as a woman, a potential friend or lover, instead of just a sounding board. That was not going to be tonight, apparently.

Before she could even respond, Cooper continued. "Maybe you could give me some professional advice. Can I grab you a drink and bend your ear?"

Harley could think of many, many things she would rather do with her evening. And many, many things she'd rather do with Cooper Brickman. There was no way she could say no, though. Because it was Cooper Brickman. And the truth was, she probably wouldn't say no to anyone. It was a problem she had, not saying no. Maybe that was why people shared their TMI with her all the time. They read her correctly that she wouldn't shut them down.

"Sure, of course. I'd be happy to." Harley figured she'd be able to gaze at will on the picture of hot he presented in that tux while she murmured appropriate words of understanding for five minutes. Then maybe they could move on from the topic of his sister to the topic of her desire to see him naked.

Forty-five minutes later Harley opened her mouth for the ninth time or so to speak, but Cooper didn't seem to notice. He was too busy venting what must be about a decade's worth of anger and anxiety and didn't seem to require any response other than an occasional nod from her. It was worse than she had expected. It was like any warm body would do, and she was it.

"Our mother is in the south of France with a twenty-two-year-old boyfriend, though I use that term loosely, and my sister is staying with me until she gets back. But you know what will happen, don't you?"

"No." She had absolutely no idea whatsoever.

"She won't come back for months. Mark my words. Who ditches their daughter like that?" Cooper stuck his finger out and lifted his glass of whiskey. "A selfish woman, that's who. I love my mother, but she doesn't always have her priorities in order."

Harley was going to give some kind of pat answer, because she did feel bad for his sister, but Cooper kept talking.

"What if Mary Jane starts her period or something? What am I supposed to do about that?"

"Uh . . ." Harley felt as appalled as he looked. He took another deep, bracing swallow of his whiskey.

"And my housekeeper said she needs a bra, which maybe she does. I don't know. I'm not going to look! But how the hell do I deal with that? I cannot take her bra shopping. I'm thirty-five. She's twelve. That's fucking *weird*, pardon my language."

Good Lord. Harley wanted another drink. "It is a little odd. But she's your sister, not a random kid you have no relation to. It's perfectly acceptable. Just take her to the store and hand her over to the clerk."

"That's all anyone ever does with her—hand her over. No wonder the kid is seeking validation online." He flagged down a passing waiter. "Can I get another Jack and Coke?" He peeled two twenties out of his pocket. "And a vodka tonic for the lady."

It would never have occurred to Harley to have the waiter fetch and carry for her. It was an open bar, which to her meant drinks were delightfully free, but you got it yourself. But she wasn't a rich and famous driver, who had staff, and clearly he expected that if he wanted a drink, he didn't have to stand up. For a minute Harley was distracted by the thought of what life would be like if she were rich. If Prince Charming really swept her away to a world where she no longer had to be concerned that the sum total of her net worth was seven dollars the day before payday.

"Thanks, man," Cooper told the waiter with a smile. "I appreciate it."

Harley appreciated it, too. In fact, that drink couldn't arrive fast enough. This was surreal and bizarre.

When it did, she sucked her vodka tonic down in record time, though not as fast as Cooper made his whiskey disappear.

He was leaning forward, forearms on his thighs, his knees bumping hers. A casual observer might think they were having an intimate conversation. Which maybe they were, just not the kind of intimacy Harley was looking for.

"Where do you live?" he asked suddenly.

"Charlotte."

"And you're a nanny?" he asked, a little longingly.

Oh, no, she saw where this was going. "Yes. I work for a cardiologist and a therapist. They have two boys, two and four."

"I don't suppose you're looking for a new position?"

He gave her a charming smile, one that made her want to kiss him repeatedly and give him everything he asked for. Except for that. There was no way she was going to quit a job she loved to monitor the Internet activity of his tween sister and go on maxipad runs when puberty well and truly hit.

Trying to channel her sister and the fact that Charity would direct the conversation to where she wanted it to go, Harley gave him a smile and went for an innuendo. "It depends on the position. Some I like more than others."

That was pretty damn good for her.

But Cooper didn't pick up on the flirt, probably because she sucked at it.

He just frowned. "Technically, I guess it would be considered a nanny position. I know that sounds odd since she's twelve and that's a little old for a nanny, but that's really what she—and I—need."

Sigh. She tried to give herself a mental pep talk. He was distraught. Possibly drunk. It wasn't that she had a complete lack of sexual appeal. "No, I'm sorry. I'm quite happy there and I couldn't leave the boys."

"Damn. You seem like you'd be great at it."

Under other circumstances it would be nice to be appreciated for a job well done. Right now, unless that job involved her riding him like the bull down at the Buckle bar, she didn't need a compliment. She didn't need polite and professional respect. She wanted to be seen as a sexual feast he couldn't wait to take a bite of.

"You seem very maternal and stable."

Yeah. What every twenty-eight-year-old woman in a cocktail dress wants to hear.

Suddenly Harley felt monstrously depressed.

It was the same old story. She was a scullery maid in the eyes of every man under fifty.

Even the fact that he was good looking wasn't making up for the fact that her ass was going numb from sitting stiffly in the chair on the edge of the dance floor or that her stomach was growling from hunger, her lips chapped. She desperately needed to use the restroom as well since she'd sucked down the two vodka tonics he'd gotten her, but wasn't sure how to interrupt him without sounding like a jerk or like she was trying to ditch him.

Which was just the most hilarious of ironies. Her trying to ditch Cooper Brickman? Not how she imagined the evening going if she ever had his hotness all to herself. But even his muscles couldn't alter the fact that her bladder was going to burst, and she felt about as desirable as Mrs. Doubtfire. She just wanted to pee, then hit the dessert table for some sugary comfort.

When "Single Ladies" came blaring out from the speakers and the DJ announced the bride was about to throw her bouquet, Harley lifted her head. If she knew her sister, she would be out there knocking down every bridesmaid she could for the honor of having a random man feel up her leg for the garter deposit. Charity had no interest in the men or marriage; she just wanted to win. Plus possibly prove that catching a bouquet in no way guaranteed a proposal.

As Imogen, slim and elegant in her lace gown, moved to the front of the stage area, Harley's sister didn't let her down, appearing out of nowhere and grabbing her.

"Come on! Single ladies, front and center. That means *you*, Harley!"

As she tugged her arm and Harley stood with an apologetic look at Cooper, her sister realized who she was talking to. "Oh. Hello. Are you going to be vying for the garter, handsome?"

Cooper, who had been earnest and serious, suddenly looked like a rooster let loose in the henhouse. He gave Charity a sly smile. "I hadn't planned on it, but if you catch the bouquet I may have to rethink that."

Seriously? Harley got him telling her about his concern over his sister's impending puberty, and Charity got flirty Cooper? What the hell was fair about that? They looked exactly the same. They were *identical* twins.

She clearly had no sex appeal. Zero. Less than zero. Negative sex appeal.

Annoyed, she didn't even try to catch the bouquet, preferring to stay a bit clear of the melee, sneaking side glances at Cooper, who was watching Charity. Unfortunately, watching Cooper meant she wasn't watching the bouquet.

It hit her in the head.

Then bounced off and fell right into the hands of her twin, who let out a whoop of triumph.

Damn it all anyway.

COOPER had no idea what had just possessed him to jaw Harley to death for the last forty-five minutes. He never talked about his personal life with strangers. He didn't even talk about his personal life with friends. But he was really worried about Mary Jane, and Harley just seemed so compassionate, he had found himself blurting out all manner of random and embarrassing shit. He suspected he was drunk.

Okay, he knew he was drunk.

When he got back to Charlotte he was going to have to send her flowers or chocolates as a thank-you for letting him monopolize her for half the wedding. Damn, the poor girl had probably been dying to dance or hit the dessert buffet and he'd been holding her hostage. Normally his manners were a little more polished when it came to the ladies, so he didn't blame her for dashing off with her sister the minute she appeared. But what was crazy was that his reaction to her twin was totally different. He didn't feel like confiding in Charity. He felt like flirting.

How could two women who looked identical inspire totally different responses from him?

And how could he be so fucking shallow?

Of course, they weren't identical, not really. Harley had

met his gaze with concern and sympathy. Charity had given him a sassy smile. Charity was also more in-your-face with a tighter dress, breasts on display and glowing with some kind of unnatural bronze glitter, her hair teased up pageant style. She was currently fist-pumping and vying for domination on the dance floor. Harley's hair was more controlled, and while her dress was very similar to her sister's, both a blue that complemented their eyes, her chest was more contained. But mostly it was her demeanor that was more contained. She hovered around the fringe, observing, and Cooper felt weird and conflicted about the whole thing.

It was distressing to realize that if you shook boobs in his face, he was that easily distracted. He was too old for that, or so he had thought. Yet now he couldn't stop looking over at the dance floor and thinking he really would love to feel the warm slide of a woman's skin against his.

The twins were both attractive, obviously, and truthfully, Harley was the type who actually interested him as the complete package, but she fell squarely in the nice-girl camp, and he felt like it would be in seriously poor taste to hit on her after she had listened to him blather on and on. On the other hand, it wasn't right to flirt with her sister either. Charity was like Harley on sexy steroids and that was appealing, he wasn't going to lie, because she was the kind of woman looking for a little fun, not much else. Harley was the girl you put a ring on, or at least settled into a relationship with, and he wasn't exactly fit for a relationship at the moment. His plate was piled pretty high. With crap.

It had been a shitty year. He'd had a piss-poor season, with his worst finish in ten years. His mother's defection, yet again, with no understanding that her boy toy was a mooch, plain and simple, and that by taking off she hurt her daughter. Then there was Mary Jane herself and her habit of trolling the Internet twenty-three hours a day and buying all manner of crap online. Every damn day the postman was ringing the bell with a mystery package for MJ and she wouldn't talk to him about it. She cloistered herself in her room, and it terrified him, he was not afraid to admit. She could be buying shrunken heads from Peru or One Direction blow-up dolls for all he knew, and he wasn't sure which was scarier.

So while yesterday he would have said that he was way too goddamn old for drunken wedding hookups, today that didn't seem like such a bad thing. Okay, so maybe not an actual hookup, because that might be pushing a boundary or two, but a little harmless flirting. Was the distraction of a pretty woman so wrong? Didn't he deserve a break from reality?

Charity caught the bouquet, after it nailed Harley in the head. Cooper thought maybe that entitled her to the claim on it, but Charity seemed determined to keep the prize. Harley didn't look like she cared one way or the other and beelined for the back of the tent.

He was on the fence about joining the bachelors or being mature and skipping the whole thing, when Ty, the groom, pointed at him. "Get out there, Brickman. You're next to take the plunge, you know. You're the last bachelor on the circuit over thirty." Ty had taken his jacket off and he was grinning, hadn't stopped grinning since the minute he'd said "I do."

Cooper was happy for him, but that didn't mean he wanted to get married himself. He figured he was like wine—he'd be better with age. Once he retired and had more time to devote to not screwing things up with a woman, he would. But he'd play along and get out there for the garter toss. What was the worst that could happen? He'd be forced to put a garter on Charity's leg. Hurt him.

"Just because you fell for this marriage con doesn't mean I will," he said to Ty, clapping him on the shoulder. "But I have no objection to showing all these young punks how to do this thing."

"I'm counting on you to be thoroughly tacky just on principle," Ty said. "Imogen was adamantly opposed to the whole bouquet-and-garter thing. It's outdated and sexist, according to her."

"It is," Imogen said dryly, coming up behind her new husband.

Ty jumped. "Damn, you move like smoke, Emma Jean."

"One of my many talents." She linked her arm through his. "But far be it from me to deny your male friends the opportunity to jostle each other for domination. Just tell whoever catches it not to fondle Charity. I'm sure she doesn't want a stranger's hands all over her thighs. The ritual really has its basis in pagan fertility rites, but I don't want to encourage conception at my reception."

Ty made a face at Cooper. "Yeah. What she said." Then he turned back to his wife. "But I think you're naïve in assuming the ladies don't want to be fondled. Probably eight out of ten are vying for a grope. It's a wedding. Everyone wants to get lucky."

"I know I do," Cooper said with a grin, because he did, and it was the expected answer.

"You're not a lady, idiot."

"Hey, I have a feminine side."

Ty snorted. He kissed Imogen's forehead. "It's show-time. I have to aim this thing right for Brickman."

Cooper wasn't sure he really wanted to catch the garter, but he was just competitive enough that now he felt obligated to make it happen. The competition wasn't stiff. At a wedding with two hundred guests, it was clear they had reached the age bracket where every male was either married or from the next generation of cousins and nephews and still in their teens. Ty was right. Cooper was damn near the only bachelor left between twenty-five and forty years old. There were a few ballsy dudes in their fifties out there, clearly having spotted the legs on Charity. The rest were young, including a precocious ten-year-old. Where the hell was that kid's mother? Cooper's sister was at home, where children should be, damn it.

At home, on the Internet. Doing God only knew what.

Shit. He wanted another drink.

Instead, he elbowed Carl Hinder, the owner of Hinder Motors, out of the way and snagged the garter when Ty tossed it. "Hah. Eat that, Carl," he told him with a grin.

That might have been his biggest earliest indicator of how truly drunk he was, given that Carl was a heavy hitter in the industry and someday might be his boss if he ever wanted to change teams. The other might have been that he found it necessary to toss back the drink the waiter brought him before he swaggered onto the dance floor to place the garter on Charity's leg.

Third, it was possible he went higher under the blue dress than he intended. The thought was to edge just past the knee and call it quits, but his maneuver had more speed than finesse, and suddenly Charity was grabbing his hand and stopping him, a look of alarm on her face.

"Whoa! Keep it PG-13, big guy. This isn't a sex club. Imogen's grandparents are here."

While he found it hard to believe anyone in their eighties hadn't had their share and then some of sexual encounters, he knew Charity was right. This wasn't prom, it was a classy wedding at a beautiful venue, and hadn't he just said he was too old to behave like that? "Sorry, didn't mean to make you uncomfortable. I think I may have been hitting the Jack a little too hard."

Standing up, he held a hand out to her to assist her off the chair, while the reception-goers all cheered. There might have been a few catcalls and snickers as well, so he figured the best way to defuse the situation was to acknowledge it. He turned to the crowd and gave a grin and a shrug to show he'd been thoroughly rejected. Everyone gave a chuckle, though he saw Imogen's mother giving him a dirty look. Whoops. The art gallery owner from Manhattan was unimpressed with him. But hey, he never claimed to be anything more than a country boy at heart, despite all the dollars in his bank account.

"Can I get you a drink?" he asked Charity, figuring he should make amends.

"No, I'm fine, thanks." She tapped him on the chest with the floral bouquet and gave him a smile. "Nice to meet you, Brickman. Keep it off the streets."

She walked away.

Just walked away.

Yeah. Shitty year. Check.

CHARITY McLain was totally ticked off, her cheeks feeling hot from the embarrassment of having Cooper Brickman treat her like a two-dollar hooker. She stomped over to her sister and tossed the bouquet down, announcing, "Just because a man has money does not mean he can mine for gold in front of two hundred people. These damn drivers are all far too used to getting their way. I feel like a piece of meat."

Harley blinked up at her, startled. "It's just a tacky tradition, Char. I'm sure he didn't mean anything by it."

She slid into the seat next to her twin and stole a bite-size brownie off Harley's plate. "That's because you work with cute kids who both adore you and respect your authority. I work for a nineteen-year-old driving wonder who thinks he's God's gift and uses every chance he gets to make it clear that he has a penis and I have a vagina." She bit the brownie hard and spoke around it. "Though I bet his penis is small. Really small. Like pencil dick."

"If you hate your job with Roger you can look for another one."

That was Harley for you. Being rational.

Charity just wanted to vent.

Most days she didn't mind her job as a handler for a cup series driver, because she actually liked being bossy and in charge, and working for Roger afforded her many opportunities to treat him like the obnoxious brat he was, but she did want to command respect. It was annoying that because a girl liked big hair and red nails, no one took her seriously. Tonight alone, she'd had her butt pinched, her lower back massaged by a seventy-year-old, and Cooper Brickman sliding his hand up her inner thigh like she'd dropped the flag and let him at it. It didn't matter that he was good looking or rich. He didn't know her at all.

"You don't understand. Everyone treats you with dignity. I get treated like a hussy because I choose not to hide my body."

"At least men pay attention to you," Harley said. "I'm like this tablecloth." She gestured to the linens. "No one notices me. Later on no one will be able to tell you what color this tablecloth is. That's me. No one remembers me. Not once does a man look at me and want to have sex with me."

"But you know a man likes you for *you*." Grumble, grumble. She had thought this wedding was going to be fun, but now her feet hurt and she felt like she and Harley were having the same discussion they'd had a million times, with no resolution. "I confess Brickman just tipped me over the edge. When I went to order a cocktail, I forgot what's in a Manhattan, the signature drink they're serving in honor of Imogen's family, and I asked the bartender. I was repeating it back to him and I mispronounced 'vermouth' by total accident, and do you know the guy next to me mistook me for Nikki Strickland?"

It had been horrifying. No one wanted to be mistaken for Nikki, who had more shoes than brain cells, at least not anyone Charity knew or wanted to know.

"Jonas's wife?"

"Yes. This dude told his friend that you can't expect beauty and brains to go hand in hand. I just tripped on my tongue! I'm not an idiot. And I am no Nikki Strickland. I have a job, for one thing."

"I guess it could be considered a compliment," Harley said.

Charity stared at her sister in amazement. "Are you drunk? How?"

"She weighs like two pounds. It makes me feel better about chowing on these desserts since we're the same size."

Charity snorted. "You know, I'm surprised Imogen hasn't invited us to be a case study for her sociology thesis on the effects of hair and makeup on men."

Harley laughed. "Don't even suggest it."

Wait a minute. Just hold the freaking phone. "I have an idea. Let's twin-swap, right now. You'll see what I'm talking about."

Harley raised her eyebrows. "Are you insane? We haven't done that since high school and it was a total disaster every time."

There *had* been an incident where Harley had taken Charity's spot in detention in exchange for Charity flirting with Robby Newcomb pretending to be Harley to get her a date for homecoming. But Harley had been too efficient at doing Charity's homework under incarceration, and Charity had been a little too efficient in flirtation, and there had been accusations of cheating all the way around. Not pretty.

But they were older, savvier now.

Just once, Charity wanted the respect that Harley enjoyed from men, even if it was under false pretenses. Plus she was bored. It would certainly serve as entertainment for the rest of the night.

And she knew just how to talk her twin into it. "We're at a wedding. It will be fun. Let's just go in the bathroom, change dresses, slap some lipstick on you, and see what happens. I can't wait to see you trying to fend off Cooper Brickman."

Harley had a crush on Cooper and it didn't take a twin connection to see that. There was no way Harley would be able to resist the idea of him hitting on her.

Harley sat up straighter.

Bingo. Charity had her.

But then she shook her head. "This is really a bad idea."

She waved her hand. "Whatever. I've had worse." Like dyeing her hair black in eighth grade. "This is totally going to make this weekend suck less."

Her sister bit her lip, a sign she was wavering. "He called me maternal and stable."

Yikes. Charity instantly felt bad for her. "Screw that. Show him the sassy side of Harley. Make him see you as a woman."

Harley put down her brownie, her expression suddenly fierce. "You're right. I can do this. I'm not a tablecloth. Cooper Brickman is going to remember me, damn it."

The wedding was about to get a whole lot more interesting.

Especially since she'd spotted Jeff Sterling, the team owner who she thought was hot with a capital *H* who had never shown her the time of day. He always looked at her like he expected her to suddenly jump onto a pole and start working it. He went for understated women. Like Harley.

Who Charity was about to become for the evening.

CHAPTER

TWO

IT was a weird experience to be Charity. Harley felt naked, first of all, and she was well aware of the half-dozen pairs of male eyes that swung in her direction when they walked back into the tent, past the bar. She was also struggling a bit to achieve that confident strut her sister had mastered, but at the same time it was an awesome feeling to be able to be so brazenly sexual and yet no one knew it was her. With each step she took, she felt more comfortable in the heels that were a good two inches higher than her own, the short skirt allowing so much cool air up under the skirt that it automatically made her aware of her girl bits, which in turn made her want to display how sexual she was feeling. So her hips started to move more easily, and her chin came up.

She found herself making bold eye contact with the men who were checking her out, staring them down. Some quickly looked away, obviously embarrassed or ashamed, but two others acknowledged her, one giving her a grin and a wink, the other letting his eyes roam over her legs. He twirled his finger in a gesture for her to turn around, his lusty gaze appreciative. Harley raised an eyebrow at him and shook her head, not wanting to encourage him and his outrageous assumption.

But for once, she wanted to be thought of as sexy, not maternal. At work, she could be maternal. At a wedding she wanted to be a single woman, a sultry, sexy single woman who could make the driver she had fantasized about for years want her. Granted, it meant Cooper actually wanted her sister, not her, but if she was Harley with him when he wanted Charity, even though he *thought* she was Charity, she was still Harley, so didn't he by default actually want her?

Yeah. Think that one through a few times and learn the definition of rationalization.

It was probably flawed logic, but then so was using hot wax to remove body hair and she did that every single month.

Funny how she was aware of Charity next to her but could tell that eyes were on her, not her sister. Male gazes were drawn to cleavage and short skirts, not sensible sweaters over conservative dresses. Which she knew, of course, since she was usually the one being ignored, but it was an odd perspective, both exciting and unpleasant. She didn't like being objectified, and it annoyed her that Charity constantly was, but at the same time, she couldn't deny there was something ego-boosting about the attention.

It was the ultimate paradox—how did you achieve interest without it becoming smarmy?

Harley had never had that problem. She was used to being indignant on her sister's behalf, and she knew that Charity tolerated a lot of ego on a daily basis in her job as handler at the track, but Harley never experienced that attention herself. She had to admit she was willing to over-look a little macho swagger just once if it came from Cooper. Because it might be her only shot at a decent story to tell her grandkids someday. *I flirted with Cooper Brickman at a wedding.* Okay, it wasn't much of a brag, but it was more than she had at the moment. Her arsenal of scandalous stories was nonexistent.

Maybe Charity was right and this was something of a social experiment.

She *could* be Cinderella tonight if she chose to be. The quiet and plain nanny who got to flirt with the prince of stock car racing.

It would be liberating, thrilling. If she could pull it off.

Her eyes landed on Cooper, sitting at the bar, his gaze fixed on her. She felt the heft of his lustful appreciation from across the room, and immediately her body responded to the intent in his eyes. But then he glanced behind her, at Charity being her, and his expression changed, became respectful. For a second it gave her pause, but then he was undressing her with his eyes again and her panties went damp and all rationale went out the door.

"Play it cool," Charity said from behind her. "Let him come to you. And remember, I just blew him off on the dance floor over the garter thing, so if you're being me, which you are, give him a dirty look."

She wasn't sure she even knew how to do that. Harley wrinkled her nose up and did a sharp turn to the right, breaking eye contact. Okay, that was the worst expression of disdain ever, but she was a novice. She'd been born with the people-pleaser gene. Blowing someone off was foreign to her.

"Oh, let's get more desserts," Charity said, pointing to the burgeoning dessert buffet. "They cleared your plate from before. Damn efficient waiters. I hate to think that those brownies went to waste."

Harley blindly grabbed a plate and threw everything within reach on it. Her heart was racing and she felt odd, like her insides had been inflated. That look on Cooper's face. Damn. If chocolate was a substitute for sex then she was going to have to stuff her face, because he had basically caused her ovaries to explode just from that one hot glance. If she didn't find something to fill her, it was going to be ugly.

"I can't do this," she told Charity, panicking.

Her sister gave her a stern look. "Did you see that look he gave you? Girl, just have another vodka tonic and get your flirt on. I'm going to have an intellectual discussion with the bride's mother about the modern art movement and enjoy being taken seriously."

Harley tugged at the dress bodice. She was sure any second her breasts were going to spring forth and she would wind up online under "Embarrassing Wedding Photos: The Nipple Edition."

"Stop touching your dress."

"Stop pressuring me!" Harley shoved a tart in her mouth and wished some of its bite would rub off on her.

COOPER was losing his charm along with everything else this year.

The whole night was a disaster. First he'd stressed about his sister getting her period to Harley, then he'd groped Charity and she'd reprimanded him like he was a kid with his hand in the cookie jar. Which, he supposed he had been, in a sense.

Maybe it was time to scrape his manhood off the floor and head back to his room at the inn. But he got waylaid by

Carl and some of the other guys and it was forty minutes before he broke free, though it did give him time to suck down a water and combat some of the effects of the whiskey. He made eye contact with Charity once, when she strolled past the bar looking like she owned it and every man sitting there. Which, if the appreciative gazes from the men left and right were any indication, she did.

It just made him feel even shittier.

At some point Cooper had torn his tie off, so he went wandering in search of it, planning to pack it in for the night. Harley was at the table with a plate of macaroons in front of her. His tie was lying next to her little purse. At least he thought it was Harley. His first gut instinct was that it was definitely her, but then he started to doubt that because she had the bouquet Imogen had thrown and Charity had caught, and she was wearing a dress that was pushing her assets up further than he remembered an hour ago. Her smile as he approached also seemed a little sassy to be Harley, but then again, would Charity smile at him at all?

He doubted it.

Plus, her eyes . . . something about the sincerity in them said Harley to him.

Damn, he was just altogether too drunk for the identical-twin thing. It was messing with his head.

"Harley, right?" he asked as he sat down next to her. "I'm ninety percent sure, but before I start talking and make a bigger ass out of myself than I already have tonight, I want confirmation."

She leaned toward him and licked the cream off of a macaroon, the tip of her tongue sliding into the pink meringue in a way that made him shift uncomfortably in his chair. Jesus.

"You had a fifty-fifty chance of being right," she told him. "But you're wrong. I'm Charity."

Hell.

This night had gone from bad to worse to naughty.

He should walk away. He really should.

He didn't.

"I apologize again for taking it a little too far on the dance floor," he said, tossing his hair out of his eyes. "I didn't mean to offend you."

That pink tongue got a tiny dot of cream off her bottom lip, thoroughly distracting him. "I didn't object to the direction your hand took, Cooper, just the setting we were in."

Hello. Not at all the reaction he was expecting, given how annoyed she had looked. Maybe the night wasn't such a bust after all. "Is that right?"

She nodded.

If you don't ask . . .

"So. If we were in private, we could try that again? Or should I say, *I* could try that again, with more pleasurable results for both of us?"

"Possibly."

It wasn't a no.

Which meant he didn't see himself going to bed anytime soon. At least not alone. He'd always liked a challenge, damn it. It was what drove him year to year in his career, what kept him in shape, what made life exciting. Sometimes made it a little dangerous.

It was a little dangerous to be flirting with Charity at McCordle's wedding.

Not a huge risk, but potentially an entanglement he didn't need right now.

But he'd feel her out, see if she was the kind who understood that a few hours of fun at a wedding didn't translate into anything more the next day.

"Dance with me?" he asked, as a slow baby-making song came over the speakers.

"Is that a thinly veiled excuse to touch me inappropriately on the dance floor again?"

The words were teasing, but her expression wasn't. If he wasn't mistaken, that was lust written on her face, not as a seasoned flirt would show it, but as a raw, naked desire.

It punched him in the gut and had his dick going hard.

Cooper held his hand out to her, hoping she would say yes. Willing her to. "I wasn't planning to put my hand up your skirt, no. Unless you'd like me to. Then I think we should arrange to do that somewhere in private."

Suddenly his thought to just flirt with Charity, convince her he wasn't a lecherous wedding guest, was overshadowed by his lecherous-wedding-guest thoughts. He was still buzzed and it had been a few months since he'd last shared his bed with a woman.

That suddenly felt like a very, very long time. An eternity. The stress of Mary Jane moving in, his disappointing year, his mother, it all had been weighing him down. But now he might have an opportunity to escape his crowded thoughts for the rest of the night.

"Don't get ahead of yourself," she said. "Let's just see how you move first."

"Is this a test?" When she accepted his hand, he stroked the warm flesh of her palm with his thumb and led her onto the dance floor. "To see how much rhythm I have?"

"I don't think swaying to R&B requires rhythm." She gave him a rueful look, but she did let him pull her close against his body, her breasts brushing his chest.

"So you're staying with your sister?" he asked, then immediately regretted it. He still felt odd about the mind freak of Harley and Charity looking nearly identical. He was attracted to both of them, clearly, and that made him uncomfortable. So he wanted to ignore that fact.

She nodded. "We get along well. So I guess you're staying here at the inn?"

It was polite conversation, nothing more, and Cooper nodded, distracted by her eyes. She had the kind of eyes that hinted at hidden thoughts, unspoken words, a compassion that belied the sassy tilt of her head. A paradox. It was both appealing and confusing.

"Yes. I have a suite with a Jacuzzi tub and a mountain view."

"A suite? Fancy."

"Would you like to see it?" he asked, leaning down to murmur in her ear, his hands low on the small of her back. He found that he didn't want to talk. He'd done enough of that earlier, boring Harley with his worries. He wanted to move his mouth over Charity's and explore all the curves of her body until his mind was empty of everything but the feel of her beneath him.

Her hands came up to his chest and she scratched her nails lightly across his shirt. "You don't waste any time, do you?"

"It's almost midnight. Another couple of hours they'll be shooing us out of here. I'm just trying to make sure an opportunity doesn't pass me by."

The song ended and transitioned into a fast-paced pop song. He hoped she didn't expect him to dance to that, because he was drunk, but not that drunk. But she just gave him a smile and said, "I want another drink."

"Your wish is my command." Cooper took Charity to the bar and ordered her a drink, then took a seat on a stool. He patted his lap. "Sit down." He wanted to feel her snuggled up against him, but mostly, he wanted to see if she would do it or not. If she did, he would wager that she was in, all in, for going back to his room with him. If she was like she had been earlier on the dance floor, annoyed and offended with his aggressiveness, then he would make sure she got safely back to her room with her sister and he would pass out alone.

Which might be the smarter thing to do.

"You want me to sit on your lap?" she asked, expression doubtful.

"Best seat in the house." The wedding music was still pumping behind them, the bass low. The lighting was dim, and Cooper put his elbows back on the bar as he waited for her answer, watching her, his legs apart.

He could see the conflict on her face. She wanted to. She wanted him.

For a minute she didn't move.

Then she stepped forward between his legs.

Oh yeah. Mistake or not, he was looking forward to seeing where this led.

SIT on his lap? He wanted her to sit on his lap.

Oh, Lord. That was both tempting and terrifying.

"Thanks." Harley stepped between his legs and gingerly rested her ass on his thigh, her feet still on the ground, very aware of every inch of him. That was the most she could handle. She couldn't just hop up on him in heels. But Cooper grabbed her around the waist and hauled her all the way up onto his lap, her legs suddenly airborne, Charity's tiny dress sliding up.

Her natural reaction was to squawk, yank the skirt down, and plant her feet back on the ground, but she resisted the urge. Instead, she crossed one leg over the other and slid her fingers through Cooper's belt loops to steady herself, heart racing in excitement.

"Comfy?" he asked.

"Horny" was a better description. Or stunned with the reality of what was actually happening. But this was her opportunity to let out her inner flirt, who was buried deep beneath a layer of sensible and shy. And he'd never know it was really her, so that took the pressure off entirely.

"Definitely." She wiggled a little to readjust so she didn't fall, but it had the added effect of arousing both of them. His nostrils flared. He didn't sit up, the very picture of casual sexiness, and Harley took a second to be amazed that she was doing this, that she was sitting on Cooper frickin' Brickman's lap.

He was so hot Harley couldn't believe she was actually being allowed to touch him, her hands intriguingly close to his abs. She found herself holding her breath, waiting for the moment to pass, for him to realize she was no Charity and gently remove her from his lap. But he didn't. And she was going to carpe the goddamn diem out of the opportunity.

The plan had been to flirt, just flirt with Cooper.

She wasn't supposed to sleep with him.

But really, why not? This was her fantasy. Why not really make it a night to remember?

Harley faked a wobble as an excuse to put her hands on his chest. She wanted to feel those rock-solid muscles she had been admiring from afar for three years in greater depth.

His eyebrows rose in question.

"I lost my balance," she told him, her voice filled with a sultriness she hadn't known she had possessed. She was so impressed with herself.

"I'm sure it was my fault," he said. "Here, let me help." As he shifted his elbows off the bar, the palm of his hand firmly cupped her ass and lifted her closer to him, so that her top half splayed completely against his chest.

Her mouth was inches from his, her breasts brushing

against his chest. Harley's breath caught and she swallowed hard, tongue suddenly thick with desire. His thigh was hard, warm. She was fairly certain she could feel the cusp of his erection, though the angle was just off enough that it might be her imagination. Or wishful thinking. But nonetheless, it was a whole lot of Cooper up close and personal and it felt as good as she had always imagined. Better, because it was real.

"Thanks," she said, moistening her bottom lip with the tip of her tongue. "That's so sweet of you. I could kiss you, you're so sweet."

She couldn't believe she'd had the balls to say that. It was amazing what not being herself did for her nerve.

"I wish you would."

Mentally fortifying herself, Harley studied his face, her hand coming up to trace the sharp angle of his jaw. He was so rugged, so manly. Being this close, hiding behind her sister's persona, she felt free to touch, to say exactly what she was thinking. It was an odd sensation, so real yet so utterly unbelievable that it was happening.

"What are you thinking?" he asked her.

"That I wish I weren't wearing panties." It was true. She was. But normally any sexy thoughts she had stayed just that—thoughts. Harley had never spoken dirty to a man, not even her former boyfriend of three years. It wasn't that she didn't think in those terms. She just couldn't bring herself to say them with any confidence so she never said them.

Until now. It just came out. Easily.

Maybe it was the fact that she was sitting on Cooper Brickman's lap. It was just so surreal that she was capable of behaving in a way she had always wanted to, without fear of repercussion.

"Holy hell," was his opinion. His grip tightened. "Kiss me. Now."

So she did. Gripping the front of his shirt, she reached up and touched her lips to his. The second she did, the desire she'd been carefully keeping under wraps for *years* exploded. This was what she had been fantasizing about, this was her chance to take what she wanted, and the kiss didn't disappoint. He was smooth and hot and talented. He was a manly man, self-assured, and good at what he did, all of which made him the perfect package for one night of pure pleasure.

Forget just flirting. She wanted to ride this wave all the way to shore. Harley kissed him greedily, leaning against him, legs moving restlessly as she tried to climb higher on him, to give her lips better access. He tasted like whiskey and sexy male and she wanted to eat him alive.

"Damn," he murmured when she pulled away, before kissing her again, harder this time, to match her frenzied pace. He thrust his tongue inside her mouth, teasing her with skill.

They were both fighting for domination. It was a new sensation for Harley, to be so aggressive, to take what she wanted, to spar with a man using her tongue. It was freeing and super, super sexy.

Finally, she broke away to breathe, putting a bit of space between them as she panted.

"Come to my room now," he demanded. "Before I shock Imogen's grandmother even further."

Could she do this? Did she really have the nerve to go for it and enjoy a night of undoubtedly hot sex with Cooper Brickman?

Harley took a deep breath and felt his chest again. Oh, hell, yeah, she could. "Okay. Let me tell my sister."

For some reason Cooper frowned. He glanced around her like he expected her twin to pop up. "Harley?" he asked, like he was unsure of her name.

Harley's cheeks heated up, feeling more than a little insulted. "Yes."

"Your sister's really sweet," he said. "We talked for quite a while."

It was weird to sit there and hear him discussing her with him, not knowing it was her. For a split second she debated telling him the truth. He might be annoyed briefly, but he had an erection. How long was he going to argue with her about it?

"I'd like to hire her as a nanny for my sister." But then he grinned, running his thumbs up her arms and giving her a cocky tilt of his head. "Now you, on the other hand, I have different plans for, all involving my bed and you in it."

So maybe she wouldn't tell him after all.

Determined not to second-guess what she was about to do, Harley leaned in, letting him kiss her again, wanting to absorb the sensation of being so up close and personal with Cooper. Wanting to have the courage to go for it, to take what she wanted. "Let's go. I'll just text my sister." Charity wasn't going to care where she was.

"She's busy talking to Jeff Sterling anyway," Cooper assured her. "Though I'm not sure why."

Harley glanced in the direction he nodded. Charity was sitting at a table talking to Jeff, looking up at him from under her eyelashes in a shy manner that Harley had to admit looked exactly how she would if that were really her. It was very bizarre. Like seeing a clone of yourself. "Maybe she likes him," she said simply, curious actually if that were the case. Charity had never mentioned it to her.

"Why? He's like twenty years older than her."

Harley laughed. Cooper sounded so certain no woman could ever find Jeff attractive, even though he was a fit and good-looking guy. "Stop talking, Brickman. Let's go." It was a very Charity response. Or maybe it was a Harley response that she just finally felt comfortable saying out loud.

"Done and done." He drained his whiskey, then gently eased her off his lap and back onto the floor.

Another minute they were out of the tent, heading over the terrace toward the inn, Cooper's hand firmly in hers. For a second, Harley paused, wanting to take in the night, the feel of the crisp air, the smell of encroaching winter. The vista was stunning and she felt so removed from her normal reality. She wanted to push the pause button and remember this moment forever, a little drunk, a lot aroused, here with Cooper with the entire estate spread out below them.

"What?" Cooper asked.

She realized that Charity would never stop to wax poetic about the trees and the mountains and she wondered for a brief moment if she really knew, understood who she was. She certainly didn't sexually know herself all that well. She couldn't define what she enjoyed or what described her type for men. Like much of her life, she had drifted along, letting it happen.

Sex had happened.

But she hadn't been proactive in bed or really, in any aspect of her life.

She left that to her twin and let the current push her through life.

"It's beautiful here." It was what they had said to each other before, but that wasn't why she said it. She wasn't trying to jog his memory or have him guess she was really Harley.

What she wanted was far more immediate, far more bold. So she gave him a voracious look, wanting him to understand her intent without her having to spell it out. "I don't want to wait until we get to the room."

His eyes widened as he took in her meaning. Then he tugged her hand, veering right and off behind a hedge, pushing her up against the cool stone of the mansion. "Can't wait, huh? How about I give you a little something to tide you over?"

Something about her back smacking into the mansion had both shocked and aroused Harley. She wanted Cooper to yank her dress down and suck her breasts, and lift her skirt and squeeze her thigh as he thrust into her hard.

She was breathing anxiously, her inner thighs moist, and he wasn't even touching her yet.

Harley had an epiphany.

Yes, she was Cinderella, the quiet girl in the kitchen who watched others live their lives to the fullest.

But what she hadn't realized was that when her Cinderella was let out to the ball, she became a kinky sex goddess.

Harley gripped the front of Cooper's shirt and dragged him to her for a kiss, her free hand stroking his erection through his pants, all rational thought gone. "Yes," she demanded. "Make me come. Now."

CHAPTER

THREE

COOPER had encountered determined women before, but none as unabashedly bossy as Charity.

His career invariably meant women showed him a certain amount of deference, whether he liked it or not. It came with the territory of fame and money. There was always an element of them wanting to secure him, the trophy, and in order to do that, they worked hard to please him. It could be a frustrating experience because he'd met very few women who would stand up to him and call him out or demand what they needed and wanted.

Some men would appreciate that, take advantage of it, but Cooper had always wanted a partner, not a puppet.

Charity had no problem speaking her mind with him.

"Now?" he asked, her edgy orders both arousing him and mildly annoying him. She'd been just hot and cold enough with him that he wasn't sure she was entitled to be calling the shots. He certainly wasn't used to it. "How much time are you giving me? Do I have at least five minutes?"

He slid his hand up under her skirt over smooth, warm skin. Normally he wasn't big on voyeurism, given he was on the public's radar, and it was easy enough to get busted even when you thought you wouldn't be, but he couldn't resist stroking over Charity's panties, unable to back down from her obvious challenge.

She bit his ear in response. Holy shit. That spurred him on to tug the lace aside and slip his finger into her wet heat. And wet she was. Damn. He felt his nostrils flare and his cock harden as he stroked her, her pleasure obvious from the way her eyes rolled back and her breath caught. Her hand landed on him, and her rhythm quickly matched his, while their mouths melted together with an ease, yet ferocity, that was new to Cooper.

He'd kissed a lot of women. But it had been a long time since he'd been this bowled over by a mere mating of his mouth with a woman's.

"As long as it takes," she murmured in his ear, knee shifting so he had better access under her skirt. "But before I freeze to death."

She wasn't playing around. "Is that a challenge?"

"It's an order."

Fuck. No one had ever said that to him. "Yes, ma'am," he said. With the pressure on, he focused entirely on pleasing her, angling his finger deeper inside her and listening for her reactions to his touch so he could adjust accordingly. With his other hand he cupped her breast and angled his body so that if someone happened upon them in the bushes they wouldn't see Charity's body or her face. No one needed to see her orgasm but him. "Does that feel good?" he asked.

"It's alright." But her breathing revealed it was way more than just okay.

He caressed her clitoris with his thumb, enjoying the

way she started to rock onto his touch, her fingers gripping his biceps tightly for support. There were a whole lot of dirty things he wanted to say to her, but he could wait two minutes, not wanting to distract her. Instead, he let his fingers do the talking. He gently pinched the swollen button before taking two fingers deep inside her, thumb still on her clit. She bit her lip, eyes closed, and popped off a tight, quick orgasm.

Cooper gave a smile of satisfaction. It felt good to beat the deadline, to know he had met her demanding challenge. He smoothed her skirt down over her thighs and gave her a rough kiss. Her grip on his arms had relaxed and she opened her eyes.

"Not bad," she said, with a saucy smile.

Cooper gave a laugh. "Oh, really? Glad it didn't totally suck for you." But it did make him want to smack her on the ass, to see her jump, to wipe that smirk off her face and replace it with renewed desire. He wanted her to lose her mind, to beg, to plead for release. At his touch.

There was a thick taste of desire in his mouth, the need to touch her further, to strip her naked, forcing all his muscles to tense.

"I want more," she said, tugging on his hand, actually pushing it back down over her thighs.

The hell with that. He was taking her inside where two could play this game. "Come on." He pulled her off the wall, aware of the goose bumps across her chest and the pink in her cheeks from both arousal and the cool air. "We're going in."

He tugged; she resisted.

"Kiss me first."

He gave a soft laugh. It was a hell of a turn-on, her demanding attitude, and he was going to enjoy battling her for domination. She clearly wanted the last word.

"I'm the one in the driver's seat, sweetheart." He tugged her again and gave her a light smack on the ass to get her moving.

She moved past the bushes and shot him an indignant look over her shoulder. "We're not on the track, Brickman. We do this my way."

As he stared at her long, long legs in that short skirt, her strappy high heels making him imagine what it would be like to take her just in those, he briefly wondered if she was into something he wasn't going to like. He wasn't interested in crawling across the floor. Nor would he let her have that kind of control.

Cooper pulled the door to the inn open and gestured for her to go in. "Think of yourself as the crew chief. You can spot for me and call out hazards, but ultimately the decision is mine whether to go low or high."

But that seemed to amuse her. "We'll see. And don't talk to me in driving analogies. I'm no pit lizard. I don't think it's cute."

Oh, she was definitely pushing her luck.

Cooper was so turned on he wasn't sure he could take another step.

But he was sure he was about to thoroughly enjoy himself.

"Where's your room?" she asked, heading to the elevator without waiting for him.

"Fifth floor." The elevator doors opened and after they were in and he'd pushed the button, Cooper crowded Charity against the wall, staring down at her, trying to read her expression, figure her out.

He'd never met a woman who responded the way she did. She acted almost like she was irritated that she was attracted to him. "Hey," he said, softly, brushing a loose hair back off her temple. He could still walk her to her own room if she wasn't totally into this. He didn't want to be just any guy who could get her off.

Which was stupid. Of course he was just any guy that could get her off. But he wanted to know that she genuinely wanted to do this. It mattered.

Her blue eyes softened. Even her posture changed, her shoulders relaxing. "Yes?"

For a second he was caught off guard. That tone of voice was different. It was comforting, made him want to share his feelings, be honest with her. "You sure about this?" he asked.

But her eyes shuttered then. "Of course. Why wouldn't I be?"

The elevator dinged and opened, but he blocked her exit. "Because you don't seem to like me all that much."

There was a pause, her tongue coming out to lick her bottom lip. Her fingers curled into the front of his shirt, her gaze dropping, breath growing louder. He felt anxiety radiating from her. But then her head rose and she wore a small smile. Her hand touched down to cup his cock and stroke up and down. "What's not to like?"

Maybe if he hadn't been drunk, he would have pulled the plug. Something felt off about what was happening. Like he was going to regret this in the morning.

But he was drunk. She was beautiful. Her hand was rubbing him into a state of arousal no cold shower was going to appease.

So he turned and stuck his hand into the door that was closing again to force it back open. Then he led her off the elevator and to his suite, mouth dry with anticipation.

HARLEY'S heart was racing as she followed Cooper into his suite, both from excitement and from nerves. For a second she had thought he was on to her. Or that he might just send her packing. She was giving him mixed signals, she knew that, and he was clearly picking up on it. The sexual desire, the physical aggressiveness—that was her. But the challenge was trying to sound like Charity, and she didn't necessarily think she was doing that great of a job. She was coming off more as a bipolar bitch than anything else.

So she figured she had him in, committed to sex with her. She was in his suite. There was no reason to keep up the pretense. She was just going to be herself. The Harley she really was. Not the Harley everyone seemed to think she was.

She paused in the doorway as he bent over to turn on a lamp. "Wow," she said, looking around, her inner thighs still moist from the orgasm he'd given her. "This suite is amazing."

"Yeah, it's not bad, huh?" He looked around, giving a little shrug. "I'm not sure what I was expecting, but this is really nice. Very traditional."

It was. A little too fancy for Harley's tastes. It reminded her of going with her mother to the beauty salon in the department store as a kid and having to walk through the crystal and china department, wanting to touch, but afraid to. She set her purse down carefully on an antique writing desk and moved through the living room area with its settees and dark wood furnishings to the windows. The gold drapes were open and there was a sweeping view of the mountain under the moonlight.

"The view is even better from the bedroom."

If that was a ploy to get her closer to the bed, she was willing to pretend otherwise because she didn't want to stop and think and get nervous. Cooper was standing in the doorway to the bedroom and he was peeling his tux jacket off and tossing it on the back of a chair in the sitting area.

His tie had disappeared earlier, so it was easy for him to undo the top two buttons of his dress shirt before moving on to unbutton his sleeves.

He looked comfortable in this suite, in the tux, yet when he tugged the shirt recklessly from his pants and finally got the shirt completely open, he looked even more in his element. Harley had heard enough about Cooper on race days to know he had been raised on a farm with his grandparents for the first ten years of his life until his mother had married a surgeon, who helped put him on the path to financial success. From nothing to everything. It must be a strange divide to cross.

Personally, it put her more at ease, seeing him kick off his dress shoes with the toes on the opposite foot. He carelessly knocked them out of the way as she walked toward him, deciding that she wanted to leave her own shoes on. It wasn't every day she wore heels that high. In fact, she never did, so she wanted to take advantage of the sexy factor and wrap her legs around him, the black strappy heels rising up off the floor each time he thrust into her.

It was that thought that had her erasing the distance between them and flattening her hand on his chest while she raised her mouth toward his, requesting a kiss. He obliged her, his arms wrapping around her and drawing her close. Before she even knew what he was doing, he had the zipper down on the back of her dress.

The man had mad skills. Harley broke the kiss and blinked. He gave her a wicked smile.

"I want to see what I'm touching," he told her.

No complaints from her.

The dress fell down to her hips at his urging, then with a soft whoosh hit the floor. He helped her step out of it and Harley moved around him, giving his nipple a squeeze before pulling her hand off his chest and strolling over to the bed in nothing but her bra and panties and Charity's diva shoes.

He made a strangled sound in the back of his throat and she heard the clink of his belt as he obviously jerked it open. The room was dark, which bolstered Harley's confidence. She turned and sat on the bed, leaning back onto her elbows, legs artfully crossed. Or so she hoped. Lightly swinging her foot up and down, she watched Cooper move past the bed and turn on the lamp in the corner, creating a soft glow across the room. It was perfect lighting. Not so bright she felt self-conscious, but preventing them from fumbling around in a pitch-black bedroom high school style.

"Told you the view was even more amazing in here," he said.

But he wasn't looking out the window. He was looking at her, gaze sweeping up and down the length of her body as he moved in alongside her. Harley sucked in her breath at the predatory gleam of appreciation he was giving her. It was unbelievable that she was here, with him, the man she had secretly cheered on week after week as she watched him on TV. She had wanted him to win because she had wanted him.

Now she had him. At least for a few hours. It was so hard to comprehend that she of all people would be in this position. The result was her emotions were swinging wildly. She vacillated between bravado and shyness and she wasn't sure which she was feeling right at the moment. So she was going to just wait and let him take control.

He didn't disappoint. He leaned over and gave her a long smoldering kiss, his tongue sweeping inside her mouth. Then he put his hands on her knees and forcibly uncrossed her legs, stepping into the space between them. "You're so quiet all of a sudden. Are you calculating ways to torment me?"

Harley sat up all the way, not liking the awkwardness of being on her elbows with her legs now spread. With him standing, he was towering over her and she didn't like it. Scraping her hands across his rock-solid ab muscles, she took the zipper on his pants down.

"I have no idea what you're talking about." She slid his pants down, intrigued by the bulge she was seeing in his briefs. Normally she wasn't one to just go down on a guy, but suddenly his cock was really right in front of her and she wanted to taste him, to hear him groan because of her.

When she sprung him free, he made a sound in the back of his throat. "*That's* what I'm talking about. I know where you're going with this and I'm not sure how I feel about it."

"What do you mean?" Harley studied his erection, lightly running her fingers over the smooth skin. His cock jumped at her touch. It was a pretty penis, she had to say. Good length, pleasing circumference. Not too big, not too small . . . the Goldilocks of cocks. Just right.

She flicked her tongue over the tip, wanting to take it slow, really enjoy the moment.

"I mean, this puts me in the passenger seat and you can guess how I feel about that." His hand slid into her hair gently. "But I think I can make an exception this once."

Her response was to open her mouth and descend onto him, enjoying the low groan he gave. She cupped his balls and stroked down low on his shaft in conjunction with the movement of her mouth. Up and down, she found a slow, steady rhythm, taking him a little deeper each time.

"Damn," he muttered.

It felt amazing to have him by the balls, literally, to be in control and confident in what she was doing. The room was

ERIN McCARTHY

warm, his arms enclosing her as he held her head. He never pushed her forward, never tried to take over the pace, he just held her for his balance, and she enjoyed the connection. He had spread his feet apart and shoved his pants and briefs down to his ankles so there was nothing but Cooper's hard body in front of her.

Wanting to explore a little more of him, she moved her hands to his hips, brushing her fingertips as she went. She continued around with her left hand, discovering that his ass was as tight as she could have imagined, and felt even better. Splaying her palm over him, she pushed him from behind, driving him deeper inside her moist mouth.

God, it felt so good. Her nipples hardened, and she shifted restlessly on the bed, her inner thighs aching. She pulled off him to take a deep breath, lips swollen, grip tight on his ass.

"Look at me," he urged, tilting her head upward.

Harley gazed up the length of Cooper's chest to see him staring down at her intently. "Yes?" she whispered, feeling suddenly shy. Maybe she'd been too aggressive. Her cheeks heated and she started to drop her eyes, but he gripped her chin and forced her to stay still.

"You look so gorgeous right now," he said. "Are you enjoying this or are you just being generous?"

"Oh, I'm enjoying it," she told him sincerely.

His thumb stroked her chin. "Now that's hot. I actually believe you."

"Why would I lie?" she asked. Then immediately realized she was lying about, oh, her identity.

"People lie for a million different reasons." He stepped back a step, dropping his hand. "Now lie down. Let me return the favor."

"You already did, so to speak. Outside." She stayed where she was, running her fingertips over his hips, follow-

44

ing that sexy muscle that acted like an arrow to his erection. His body was fascinating to her. She'd never seen a man so in shape naked before. Well, in person anyway. She had a friend who frequently sent her images of hot guys lounging around naked. Never full frontal, though. But this was real and she was touching him.

"Uh-uh." He put his hand over hers to stop her movement. Then he put his knee on the bed and she had to either move or be crushed by a wall of man muscle. "Down. Now." Then he smiled, a charming grin that had made him a favorite for interviews and guest appearances. "Please?"

Like she could resist that. It was one thing to stand up to him being bossy, another to be demanding when he was so damn cute. "You use that smile to get what you want a lot?" she asked, even as she scooted up on the bed and went back on her elbows again.

"I have no idea what you're talking about," he said, propping one hand on either side of her. "Though my gran always told me if God gave you dimples you're obliged to use them."

Harley laughed softly. "That's a good point. I could just lie here all night and stare at those adorable dimples," she teased.

He pretended to wipe the grin off his face and gave her a mock serious expression. "Hell no. Where my head is going you're not going to see my dimples." His hand cupped her mound and he stroked her over her panties. "But feel free to gaze at them as long as you like when I'm inside you."

Harley wasn't sure what was happening exactly, but it wasn't the hot and fast sexfest she had been anticipating downstairs on his lap and on the terrace. There was something sweet about Cooper. He seemed to be enjoying her company, the companionship, as much as he was anticipating the sex. Thinking back to their earlier conversation, she had to wonder how many people a guy like Cooper had in his life to talk to on a real, honest level. Maybe not many.

"I can do that," she told him with a smile of her own.

Cooper gave her a kiss, the kind that made her toes curl, a sigh escaping her mouth as he pulled away. Then he peeled the straps of her bra down, one at a time, slowly, sensually, and she shivered. As it slid a little on her chest, he kissed a path across the swell of her breast, dipping his tongue down into the cleavage before moving on to the other one. He seemed in no particular hurry, thoroughly exploring, sucking flesh into his mouth gently and slipping his tongue under the fabric in a teasing touch that came close to her nipples but not close enough.

Finally, when she thought she might scream from just lying there while he skimmed over her chest, he reached under her and undid the hook on her bra. Then he pulled it off her with an appreciative sound before folding it in half and setting it on the nightstand. He was tidy with her bra. That struck Harley as oddly adorable. But then the urge to giggle promptly disappeared when he drew her nipple into his mouth and sucked.

"Oh," she said, arching her back. It was about time. And she had already had an orgasm. She couldn't imagine how he was staying so calm and in control. "Cooper."

"Yes?" He flicked his tongue over her. "You have very nice nipples, you know."

"I didn't know that actually." Harley was having trouble breathing and she was fighting the urge to squirm as he slowly teased over her tight buds again and again, like he had hours and zero sense of urgency. Was she supposed to say thank you? No one had ever complimented her nipples before. Men usually just took them for granted and so did she. "Thanks."

Cooper gave a soft laugh, his warm breath tickling over her bare skin. He started to move lower, nuzzling her as he went down. "Did you want to ask me something?"

She wanted to know why he was torturing her. She wanted to know if he knew what he was doing to her. But she knew the answer to both. He knew exactly what he was doing and he wanted her limp and begging. The driver's seat. He was definitely in it.

He took her panties down, setting them next to her bra, and without any hesitation whatsoever took her with his mouth. She wasn't even sure what he was doing, logistically, she just knew he seemed to be everywhere all at once and his touch was light, warm, moist, and she was suddenly moaning, fingers reaching for his head to grip.

Then just as suddenly he stopped. He looked up at her, dimples on display. "You had a question, darlin'?"

She shook her head. "No. Don't stop. Please."

"Happy to oblige." Cooper stroked up and down her labia with both thumbs before sliding his tongue slowly up and down, up and down, in a torturous trail.

The lack of sex in the last year had her easy to please, definitely, but it was more than that. It was the way Cooper was focusing on her with such easy confidence, the way he caught on to her reactions and increased his tempo when her fingers dug harder into his hair. He was listening to her body, to her breathing, to her soft moans of encouragement, and pleasuring her with generosity and serious skill.

Just when she thought she couldn't enjoy it any more, he slipped his thumb inside and pressed her in the perfect spot with unerring accuracy. Harley came hard, the orgasm hitting her without warning, her legs jerking as her body found release a second time. It was far more intense than the one outside and she cried out louder than she meant to, or was comfortable with. But she couldn't stop it, nor could she stop herself from holding on to his head for dear life, grinding his tongue further into her.

He probably couldn't breathe. He was probably right then and there smothering to death in her girl bits, yet she didn't release him until the last wave of pleasure subsided. When she did finally free him from the death grip, she immediately relaxed on the bed and murmured an apology, throat raw from her moans, mouth still hot with desire. "Sorry, sorry."

"Sorry for what?" he asked, wiping his mouth as he moved up the length of her. He reached over to the nightstand and opened the drawer. He pulled out a condom.

He kept condoms in the hotel nightstand? That was bewildering. "For holding your head prisoner."

Cooper grinned as he rolled the condom on. "I appreciate the enthusiasm. And I can handle a little roughhousing."

"I didn't mean to be rough. I just . . ." Couldn't control herself around him. The words died on her lips. She wasn't sure what she wanted to say to him, share with him. This wasn't a night for growing intimacy or fostering trust or a friendship. This was about sex, plain and simple.

"Never mind," she retracted lamely.

He paused, his hands on her knees. "Charity."

Oh, God, he was calling her by her sister's name. She had almost completely forgotten that he thought she was her twin. She sucked in a breath, heart racing, goose bumps rising on her bare flesh. She could smell him, a mix of cologne and soap and the sharp tang of her own arousal on him, and she felt the enormity of what she had done.

She had to tell him the truth.

She had to confess.

She opened her mouth.

"Shh," he said, leaning over and giving her a soft, delicate kiss that shocked her in its sweetness. "If it feels right, don't apologize. Just enjoy it."

Before she could respond, he lifted her leg and rested it on his hip. Then he thrust and the truth was smothered under a soft groan as the feel of him buried inside her had her biting her lip.

Later. She could tell him later.

After she finished rolling her eyes back into her head.

CHAPTER
FOUR

COOPER hadn't come to this wedding expecting anything. He certainly hadn't planned on finding himself buried inside a woman who was as puzzling as she was intriguing. He swallowed hard, his cock throbbing, as he watched her squirm beneath him, making soft cries of distress and arousal. Her lack of pretension excited him, made him mad to tease her, then please her, alternately.

This wasn't how he'd seen this going down. He had expected a bossy, dominant tug-of-war between himself and Charity, tearing clothes and sex against the wall. That would have been fun. But this was better.

He started to move, pulling almost all the way out of her, before sinking back into her moist heat. Hair falling in his eyes, he concentrated on gauging her reaction, testing how fast she wanted him, how deep, a slow slide or a quick thrust, wanting to make sure she eked out every bit of pleasure from him she could. That mattered to him, that it was worth her time to be with him. He was going to enjoy it, no matter what, that was clear given the way he was already straining to hold back an orgasm, his balls tight, mouth thick with desire.

But there was something about her eyes . . . something that spoke of trust.

It shouldn't be there.

There was absolutely no reason for it, no way he had earned it.

Yet it was, and so he felt compelled to live up to her obvious expectations.

It brought out a tenderness in him he hadn't expected to feel. Not for the balls-to-the-wall woman who had put him in his place on the dance floor.

Her breathing was getting anxious, her fingers digging into his back. He could feel the tight squeeze of her body onto his cock, forcing his eyes closed for a split second before he regained control. She was so close to an orgasm he thrust harder, amazed that she could come again so quickly. Amazed, and damn grateful. There was nothing sexier than a woman who got off on his cock.

Her eyes were glassy, the skin above her chest flushed a bright pink, her breasts giving a hot little bounce with each movement he made. Her leg moved restlessly across his ass, and her head shifted back and forth. Cooper shifted his fingers into her hair and held her still. Those blue eyes widened in surprise as he leaned down, wanting to kiss her.

But right as he was about to brush his lips over hers, she came with a soft cry.

He swallowed it, sweeping his tongue inside her mouth as she arched toward him in an explosive orgasm. It sent him into his own release as he stopped holding back and finished strong, his forehead resting on hers.

"Oh, God," she breathed.

"Just call me Cooper," he said with a grin, lifting his

head to snag a lungful of air and shake his hair back off his face.

She gave a soft laugh, which caused her inner muscles to clamp onto him a little tighter.

"Damn," he groaned. Kissing her softly, he pulled out and rolled onto his back, wiping his forehead before carefully rolling the condom off and tossing it on the wrapper on the nightstand.

"Why did you have condoms in the nightstand?" she asked, shifting onto her side, her fingers brushing over his lip.

It didn't sound accusatory, just curious. Immediately she lowered her eyelashes. "Sorry, that was tacky."

He shrugged. It didn't offend him. "I think I have a touch of OCD. I unpack when I travel because I don't like living out of a suitcase. Maybe it comes from being on the road so much. There were condoms in my travel bag, so, well, they went into the nightstand."

"It probably saves time in the long run. Twenty minutes to unpack, no time spent digging around."

"Exactly." He was stupidly pleased that she got it. His friends tended to rib him about his quirks and lack of clutter.

"I'm the same way. I like everything to have a place. My sister is the total opposite. She can never find anything and her room looks like a unit on *Storage Wars*."

That surprised him. "Harley is that messy? For some reason I didn't expect that." Though he wasn't sure why. It wasn't like he knew either one of them, really.

"Oh!" She pursed her lips. "Yeah. I mean, I guess I shouldn't criticize. To each their own, right?"

Her reaction was a little puzzling, but Cooper yawned, the whiskey and the sex catching up with him. He pulled a blanket up over their naked bodies and wrapped an arm around Charity. "Uh-huh."

Her breasts were pushed up against him, her lush body warm, her hair tickling his shoulder. Cooper felt his eyelids growing heavy, so he squeezed her arm and murmured, "Kiss me."

HARLEY did as Cooper asked, her throat tight with fear as she leaned over and gave him a quick kiss. His eyes were closed and his breathing was evening out. He was seconds from sleep and she was wide awake. God, she couldn't believe she had started talking about her sister. She'd been so relaxed, so satisfied that she had just spoken without thinking.

That had almost been a complete and total disaster. Naked was not the time to tell someone you were a big fat liar and not the person they thought you were. There probably wasn't any good time for that, but this certainly was not the optimal time.

It hadn't seemed like such a big deal when she had been flirting with Cooper in the bar at the wedding reception. Now, it felt . . . oppressive. Wrong. It shattered the easy contentment she'd immediately had after he pulled out of her. The sex had been amazing. Very easy, very much focused on her. Nothing kinky or unnerving, like Charity's last lover, who had asked for a rim job five minutes into the proceedings. Harley could not have dealt with that kind of expectation.

Cooper wasn't selfish or rough. He was nice, thoughtful. Sexy.

He'd made her feel important. Special.

She stared up at the ceiling, his arm heavy on hers. She

didn't want to regret this. But neither could she hang around and pretend nothing was wrong. If she stayed, she had to tell him the truth. Or she could leave. There were no other options. She couldn't stay and sleep in his arms, then wake up together, share a room service breakfast, have some morning sex, and not feel like a total jerk if she kept her secret. If she told him, likely he would just ask her to leave. It was that simple.

Reasoning with herself, she turned and studied him sleeping. She'd gotten what she had wanted. More than she had expected. All she had wanted was the fantasy sprung to life for just a brief moment in time. It wasn't like a man like Cooper Brickman would want to date her, as herself or as Charity. It was a wedding hookup, nothing more, and it had been a damn good one.

It was her little secret, something to look back on and smile.

She couldn't stay and not be honest, and she couldn't stay and want something more. Which she would. She knew herself well enough to know that the longer she was with him, the more deep kisses and charming smiles he gave her, the more she was going to wish that it could be beyond one night. She was going to wish she truly were Cinderella with her Prince Charming, and that was really just ludicrous.

Wanting that was about as senseless as a screen door on a submarine.

It felt like a decision, so she eased herself out from under Cooper's arm, heart racing at the thought of him waking up. She wanted to touch him one last time, but she settled for one final glance at his strong jaw, his messy hair, his amazing muscular chest exposed above the blanket. Crawling out of the bed, she grabbed her panties and stepped into them. She grabbed the bra but didn't bother to put it on. It would take too much wiggling. It was a challenge to zip her dress back up, but she managed to get it almost the entire way up.

Her purse was in the living room, and she checked inside to make sure she had her room key. Next to her lipstick was a tiny box of chocolates that served as an elegant wedding favor. She tried to shove her bra in, but it wouldn't fit with the chocolates. Abandoning the bra wasn't practical, but it was easy to replace and she wanted the tiny box as a reminder of the night, and she was not about to stroll down the hotel hallway with her bra in her hand. There was a writing desk and she dropped her bra there. On the pad of paper she wrote in her left-slanting bubbly handwriting, "Thanks for a great time." Since she couldn't sign her name, she put a smiley face instead.

Lame? Probably. But she couldn't just sneak out without saying *something*. Yet she couldn't give him a phone number without telling him she wasn't Charity, and who was to say he would want to call her anyway? What they had done had clearly been intended to be a one-night stand, and this way she was leaving it as is. Uncomplicated.

Padding barefoot across the room, she slipped out into the hall and put her shoes back on as she eased the door shut carefully behind her. With a sigh, she headed back to her shared room.

Charity was awake, watching TV, still wearing Harley's dress under the covers of her bed.

"Hey," Harley said. "How did the rest of the reception go?"

"It was fine," Charity said, looking like it was anything but. "It turns out that no matter what dress I'm wearing, Jeff Sterling just doesn't like me. Hard truth, but there it is."

"Oh, I'm sorry." Harley tossed her purse on the dresser and bent over to pull off her shoes. "Maybe he's dating someone. Or maybe he prefers women his own age."

Charity rolled her eyes. "Please. What man prefers

women his own age? None, that's who. But whatever. How was your night?"

"It was . . . good." If that was the right word for mind-blowing sex with the man you'd only seen on TV before. "We went out on the terrace and talked."

"You talked?" Her twin's eyebrows shot up. "You had a hot guy in a remote location and you talked? Please tell me you at least made out with him."

For some reason, Harley shook her head. "Not really. Just a few kisses." Why the hell was she lying to her sister?

Maybe because Charity would spend the next hour grilling her for every last detail and she didn't want to share. She wanted it to be private. "I don't think he is really attracted to me that way."

Which was true. He wasn't attracted to her, Harley. He was attracted to Charity. Ack. What a mess. But she didn't want to think about it that way. It was what it was—a few short hours of amazing.

"Well, I think this was an epic fail." Charity clicked the TV off and pulled the covers up to her chin. "I'm going to sleep."

"In my dress?" Harley went into the bathroom to change into her PJs.

"Yes."

Charity was obviously disappointed and determined to be obstinate, so Harley dropped it. The dress could be dry-cleaned, and on the list of things she gave a shit about, it wasn't in the top ten.

"You didn't tell him I was you, did you?" Charity called from the room.

Harley paused and poked her head out the door. "No. Why?" She could still feel the weight of Cooper over her body, his erection sliding in and out. Did Charity suspect anything?

"Because since nothing happened it's pointless to tell either one of them. We'll just look like idiots. Night." Charity flopped over toward the window.

Right. Idiots.

COOPER turned his head to check two things when he woke up. One, if he was hungover. Two, if he was alone.

The answer was yes to both.

He groaned and forced himself to sit up, his mouth dry. He knew from experience that the longer he lingered in bed, the worse his head would pound. He needed coffee pronto. In the bathroom, he looked for signs that Charity had been there at all, but there were none. She must have taken off the minute he had fallen asleep.

Or maybe he had imagined the whole thing. He had been pretty damn buzzed.

But he didn't usually have dreams that vivid. He distinctly recalled the feel of her smooth skin, the soft look in her glassy eyes, the way he had felt oddly protective of her and intent on driving her wild. She had come three times and he remembered the taste, touch, and sound of each one.

No, sex with Charity was real. It had happened. She had just left him in bed and taken off without a good-bye.

That was a bit of a lowering realization. He hadn't had that happen often in the last fifteen years. In fact, it had never happened. His celebrity status shielded him from rejection and a lot of dating awkwardness because most women wanted to stick around to please him. He had never felt that so obviously as he did strolling into the living room of his elegant suite naked, face swollen, mouth dry, in search of the coffeemaker, all alone.

It was not a good feeling. It made him wonder if she hadn't enjoyed herself as much as he'd thought.

Charity's bra was lying on the desk. He remembered putting it on the nightstand in the bedroom, so he wasn't sure why it would be out in the living room. Running a finger over the black lace, he debated calling her room in the inn to tell her she'd forgotten it. It seemed a little weird to call to tell her he had her bra, but then again, he thought most women seemed possessive about their undergarments. The shit was expensive, he was well aware, having bought more than his fair share of it over the years.

Then he saw the note lying next to it. She must have set the bra down to write, then forgotten it. It just said, "Thanks for a great time." Smiley face. That was it? No phone number? No xo? No signature?

Wow.

That felt like a complete and total dismissal.

Grabbing the bra, Cooper went and fumbled with the coffeemaker. He didn't understand how it worked and after two frustrated minutes, he pounded his fist on the top of it and gave up, thoroughly irritated.

Charity had left, leaving her bra like some kind of sexual Cinderella.

His phone was ringing urgently next to his room key. It was his housekeeper, Rosa.

"Yeah?" he said, not caring that he sounded grumpy. He was grumpy. He wanted coffee.

"A llama is here. In your house. Your sister ordered it."

"What? A *llama*? Are you fucking kidding me?" How was that even possible?

"Mary Jane says you told her she could have a pet. Why would you let her buy a llama?"

Every inch of his head and face throbbed. "I meant a dog. A cat. A goddamn gerbil. Jesus fucking Christ, how could this happen?"

The minute the words were out of his mouth, he knew he

had offended Rosa, a devout Catholic. She sucked in her breath and he could practically feel the air around her stirring as she gave the sign of the cross. "Don't you take the name of the Lord in vain, Mr. Big Shot, or I'll quit. I may quit anyway. There's a llama in the mudroom! *No es bueno.*"

Cooper rubbed his forehead with the heel of his hand. "I'm sorry for swearing, Rosa. Can you have MJ put it in the garage? And just keep the door closed until I get there. I'll call you when I'm on the road. Thanks, Rosa. I'm sorry for the inconvenience." *Don't quit. Please, God, don't let her quit.*

Her response was to say something in Spanish he didn't understand and hang up on him. Cooper picked up the hotel phone and ordered coffee and eggs. They would be there by the time he was out of the shower. Then he called Eve Monroe. She didn't pick up, but he left her a message.

"Hey, Eve, can you give me a call back? I want the number for your friend Harley. I need a nanny for MJ now before she ends up doing something illegal." Something needed to change and he wanted to stabilize his sister's life before she totally went off the rails.

Cooper wanted Charity's number, too, but he wasn't going to ask for it. If she wanted him to have it, she would have written it down for him. No, she was clearly satisfied with just one night, and he was going to have to be, too.

Which felt really unsatisfying.

CHAPTER
FIVE

"I can't believe I'm doing this," Harley told Charity. "This can only end in disaster."

She put her cup of coffee down. She already had the jitters. She did not need to caffeinate.

Charity was spooning the innards out of her grapefruit, wearing black pants and a cute sweater, ready to head to her job as a handler at the racetrack. "I don't know what you're so worked up about. You need this job, and I'm sure the salary will be way higher than any other nanny gig in town. It's Cooper Brickman. He makes bank."

Yes, it was Cooper Brickman. That was the problem. It had been two months since the wedding reception. Two months since she had stupidly indulged in sex with him as her twin sister. Two months of repeated phone messages from Cooper to her, the real her, asking her to reconsider the job offer he'd made, as he'd been unable to get a nanny to stay for any length of time.

Which meant his sister was a nightmare.

It had been easy enough to call him back and leave polite messages in return declining the offer. Until her job had disappeared when her family had been transferred to Seattle. She could probably find another job fairly quickly, but it might takes weeks, involve multiple kids, and pay next to nothing.

"He offered me almost six figures."

A piece of grapefruit fell out of Charity's mouth. "Are you kidding me? Oh, my God. If you don't take this job I will pretend I'm you and take it, and I don't even like kids. That is crazy good money."

It was. She'd been unable to resist it, frankly.

More to the point, she'd been unable to resist the idea of being around Cooper, even if it was just a little bit. Even though he would never know the truth.

But she was nervous, because she didn't like to lie, and saying she was Charity had been a big one. Even her sister didn't know the full scope of what had happened that night, and Harley had never kept something that huge from her twin. It was stressing her out totally.

"I feel like I'm going to puke."

"Why are you so nervous? You've been a nanny for five years. This is only one kid and she's half grown already. You're overqualified."

"You know I have a crush on Cooper. I can't help it," Harley said, her palms sweating at the memory of his tongue sliding over her body. "I'm going to embarrass myself by drooling."

Her sister shrugged. "He is a smexy bastard, isn't he? But also a total tool. Keep in mind he's probably slept with hundreds of women. You don't want to be a notch on his bedpost. Hell, that bedpost is probably whittled down to a stick at this point."

Wonderful. "I thought you wanted me to hook up with

him at the wedding. I did kiss him. As you, you know." And then had done a whole lot more than kiss him, but she wasn't prepared to admit that.

"So? He doesn't know that so what difference does that make? As for me suggesting you sleep with him, that was then. This is now. You're talking a serious humongous paycheck here. That is better than a couple of hours flat on your back for Cooper the Cunny King Brickman."

Harley's cheeks got hot. "The *what*?"

"That's what they call him. Seems he has no issue going down on a woman." Charity licked her spoon as a visual aid.

No. No, he didn't. Harley suddenly felt like she had been scammed. That his moves had all been choreographed, designed to force a woman to let down her guard. Make her feel like his focus was totally on her, and her alone.

Only to hear that she was one of a cast of thousands. "Thanks for the pep talk, this has been very helpful."

"You're welcome. Good luck!" Charity called, voice sunny.

Luck? It wasn't luck she needed. What she really needed was someone to slap some sense into her. Then she needed to stay the hell away from Cooper Brickman.

SHE didn't.

Standing on the front step of Cooper's mansion, ringing his doorbell, she debated whether it was too late to call him and cancel the interview. She was torn between desperately wanting to see him and not wanting to see him ever again. Swallowing hard, she glanced around the circular driveway, her little sedan looking a bit like a bumper car next to several enormous Ford-tough trucks and a glamorous fountain that sat quiet in the January cold. Shivering against the wind, she stuck her hands in her pockets and peered through the glass side panel next to the giant mahogany double doors.

Then was immediately sorry she did when she made eye contact with a woman. A tall, blond, beautiful woman. Harley jerked back, cheeks burning, as the door was flung open.

"Can I help you?" the woman asked, buttoning up a stylish trench coat, pulling leather gloves onto her hands.

Who the hell was this chick?

"I have an appointment for an interview with Mr. Brickman," Harley said, her breath misting in front of her.

"Oh, are you the new maid?" The woman eyed her up and down. "Thank God, because that old heifer he has now is so annoying. She had the balls to tell me I should take my makeup off before bed because I ruined the pillowcase." She stood back and gestured for Harley to come in. "Like seriously? Go screw yourself, old lady. What, like I'm going to let Cooper see me without makeup? Please." She gave a laugh.

Oh, my God. This was a girlfriend. Cooper had a girlfriend. In the two months since they'd slept together he'd made no effort whatsoever to get in touch with her as Charity, and he had started dating a blonde who looked like a sexy Swedish lawyer who modeled on the weekends. She had not been expecting a girlfriend. Harley stepped in, not wearing makeup, her hair pulled back in a ponytail, feeling plain. Stunned.

Why, she wasn't sure. What had she thought? That Cooper would be pining for her?

The woman swept her eyes over Harley then seemed to realize she wasn't speaking to a fellow cosmetics lover.

"Anyway, Cooper is still in bed. I'll text him and let him

know you're here. I have to run to an appointment with my personal trainer. Maybe I'll see you around." She stuck her hand out. "I'm Holly."

"Harley." She shook her hand and gave a wan smile as Holly left, commanding her phone to "text Coop." When the door closed, Harley shivered, silence settling over her in the giant foyer.

She was right on time for her eight a.m. appointment with Cooper. She rocked on her heels and wondered what she was supposed to do if he didn't respond to Holly's text and come downstairs. She wondered how much time Holly spent there, and if she could stand to be in the same house with her, knowing she was in Cooper's bed. Where Harley wanted to be again.

Damn it. This was such a bad idea.

She had a lump in her throat the size of a grapefruit and was debating just fleeing and texting him an apology. Telling him she had another job or a fatal illness. Like idiot-itis.

"Harley?"

Too late. Shitballs. She swung her gaze up to the top of the marble staircase. Seriously, who had marble stairs? But that thought quickly vanished when she saw Cooper, jogging down them, jeans unbuttoned and sliding down his hips, his black briefs clearly visible. His shirt was in his hand, leaving his chest bare, washboard abs defined and obvious even from twenty feet away. His hair was a little longer than before, falling in his eyes, and as he came closer, she saw the five-o'clock shadow and a slumberous look in his eyes. He was gorgeous. Sexy. Sleepy.

Baby Jesus in the cradle, he looked even better than she remembered and she had a damn good memory. But seeing him there, bare chested, made her all too aware of how she had touched every inch of him. Had taken him inside her. Had orgasmed at the hands, or tongue, of the so-called

Cunny King. Her whole body felt like she'd gotten a wicked sunburn. It itched and burned, and her skin felt too tight.

"Hi," she said inanely, followed by a closed-lipped smile.

"Sorry to keep you waiting. I think I must have hit the 'go to hell' button on my alarm when it went off this morning." He grinned as he reached the bottom step and stopped to pull his shirt on over his head.

"No problem." It made her feel better to have his chest covered, but she still felt ludicrous standing there in her coat. She wasn't sure what to wear, so she had gone for a cute dress with a sweater and knee-length riding boots. Now she felt overlayered and overheated next to him, especially considering he seemed in no hurry to zip his pants.

"How have you been? It's really good to see you." He stood in front of her and smiled.

She'd been better. Though he sounded genuine. She wanted to believe him. But now she wasn't sure what to believe. Her tongue seemed superglued to the roof of her mouth, but she forced herself to speak. "I'm fine. You?"

He shrugged. "I guess I can't complain. At least the llama is gone now."

"The llama?"

"Mary Jane ordered one online."

"Oh. Wow." Harley was suddenly afraid for what the nanny position entailed. She had no zookeeping skills.

He ran his fingers through his hair and yawned. "Come on into the kitchen. I need some coffee or I won't be able to think." He gestured for her to follow.

They went left and toward the back of the house, and the foyer suddenly opened into a massive two-story family room and gourmet kitchen. It was Italian influenced, with the marble floor continuing, and the kitchen featuring dark cabinets on bottom, white on top, with lots of wood-carved details and a massive mosaic in white, black, and pops of yellow behind the six-burner stove. It was a more formal environment than she would have expected and it was sparkly clean, most of the marble countertops free of appliances and décor.

The house and the man didn't seem to go together.

Then again, she remembered him carefully folding her bra and panties on the nightstand. His explanation for the placement of the condoms. It made sense his home would be pristine.

"Have a seat," Cooper said, as he went over to the coffeemaker and studied it for a second, like he wasn't well versed in using it.

Harley perched at the kitchen island on one of eight stools. Yes, eight. This was a big-ass house. Her last employer had been a cardiologist, but that wealth couldn't even touch the millions Cooper likely had. She thought about the salary he had offered her and wondered if it was just a little bit sketchy to be taking money from a man she had slept with.

"How the hell does this work?" Cooper asked, pushing buttons and lifting the lid. "This is new."

For some reason the fact that he didn't know how to use the coffeemaker made her feel better. Like they were on more equal footing.

The appliance was the same kind of single-serve model that she had, so she told him, "You put the cup in, then close the lid. When the light comes on you push the brew button."

He kept trying to put the cup in wrong and Harley got back off the stool and went over and gestured. "No, the other way." It was a mistake to get close to him. She could smell his scent, and it was familiar. The memory of him leaning over her, kissing her, assaulted her.

Cooper handed it to her. "Will you do it for me?" He gave her a charming smile. "Pretty please?"

He'd said something very similar the night she had slept with him. It made her both tense and aroused. Steeling herself against that grin, Harley took the cup and efficiently popped it in the machine and hit the brew button. A second later his mug was filling with coffee.

"Ah, thank you," he said. "You're an angel of mercy. Here, let me take your coat. Would you like some coffee, too? Of course, you'll have to make it, but feel free. God, what a douchebag of a host I am."

He moved behind her and slid her heavy coat down her shoulders before she could protest or do it herself. His body was too damn close for comfort. Harley shivered. The hell with all of this.

She wanted this over, and she sure wasn't there for coffee and a casual chat. She was there for the job and the gratuitous ogling. "I'm fine, thanks. So what exactly are your needs with Mary Jane? Besides llama purchase prevention."

"Right down to business, huh?" He hung her coat on the back of a stool and reached for his mug, now filled to the brim with coffee. He took a sip. "Ah. Nectar of the gods. Okay, so I don't know what you remember of what we talked about at the wedding."

Everything. She remembered everything. Every word. Every touch. "You told me you were worried about your sister."

He nodded. "I am. She's been allowed to run totally wild by our mother. She's been living here with me for the past six months. She is homeschooling herself and spending huge amounts of time on the Internet running her own gossip and fashion blog and doing God only knows what else.

Well, ordering llamas for one thing. Can you believe a llama costs a grand?"

Harley felt her eyebrows head north. She couldn't help it. How did a twelve-year-old get a thousand dollars to spend on a farm animal? "What happened to the two previous nannies you hired?"

"They didn't stay long. From what I understand, Mary Jane is not difficult exactly. She doesn't argue. She just basically ignores them." He made a face. "I'm not selling this job, am I?"

Not so much. "I can't guarantee I can get any better results."

"Maybe not. But you're younger. Maybe she'll see you more as a friend than as a cop." Cooper leaned back on the countertop. "I tried to take her on the road with me when this season started up, but she got busted in a casino in Vegas. It wasn't good. I think she's bored. I'm okay with the whole blogging thing, but I want to make sure she's actually getting an education, too."

"What is her blog about?" That intrigued Harley, that a twelve-year-old had that kind of initiative. She had run her own blog for book lovers for a while and she knew it was time-consuming and complicated.

He shrugged. "My assistant said it's a fashion and gossip blog."

Caution flag on the track. "But you've never looked at it?"

"No."

Harley pulled out her phone. "Do you know what it's called?"

"No." Now he looked a little sheepish. "My assistant does."

She wasn't trying to be judgmental; it just seemed like common sense that if he was concerned about how Mary

Jane was spending her time, he should see what she was posting online. "If you are interested in hiring me, I think we need to explore her content."

"Now I'm curious," he said, pulling his own phone out of his pocket. He hit some buttons and put it to his ear. "Hey. Yeah, what is the link for MJ's blog? I want to take a look at it."

There was a pause then he said, "I know. I know. Got it. Two o'clock." Another pause. "Can it wait until I've had more coffee? I'm interviewing for the nanny position. I know. God. Fine. Thank you." He hung up and rolled his eyes. "Cami is a total nag but she keeps me from being at the wrong place at the wrong time."

His phone dinged. "Here's the link." He pulled the blog up and started reading, pinching the screen to make it bigger. His eyes widened. "Holy crap."

That didn't sound good. "What? What's on there?"

Cooper held the screen out for her to see. "My baby sister is like the TMZ of the racing world. Holy hell. How does she know any of this stuff?"

Harley read the top post out loud. It had a time stamp of 11:47 p.m. the night before. "Love at First Fetish Club? Sources suggest that Eve Monroe, the rookie truck series driver and former PR rep for the Monroe brothers, was at the local fetish club, The Wet Spot, last Saturday night, when she ran into her brother-in-law, Rhett Ford. In the company of her book club friends including Shawn Hamby, of Hamby Speedway and former teen racing star, Eve didn't stay long, but it was long enough for Rhett and Shawn to apply for a marriage license four days later. What happens in the fetish club goes to the courthouse. YOLO, people. You only live once, so you might as well tie the knot. Or tie each other up."

"She's *twelve*?" Harley was horrified. She hadn't even

known what a fetish club was at twenty. At twelve, she'd still been playing with Barbies. Though on reflection, she seemed to remember she and Charity had their Barbies working as strippers from time to time. It had seemed glamorous and apropos given that Barbie's feet were perennially in pole position. But a fetish club? No way.

"It doesn't seem natural, does it? Did you know anything about Eve going to a fetish club? How do you think MJ would know about that?"

Well. The thing was. "Uh, I was there. It was a book club field trip. We were just curious, honestly." Why did she feel like she needed to explain her actions? She was a grown woman.

Cooper looked aghast. "*You* were at a fetish club?"

Okay, so it was a stretch, but geez, did he have to sound so damn skeptical? She wasn't a sexual amoeba, despite her inability to flirt. "It tied in to our book club selection. That's not the point!"

"No, I don't suppose it is." Though suddenly he was looking at her differently, like she might pull a crop out of her boot and whip him. Which reminded her of how she'd dragged him off into the bushes and demanded he make her come. And how he had. In mere minutes.

Which was totally irrelevant. "I have no idea how Mary Jane could know something like that. I guess I could see how she could find out about the marriage license if she checks public records frequently, though I can't imagine why she would do that. But I really don't see how she would know about the club."

Cooper was scrolling down through the blog on his phone. "She has an unnatural preoccupation with track romances. My God. This is disturbing. And she knows I've been sleeping with Holly. That was last week's entry." He shuddered and tossed his phone on the kitchen counter like he couldn't stomach the sight of it anymore. "She's like the best of her father and the worst of her mother all in one."

Harley decided then and there she was going to start following Mary Jane's blog. Both to learn more about her and also to learn more about Cooper. Not that she needed or wanted a reminder that the man was sleeping with a gorgeous and confident woman.

"How so?"

"Her father was a charming and smart businessman, with a gift for words. Our mother is a gossip and a manipulator." He drained his coffee mug and put his fist to his chest, like he had a sudden pain there.

"Listen to this—'Cooper Brickman has a new FWB, Holly, who has a hobby of dating stock car drivers.'"

Cooper looked at Harley blankly. "What does that even mean, FWB?"

"Friends with benefits." She cleared her throat. "Have you been hiding Holly from Mary Jane?"

"I thought I was. I don't want her aware of every woman I date. It just seems like that's not right, you know? But it seems you can't hide anything from MJ."

There was one thing that was likely a secret from Mary Jane. Not even the tween gossip could know that Harley was the one who had slept with Cooper at the McCordle wedding. Or that she was also the woman who was currently jealous. He hadn't come right out and said that Holly was his girlfriend, but no matter who she was, she was getting Cooper's attention and for that reason, Harley hated her on principle.

"So I take it your mom is still out of town?"

"Yep. Now she and what's-his-nut are in Italy. Must be nice."

Harley winced, feeling sorry for his sister. "Where's her father? Out of the picture completely?"

"He passed away five years ago. My mother married Bud Rawlings, of Rawlings Racing, when he was seventy and she was forty, when she turned up pregnant with MJ. He loved his daughter and I think MJ still misses him a lot. I try, honestly I do, but I don't know what the hell I'm doing. But lucky her, I'm all she's really got."

It was better than nothing, and yet again, she was impressed with him. He might have no clue how to handle his sister, but the worry over her showed Harley he was a decent guy who just wanted to do right by Mary Jane. "It's obvious you care about her. That means a lot to a child."

"What's also obvious is that I am not qualified to do this. She's posting about fetish clubs. Oh, my God. What am I supposed to do?"

Harley had no idea. She was used to watching toddlers and preschoolers. "I think there needs to be some fact gathering first. Make sure you truly know everything that she is doing. Then you can formulate a conclusion and/or a plan."

He put the mug down. "You're right. It's just that I want her to be happy and productive, but most of all I want her safe, you know? I feel like she could be doing God only knows what and talking to God only knows who. It's scary out there online and she's just a kid, despite what she'll tell you."

Harley felt her heart soften. She wanted to soothe his anxiety with a soft kiss. She wondered how he would react to that. "You're right to be concerned, and ten years from now she'll be glad you were looking out for her." She leaned against the island and studied him. "So I'm assuming the job description includes giving you full disclosure on her activities? Or at least the pertinent highlights?"

Damn it. She was going to accept this position. How could she not? Even though she looked at Cooper and wanted nothing more than a hotel suite sex repeat. Even though he had no idea the nanny he wanted to hire had begged him to make her come. Even though the thought of him cuddling with Holly Hobbie made her want to hurl.

All of that was irrelevant as she listened to him speak about his sister. This little girl, who wasn't such a little girl, needed her. Harley wasn't sure she was any more qualified than Cooper was to handle Mary Jane, but she needed to try.

Besides, she was clearly just a masochist.

He nodded. "You know what life is like for a professional driver. It's a time-consuming job, and this is, of course, a live-in position."

Oh, sweet Jesus. She'd known that in theory, but hearing him say it out loud made her girl parts flutter like a hummingbird.

"You will have your own suite and you can use the kitchen whenever you want. No one is really ever in here except Rosa, my housekeeper, anyway. I'm only here two days a week, so you should feel free to make yourself totally at home. You can have friends over in the evenings, but I have to ask that you don't have any overnight guests, if you know what I mean. You can have Mondays and Tuesdays off when I'm home."

It sounded horrible. Like nothing any sane person would ever agree to, frankly. Living in her one-night stand's house as virtual strangers? Fully responsible for a preteen? Never have a date or sex on anything other than a Monday or Tuesday? Not that the men were beating down Harley's door for dates, but the possibility was there. Could be there.

"Basically, MJ needs a tutor, a driver, someone to guide her morally, give her affection, and help mold her into a proper Southern girl."

"So you want me to be her mother?" Harley asked, wanting to truly understand what was expected of her. It was what she'd taken away from their conversation the night of the wedding, and this interview confirmed that.

Cooper looked startled. "Well, shit, I never thought about it that way. I guess you're right. Damn, that's a lot to ask of you." He sighed. "Maybe we can just start with Internet cop? I don't want my baby sister looking at porn or talking to men old enough to be her father."

He rubbed his temples and turned back to the coffee-maker. "Why does this damn thing only give me one cup of coffee at a time? Jesus. Who only drinks one cup?" He jammed his mug back under the machine and frowned at it.

Harley nudged around him and took out the used cup of grounds and replaced it with a fresh one from the tower of flavors sitting next to the coffeemaker. She added more water and hit brew. "I'll take the job if you're officially offering."

"Really?" He sounded almost as surprised as she felt. "That's fantastic."

Harley nodded.

"Is the salary I mentioned acceptable?" he asked. "I could probably go a little higher, but I need to discuss it with my financial advisor."

It was more money than she'd made in the last three years combined with her previous family, and they'd had two kids under the age of five. "I think that is more than generous." She swallowed, wishing she had made herself a cup of coffee. Her mouth was dry. "I'm sure we'll need to discuss Mary Jane's personal expenses and what her allowance is."

"If you can keep it under fifty grand a year, I'm happy. Let's not get ridiculous."

Harley blinked. Oh, he was already ridiculous. That was a lot of cheddar.

But Cooper Brickman was thirty-five years old and had been driving professionally since age seventeen. After an eighteen-year career he probably had more money than he knew what to do with.

Every middle-class bone in her body balked, and she decided she was going to teach Mary Jane a thing or two about budgets. The girl never needed to know how much she was allowed to spend. And someone was about to have her llama-buying button taken away from her.

"I don't think we'll need that much," she said. "I was thinking more in terms of enrichment activities like museums and foreign films."

Cooper made a face. "I'm going to have to take away her credit cards, aren't I?"

Harley nodded. "That's a great place to start. I think all purchases should have to be made out of her allowance, which we can decide on together after I do some number crunching."

"She's going to be pissed at me." He looked very uncomfortable with that idea.

"Probably. But you know it's the right thing to do. She needs attention, structure. Not designer clothes and farm animals." No one needed farm animals, in Harley's opinion, unless you were a goddamn farmer. It was craziness.

"I want to be her buddy. I don't want her to hate me." He looked miserable at the thought.

"No one wants to be hated," she told him, feeling sympathy for him. That was why she was such a people pleaser. Or doormat, according to Charity. She liked to be liked. She wasn't a parent, but even as a nanny she'd learned there were days she was going to be less popular than others because she had to be the boss. "But Cooper, I can't be Mary Jane's mother. I can only be a mentor, a friend. I'll keep her safe and provide structure and compassion. But you have to be her mother, father, brother, all in one. And that means some days she's going to hate you."

He sighed. "God help us all. I'm going to fuck this up."

It killed her to see him so worried. Harley touched his arm. "Hey. You'll do fine. You're a good man."

He gave her a small smile. "How do you know? Maybe I'm awful."

She knew that he was an unselfish lover. And that he clearly loved his sister. "Just the fact that you worry about Mary Jane tells me what I need to know."

Cooper was looking at her with an odd look on his face.

Harley wrinkled her nose, wondering if she had something hanging out of it. She couldn't have anything in her teeth. She hadn't eaten breakfast. Her nipples couldn't be showing because she was wearing a cable-knit sweater. Did he know something? Could he tell she had lied to him? Immediately, all the ground she had gained feeling comfortable around him disappeared. She put her arms across her chest and crossed her ankles. "When would you like me to start?"

"Huh? Oh." His face cleared and he said, "If you can start tomorrow, that would be fantastic. And how about I have Cami arrange a mover for you? They can do all your packing and get everything over here into your room in a matter of a few hours."

Just like that. He could make one phone call and magically she would be living with him. As his nanny. Probably about eight hundred miles away from his bedroom, which was a good thing. She did not want to hear the sounds of passion between him and his friend with benefits.

"That should be fine." He was paying her such a generous salary she could pay her portion of the rent until Charity found a new roommate. "I don't have a lot of stuff."

"Perfect. I'll give your number to Cami and she can

76

work with you on it, and all the paperwork for tax purposes." Cooper reached for his second cup of coffee. His voice shifted, became curious. "So, uh, what was at that fetish club?"

Oh, no he didn't. "What do you mean?" she hedged.

"Did you . . . participate?"

Say what? Harley felt her cheeks burn with embarrassment. Why was he asking her that? And why did he look so intrigued? From her personal experience with him he had liked the idea of her being bossy, but in the end he had taken over control. So it wasn't like he had a dominatrix fantasy. Besides, she was Harley, and he didn't see her that way.

"I have no idea what you mean," she said. Because what else was she supposed to say? But her face gave her away. Her cheeks flushed with heat.

Cooper laughed. "I'll take that as a yes." He winked.

"What? No. No. No. I did not participate. It wasn't really that big of a deal. It was just some people doing . . . things. But everyone still had clothes on and I just stood at the bar and watched." That didn't sound right either. She didn't make a habit of being a voyeur.

But he just chucked her under the chin.

Like she was five.

"Relax, I was just teasing you. I can't imagine you going hard-core."

Of course he couldn't. He saw her as maternal and stable, after all.

He was convinced she was thinking about kittens and unicorns and sunshine.

"Was your sister there?" he asked, as an afterthought.

Damn it. "Yes."

He smiled, and it was a naughty smile. The smile of a man who knows something. He was thinking about sex with her, remembering it. She could tell.

It was flattering to see his positive reaction to the memory, knowing he wouldn't allow his expression to be so honest if he thought he was looking at his hookup.

But while it got her more than a little hot under the collar and made her want to prove to him that she wasn't always the sensible twin, she knew that she already had. He just didn't know it.

That was called a cruel irony.

"Tell her I said hi."

As if. Harley just nodded. "Sure."

Crossing her arms, she promised herself she would suppress the urge to show Cooper a thing or two about hardcore.

CHAPTER
SIX

HI? Tell her he said hi? Smooth. Butter would be fucking jealous of him, that's how smooth he was. Not. Cooper mentally kicked himself in the ass. He sounded like he was fourteen and desperate besides. He wondered if Harley knew about him and Charity. He assumed she did, because in his experience women in general shared everything with each other, and they were twins. So it was highly likely she knew. Which also meant she knew why Charity had chosen to not leave her number when she had bolted from the suite and keep it at just a simple wedding hookup.

That night had popped up in his thoughts multiple times over the past few months and he wasn't sure why he couldn't shake it. It wasn't like he hadn't had his fair share of one-night stands. Hell, he was sleeping with Holly and she was attentive without being clingy, the perfect no-strings-attached relationship. Yet when he least expected it, the look Charity had given him during sex, her eyes huge, glassy, rose up in his mind, and it was distracting. Frustrating.

Now here he was with Harley, who he had fixated on as some kind of savior to his MJ problems, given how calmly she had discussed his sister with him at the wedding. And yet he was suddenly having inappropriate thoughts about her. It wasn't right. He knew it wasn't right.

He was hiring her to be maternal toward his sister, and he had slept with her sister. It was totally dog-in-the-dirt of him to be conjuring up sexual images of her, but he couldn't help it. Maybe it was because she looked exactly like Charity.

Or maybe it was the good-girl thing. It was the fact that she looked at him and expressed no interest whatsoever in him as a man. She didn't flirt and the few times they had interacted in person, she had mostly stared at him, like she didn't dare to say what she was thinking. He couldn't figure out what was going on in her head, and damn it, that was hot.

Besides, he kept picturing her standing at a fetish club, watching everyone with big, serious eyes, her arousal growing and growing . . .

It was driving him insane, the idea that she was a shy girl who would shatter beneath him in bed, which made him feel like the creepiest douchebag in Charlotte. He'd never had a twin fantasy, so what gave? Why were the McLain twins doing such a number on him?

"So when do I get to meet Mary Jane?" she asked.

Oh, yeah. His sister. "Right now if you're good with it."

She nodded. "I think that's a good idea."

"Okay, cool." Cooper picked up his phone and started to text MJ.

Harley raised an eyebrow. It was a look of complete disapproval. "No?" he asked.

She slowly shook her head. "You need to go get her in person."

If anyone else had told him that, he would have resented the criticism. But there was something about Harley that was gentle enough he didn't feel like she was judging. She was just suggesting. And she was right. Having someone to guide his actions with his sister was exactly what he needed.

"Give me five minutes," he said. "And please help yourself to some coffee, or there is bottled water and juice in the fridge."

With a fortifying sip of his coffee he went off in pursuit of his sister, up the marble staircase. His feet were cold and he wished he'd put socks on. The marble wasn't a cozy stone, but he liked that it gave the feeling of cleanliness to his house. It was tidy, sparkling, and he dug that. It was the aftereffect of growing up on a farm. There had been altogether too much dirt and chaos in his early childhood. Not that he wasn't grateful to his grandparents, because they'd raised him well, with lots of love, but he had an aversion to clutter now.

Knocking on MJ's bedroom door, he checked his phone for e-mails from his team, his boss, and his assistant, and he checked the predicted weather for the weekend. It was Daytona prep and he couldn't afford to be distracted. He was grateful Harley could start right away; otherwise he was going to worry about his sister all week.

The door opened a crack and his sister's head appeared. "How may I help you?"

His sister was blond and willowy, her eyes still too large for her head, neck too long, as she maneuvered her way through puberty. She was a beautiful girl, and she looked older than she actually was, which apparently was thirteen, not twelve, as she had informed him a few days earlier. He'd lost a year somewhere in there. Until six months ago he had never lived with MJ and he knew exactly nothing about raising kids. He didn't even really remember a whole lot about being thirteen himself.

He did remember, however, that he would not have said, "How may I help you?" at that age. MJ was a forty-year-old in a tween's body, who occasionally threw the temper tantrums of a three-year-old. It was confusing as hell and he was still learning his way around her. He hedged on telling her about Harley. "I'm leaving in a few hours. Going to the track, then heading to Arizona. I'll be back Sunday night."

"Got it." Mary Jane stayed behind her door, which was now only cracked, and looked at him like she couldn't wait for him to leave. "Good luck doing what you do."

"Thank you." Resisting the urge to force the door open, he asked, "Do you have everything you need?" He understood the need for privacy, but she acted like she'd been cutting rocks of crack in there.

"For the most part." Her expression turned calculating. "So what do you think of Eve Monroe's brother-in-law Rhett Ford marrying Shawn Hamby of Hamby Speedway? Rather scandalous, don't you think?"

"Uh . . ." Cooper was so caught off guard he just stared at her for a second. He was surprised she was bringing it up to him directly. "I actually didn't even know they got married. But why is two people getting hitched scandalous?" He went way back with Eve and her brothers, but he didn't really know Eve's husband, Nolan, all that well. While he had known Shawn in his late teens, he hadn't seen much of her in recent years. Not to mention he didn't pay much attention to gossip.

"Because they met on a Saturday and married the following Friday. What do you think that is all about?"

Insanity. That was what it was. "I have no idea." He took a stab in the dark because she clearly wanted an answer and he wanted to foster some sort of friendship with MJ. "Love at first sight?"

"You don't really believe in that, do you? I mean, we all know that is really lust."

"We do?" Well, he did, but damn it, how did she know that?

She scoffed. "Mom has been in love at first sight about twenty times. You're not going to decide to marry a chick on Friday you met the Saturday before, are you?"

So that's what this was about. She didn't want him bringing a wife home randomly and disrupting her life yet again. "No, of course not. You have my word on that."

"You're not going to marry Holly either, are you? She's all wrong for you."

It really made him uncomfortable that his sister knew about Holly. She had only stayed over twice, maybe three times, and Cooper had thought they were being discreet, when clearly MJ had been on to him. Awkward. But he wasn't going to pretend not to know what she was talking about. He was not going to be having Holly over anymore, that was for damn sure. "No, I have no plans to marry Holly."

"Good. She's put together, I'll give her that, and classy enough, but she's still just a pit lizard. She'll take any driver she can get her hands on. Did you know she has dated Ty McCordle and Elec Monroe in the past?"

"Uh . . ." Cooper wasn't sure what to say to that, and the truth was, he had no idea who Holly had dated before him.

"But that was years ago and she's been on a driver dry spell, so I imagine she is looking to really hook her claws into you."

Who the hell was his sister? My God, she was like Nancy Grace in a child's body. Enough was enough.

"I appreciate the warning. But I am not discussing my

personal life with you. And I'm going to suggest you find a hobby, because your knowledge of track romances is frightening."

She made a face at him. "Knowledge is power, Cooper."

Whatever the hell that meant. "Come on downstairs. Your new nanny is here."

"Really? Must we persist in this farce? I don't need a babysitter."

She clearly did, but he wasn't going to have this argument yet again. "You're lucky I don't have you doing chores like Grandma had me doing at your age. I had to muck out the stalls."

At the same time, it made him sad to consider how he had been taught values and hard work by his grandparents, and MJ was being taught what? She didn't even remember their grandfather, who had passed away ten years earlier, and their grandmother was in an assisted-living facility Cooper paid for. His sister had grown up in a world of sterile privilege.

"I would have cleaned up after the llama if you had let me keep him."

They were back to the fucking llama. "You know what? Let's lay down some ground rules for the next six months. If you can stay out of trouble and cut back your spending, we can bring the llama back." Didn't all kids need rewards? Goals?

"It won't be Serge, though. It will never be Serge again."

"You named the llama Serge?" That amused him for some reason. "We can find Serge, I'm sure. Cami knows where he went." He nudged her door open with his foot. "Come on. Downstairs."

MJ was still in her pajamas, but she did comply, sniffing contemptuously at him. She pushed her hair back and he noticed her nails were done, with little bows on each one. He wondered when she had done that. It scared him to think how little he knew about her and what she did with her time. Cooper slung his arm around her, wanting to be close to her. "You want to go out to breakfast?"

"Really?" She sounded surprised. "Okay. Pancakes?"

"Sure. We can do that."

Harley was waiting patiently at the island as they entered the kitchen and Cooper muttered under his breath, "Be nice to her, okay?"

"I'm always nice," Mary Jane said.

The truth was, he couldn't argue with that. She was never rude. She just did precisely what she wanted all the time.

Harley stayed sitting, which Cooper thought was interesting. She smiled at Mary Jane and said hello, but she didn't start in immediately with questions and false interest the way the others had.

"Have I seen you before?" Mary Jane asked her. "You look familiar."

"No."

His sister went into the fridge and pulled out the orange juice. "It will come to me. I know I know you."

God, he hoped it wouldn't click since he did not want his sister to know her new nanny had been in a fetish club. Who would have ever guessed Harley would have done that? Or that his sister would know? What a disaster.

"Harley will be moving in tomorrow," he said.

"Got it." MJ reached for a glass. "She moves in, you leave. Though I've told you like nine million times, I don't need a babysitter."

"I won't be here to babysit you," Harley said.

The hell she wouldn't.

"I'm here to babysit your brother, in truth."

Um . . .

Mary Jane looked as startled as he felt. "What do you mean?" she asked.

Yes, what did she mean? If Harley was going to do anything to him, it sure in the hell wasn't going to be handing him a curfew.

"I mean that Cooper doesn't know anything about acting as a guardian and I'm here to both teach him and make sure he's doing it right. He wants to make sure you're happy and healthy and he doesn't necessarily know how to do that."

Cooper wasn't sure about this strategy. He was assuming it was a strategy. But it made him sound like a moron. "It's not like I have *no* idea at all," he hedged.

Harley shot him a look of admonishment.

MJ looked intrigued. "That's true. He means well, but I don't think he understands teenagers."

"He's also standing right next to the both of you," Cooper said, annoyed. "And I do so understand teenagers. I was one, you know."

"Like a million years ago."

Now that was more than he could tolerate. "Mary Jane, I am not that old. I was a teenager only a few years ago."

But Harley made an incredulous expression. "Sure, when Kurt Cobain was still alive and before Al Gore invented the Internet."

Smart-ass.

Mary Jane let out a laugh.

"You don't even know what any of that means," he told her, exasperated. "So what are you laughing about?"

"I do so. Kurt Cobain was the lead singer of the grunge band Nirvana, and he committed suicide. Al Gore is a Democrat who ran for president who made some statement claiming he created the information superhighway." Smug, she drank her juice.

She was well informed, he'd give her that. "Y'all are ganging up on me. I'm not sure how I feel about this."

But actually, despite the reminder that he was damn near ancient, he was relieved. Excited, even. Mary Jane was responding well to Harley. Plus his new nanny was right—he needed to be trained, not his sister. He needed to learn the ropes of parenting and how to set boundaries for her.

It wasn't going to be an easy road, but he felt hopeful for the first time since MJ had moved in with him. He might not fuck this up yet.

"You're tough," Harley said with a sweet and somehow sexy smile. "You can handle it."

Then again, speaking of fucking . . .

"Thanks. I think."

"Cooper doesn't get told no by women very often," MJ said to Harley. "I would be careful if I were you."

But Harley just gave her a smile. "I may look sweet, but I can handle your brother."

Cooper cleared his throat. That statement was meant to be totally innocent, he was sure, yet somehow he felt it in his dick. Damn. Not good.

"I'm going to head out now if that's okay." She nodded, looking to him for confirmation. "I have a lot to do."

He nodded. "Sure. I'll have Cami call you this afternoon after everything is set up."

"Thanks." She gave him a look he couldn't decipher at all. Pulling her coat off the chair, she slipped into the sleeves.

"I'll walk you out." He put his hand on the small of her back to guide her, but Harley stepped away, out of his reach.

"See you soon," she said with a smile at his front door.

Cooper was distracted by how sweetly attractive she was. How kind her eyes were. "Thanks, Harley. Seriously. For everything. I know you didn't want to lose your other job, but I feel lucky that you did."

"I guess we'll see. Hopefully I can help." With that she left, the door closing on her, a cold draft sweeping over him.

Back in the kitchen, Mary Jane looked at him, her eyes wide and knowing. Far too mature for her age. "Mom's never coming back, is she?"

Be honest, that was what he needed to do. Harley was right. It didn't do his relationship with MJ any good to pretend. "I don't know, kid. I really don't know." But there was one thing he was certain about. "But even if she does, I want you to stay here." He loved his brilliant and quirky sister. He wanted her to know she was wanted.

"Really?" She looked young suddenly. Vulnerable, her face pale.

For the first time ever he realized how big and sterile and underused his kitchen was. How often was he even in there? Couple of times a week? The counter his skinny sister was leaning on looked very cold.

He threw his arm around her and kissed the top of her head. "Really."

The corner of her mouth turned up before she caught herself and went sour again. "Okay. Cool. I can deal with that."

That felt better than a win at Daytona.

AFTER only three days, Harley was finding her new job way more interesting than she had anticipated. Cooper in no way had prepared her for how unique of a thirteen-year-old Mary Jane was. She had the entrepreneurial spirit of a young Donald Trump and the style savvy of an A-list actress. Harley found her equal parts fascinating and terrifying. She did nothing without a purpose, and from the luxury of her large bedroom in Cooper's house, she was running a successful gossip blog and planning her future social media domination. She already had paid advertisers and was hoping to secure herself a spot with a major fashion magazine as a consultant.

The business plan she had shown Harley was astonishing and brilliant for a thirteen-year-old. Harley was impressed with her. Mary Jane had also shown herself to be witty and incredibly talented at reading people. It had been an easy transition for both of them, she thought, because they clicked and shared a mutual respect for each other.

"So what do you think of my brother?" Mary Jane asked, digging through her closet, for what Harley didn't know.

It felt like a trick question. They hadn't spoken much about Mary Jane's family in the past few days. Mostly they had focused on the blog, establishing a routine, homeschool work, and discussing Mary Jane's personal finances, which were impressive for a teen. Mary Jane had already told her she had a million-dollar trust fund inheritance from her father that her mother couldn't touch. Plus Cooper let her buy whatever she wanted, and her father's former stepson, Jeff Sterling, gave her extravagant birthday and Christmas gifts, so she had no financial concerns. On that score, Harley had to say she admired Mary Jane. Instead of sitting back and taking advantage of her inherited wealth, she wanted to build her own fortune and her own success. Though she definitely did overspend. Harley was planning to give Cooper a suggested budget to enforce when he got back.

Harley sat on the zebra-striped chaise in Mary Jane's room and tucked her feet under her. "I think your brother is trying very hard to make sure you're happy."

"I don't mean that." Mary Jane came and sat down next to her and inspected her manicure. "I know that. I mean, he's totally a nice guy. Mom ditched me with him and he like barely knows me, because he's so much older than me and he travels all the time. But he's trying to be some kind of brother and father figure, which is cool. That's not the point, though."

Harley was pretty sure she didn't want to know what the point was. "Are you glad to be here with Cooper? Or would you rather be with your mom?"

It was a personal question and Harley didn't want to push, but the one thing she absolutely thought was lacking in Mary Jane's life was a confidant. The girl was smart, shrewd, savvy. But she had no real-life friends, and despite their differences, Harley had always had a built-in best friend in Charity. She could tell her sister anything and her twin would always be there for her, no questions asked. Which was part of the reason she felt so guilty for not admitting she had slept with Cooper as Charity. Harley wanted to give Mary Jane the opportunity to share if she wanted to.

"Are you kidding? Living with my mother is a nightmare. How many boy toys does one woman need? Seriously."

One was more than Harley had ever had. "I don't have an answer for that. I'm not exactly a boy-toy kind of woman." Though maybe that was what she needed, a man who had to do what she said. Though that wasn't really her. She'd found her inner dominatrix with Cooper but then had quickly handed control back over to him. So multiple boy toys boggled the mind.

"What kind of woman are you?"

Desperate. Undersexed. In lust with Mary Jane's brother. "I'm a plain Jane. You're Mary Jane. I'm Plain Jane."

"Is that true or is that an excuse?"

My God, it was like being with a therapist. Sometimes Harley wondered who the adult in the room was. "Call it what you want. I don't like being flashy. That's not me."

"Then we're back to the same question. Who are you?"

Mary Jane stretched out her legs next to Harley and reached over to finger her *H* necklace. "This is pretty."

Harley put her arm around Mary Jane's slim shoulder and pulled her in for a hug. "I'm maternal. I like kids and books and flowers. Boring, huh?"

Mary Jane seemed to like the physical contact. She leaned in to Harley. But then she looked up and gave her a coy smile. "Do you like guys?"

"Some of them."

"What do you look for in a man?"

She knew what she should look for. "Stability. Integrity."

"What? Are you cray-cray?" Mary Jane asked. "You make it sound like you're building a bridge or something. You have to feel like squishy inside about somebody, too. Right?"

Except that men who made Harley feel squishy inside were usually all wrong for her. Because squishy was actually lust, and it seemed that brazen, cocky guys would light her fire, and they probably would. But they would also overpower her personality-wise. She knew that. Like Cooper. It was one thing to be with him under the guise of her twin. It was another to hold her own as herself.

It was the ultimate irony that she was wildly attracted to men who would be all wrong for her.

"Squishy only takes you so far if he's a tool. I want a man who I can trust not to fool around. Who comes home every night. Who is going to think I'm exciting, even when I'm boring, you know what I mean?"

Someone *not* Cooper. That was what she meant. He would definitely find her boring. That had been proven at the wedding reception. Though if they weren't talking about an actual relationship, Cooper was her type, obviously. The type that she had always secretly fantasized about tearing the sheets up with while she was waiting for Mr. Right to come along.

Who was taking his sweet-ass time, she might add.

But hey, she'd gotten her fantasy and she should be grateful for that one night, not wishing she could have part two.

"Do you think I'll ever have a boyfriend?" Mary Jane asked.

It was one of the few times Harley had heard her actually sound like she was thirteen. She sounded vulnerable and melancholy. Harley hugged her closer.

"I can one hundred percent guarantee that."

Mary Jane was silent for a second, then reverted right back to mini adult. "Should I call my bookie on that one if you're guaranteeing it?" she said.

"You have a bookie?" Harley was almost sure she was joking. But not entirely. "Please tell me you're joking."

"It's not illegal because it's an international broker. Don't worry about it."

She had a feeling that was akin to having lifeboats on the *Titanic*. It might save a lucky few, but the rest were going to go down with the ship.

"Tell me you don't bet on races."

Mary Jane stayed silent.

"Why aren't you saying anything?"

"Because you told me not to tell you I'm betting on races."

Harley winced. "Oh, God. Does your brother know?"

"I don't know. If he does he hasn't said anything. I used to play online poker, but that's illegal in the U.S. now and I haven't been able to figure out how to redirect my server internationally so it's untraceable, so I quit. It's not worth prison time, even though I do like to win."

That was reassuring. Not. "Good call."

"Thanks. Can we go to Daytona next weekend? I'm sick of freezing my butt off and I need some color. I've lost my summer tan."

"We can't just go to Daytona on five days' notice."

"Why not?" Mary Jane blinked innocently up at her.

Hell if she knew. It just seemed wrong. "I don't think your brother would approve."

"Lame. I can call him and ask him. He has a condo there, you know."

No, she didn't know that. As much as she wanted to have an argument against a trip, she didn't really have one. "I suppose the decision is his to make, not mine."

"What, like you don't want to go to Florida?"

Not really. Somehow it made her feel like a Cooper Brickman groupie. Like she was following him. Which was stupid. She was Mary Jane's paid companion and she would likely never see him the whole weekend. And it was damn cold in Charlotte this winter. "Yes, I would like to go to Florida."

"Sweet. Let's do it."

"Fine. I'll ask him tonight at dinner."

"You're going to dinner with my brother?"

Harley laughed. "No. I mean dinner, here, at home."

"We don't do that." Mary Jane looked disturbed by the very concept.

"You do now. When Cooper gets home we're going to the grocery store, then cooking dinner."

"OMG. Does he know?" Mary Jane looked horrified and giddy all at the same time.

"No. But he said he is willing to make some changes."

"Yeah, but grocery shopping? I don't think he's ever been in the grocery store." Mary Jane tilted her head. "Actually, I don't think *I've* ever been in the grocery store. Not for real. Just when my mom ran in for wine."

Oh, Lord. This was going to be interesting then. "It will be fun." Or hell, Harley wasn't sure. But it just seemed like if she was going to bring brother and sister together, they should break bread at the same table when Cooper was home.

"What would you like to have for dinner?" Harley asked Mary Jane.

"I get to pick?"

"Yes."

Mary Jane stood up and went for her tablet. "Sweet. I'm going to look up recipes. Usually I eat a cheese sandwich for dinner. Or cereal."

No wonder Mary Jane looked like she would disappear if she turned sideways. "Do you like pasta? That's an easy place to start when you haven't cooked before."

"I want something with goat cheese. I heart goat cheese. I would marry it if I could."

Harley laughed. "Okay then. But I understand. I feel that way about bell peppers."

Mary Jane tapped and swiped, her eyes lighting up. "OMG, quesadillas. That's what we'll make. I'm calling Cooper to tell him and to ask him about Daytona."

Mary Jane looked so excited that Harley didn't stop her. Cooper was probably either traveling or busy, but if he truly wanted to make changes he was going to have to expect that he would be hearing from Mary Jane or her frequently. In fact, she'd been firing e-mails off at him on a regular basis whenever a thought came to her.

It was a fair bet that Cooper had no idea what he was getting into when he'd hired her.

And he didn't even know the full truth.

But when it came to nannying, Harley was in charge.

CHAPTER
SEVEN

COOPER was on his plane, headed back from Arizona. Normally he would just stay out west and move on to Florida for the following week's race, but with MJ, he wanted to go back home for three days. It was reassuring to have Harley there now, but he still found himself worrying about his sister. In fact, he was almost more worried now that he was processing the barrage of information coming from Harley. She'd found out more about the kid in three days than Cooper could in three months. Hell, three years.

Harley had been quiet both times he'd met her in person, but in e-mail, she was anything but reserved. She was methodical, organized, and very detailed in telling him what she and Mary Jane were doing each day, along with school reports, a screen shot of MJ's Internet history, and suggestions for limiting her spending to an allowance and monitoring her social networking. It made his goddamn head spin, but he appreciated the effort she was putting into the job and frankly, he did not have the time to accomplish on his own what she was doing.

He would call it an early success except for the fact that he couldn't stop picturing Harley in a fetish club. It just seemed so damned intriguing. The more he tried to tamp down those thoughts, the more they seemed to pop up, along with frequent erections. The only saving grace was that he was busy working, but he was worried the affliction was only going to get worse at home. There he would be moving around his bedroom, his bathroom, aware that she was under the same roof. His plan was to avoid her at home, but that didn't stop him from visualizing her naked, which was nuts.

Harley was a nice woman, taking care of his sister, and speaking of sisters, he had slept with hers, to his great satisfaction. So why was he suddenly hot for Harley? It was crazy.

She stood up to him just as much as Charity had, if not more. Sure, it was different in that she was telling it like it was with MJ, but it was still a turn-on that she had the nerve to do it. She'd been e-mailing him nonstop for three days.

Scheduled Mary Jane's physical and eye exam for next Monday. Will you be picking her up or should we meet you there?

I can't go that day. Business meeting.

It's not optional. I'm sure you can reschedule your appointment.

He had practically felt the whip coming through the computer and cracking him. Damn.

Then she hit him with the guilt.

Your sister needs to know she is a priority to someone. Anyone.

Fuck. He knew she was right. So he was going to the goddamn doctor's appointment, which sounded like all kinds of awful. He didn't want to talk about his sister's physical development because they were dangerously close to the whole puberty issue. He would rather have his car dropped on him than think about her as a future woman. About *changes*. The thought made his stomach sour.

No one else would have been able to get him to go, but Harley had a certain gift. Her brilliance with MJ only increased his attraction to her, which was just a kick in the nuts. He didn't like having carnal thoughts about a woman he could not touch. Yet knowing she was under his roof, and was Charity's twin, made him realize that he had to end things with Holly because she was one woman too many to have occupying his thoughts. He already had a set of sexy twins stuck in his head. He couldn't juggle Holly as well. It wasn't fair to her or good for his sanity.

Dialing Holly, he shifted in his seat, glad he had a private moment on the plane to make the call. Traveling alone was one of the few times he had any privacy.

"Hello, darling," Holly said cheerfully. "I didn't expect to hear from you tonight."

"Well, I wanted to talk to you about something."

"Uh-oh." Her tone immediately changed to wary.

Cooper tried to think of the easiest way to put it. "Holly, I just don't think the timing is right for us to be involved." The last thing he needed to do was add someone like Holly into his already complicated life.

Despite what Mary Jane seemed to think, he wasn't now and had never been a player. He didn't take any sort of pleasure in dating multiple women or stringing a woman along. He was always very honest about his intentions and, he had to admit, he chose women who didn't expect a commitment from him, because he couldn't realistically give it. Sure, a lot of his fellow drivers were married and made it work, but Cooper didn't want to be in love and never able to see his wife. Nor did he expect a woman to trot around the country with him. He had always figured once he retired he would get down to the business of finding a woman to spend the rest of his life with and together having some junior drivers to raise.

It had never felt wrong to indulge in a fling or two here and there with consenting women who knew full well what the outcome was going to be.

But what Harley had said had gotten under his skin, he had to admit. He needed to focus on MJ, and for the first time in a long time he felt uneasy with his reputation. He didn't want his sister thinking he treated relationships as casually as their mother did.

All of it hurt his head.

"I see," Holly said. "So this is a dismissal? I didn't expect a ring, but I thought I'd have a better run than three sleepovers."

"It's not you, it's me." My God, had he really just said that? He hadn't said something that insulting since he was a rookie. "I mean, having the responsibility of my sister is just about all I can handle right now. She saw you leaving a few weeks back and that makes me uncomfortable. What kind of an example am I setting, you know?"

"I can respect that. I don't like it, but I can respect it."

"Thanks." This was where he usually offered the women he ended things with some sort of consolation prize, like track tickets or use of his condos in Daytona or Vegas for a weekend, but it felt wrong. Like he was buying her off. Their involvement had really been short and sweet and doing anything other than saying a friendly good-bye smacked of guilt.

"This doesn't have anything to do with your new nanny, does it? I know a lot of men like that shy act."

"What?" He felt offended that she was even mentioning Harley. "I don't know what you're talking about. She's here to take care of my sister, not me."

"She might have an ulterior motive."

That made Cooper laugh as he reached for his sweet tea, seat belt cutting him across the gut. "Yeah, not this girl." Harley couldn't get away from him fast enough. "You take care of yourself, Holly."

"Thanks, you, too."

He had barely hung up when his phone rang again. It was MJ.

"Hey, what's up?" She rarely called him, so it immediately gave him cause for concern. "Everything okay?"

"Yes. Can Harley and I come to Daytona next weekend? I need to work on my tan. You can get us tickets to the race."

"What?" She had never asked to attend one of his races. Or to travel with him. In fact, she had complained about it when he had previously dragged her on the road with him. It made him feel suspicious, though he wasn't sure why. "Let me talk to Harley."

"Why?"

"Because I want to talk to Harley," he said firmly.

"Fine. God. Chill."

Cooper sighed. His face hurt to go along with his head hurting.

"Hello?"

"Harley, why does MJ want to come to Florida? Is there something I need to know?"

"No. She's just tired of winter, that's all. I also think she would like to be on site to have some material for her blog. If it's an inconvenience or an unnecessary expense, you can say no. I told her the decision was yours to make."

Even though it seemed like he should say no, he couldn't

actually think of any reason why. Harley would be with her and they could stay at his condo with him. It might actually be nice to have the company.

But there was the problem. How distracting would it be to have Harley in his condo all weekend?

Uh, very.

But if his sister wanted to spend time with him, he just couldn't bring himself to say no. "It's fine. Y'all can come down."

"I'm sure Mary Jane will be thrilled." There was a rustling sound, and then she said, "He said yes."

MJ gave a whoop in the background, which made him laugh. "I'll have Cami make the arrangements."

"What time will you be home?" Harley asked.

"In an hour or so. Why?" No one ever asked him that. It felt odd. Good. Like someone gave a shit where he was and what he was doing.

"Mary Jane is going to learn her way around the kitchen, and she has her heart set on goat cheese quesadillas. I just wanted to gauge what time we should plan on serving dinner."

Cooper didn't even know what to make of that. "MJ is cooking? For real?"

"Sure. It's a great skill to have. So we'll wait for you and then go to the grocery store together."

Hold up. "You want me to go to the grocery store?" Why did the thought of that seem both intriguing and horrifying?

"Of course. Mary Jane says you don't know how to cook either, so it will be a good lesson for both of you." She seemed totally confident in his inability to say no to her or his sister.

She was right. "I don't have to wear an apron, do I?"

Harley laughed. "No. Only if you want to."

"I don't." Though he wouldn't mind seeing Harley in one. Surprisingly, he didn't even mean naked. He just found the idea of her, in his kitchen, attractive.

God, he was fucked up in the head.

He said good-bye and hung up the phone, taking a long sip of his sweet tea, shaking his head at himself. Was he having some kind of midlife crisis?

Whatever it was, it sucked.

WHEN Cooper got home, he dropped his bag in his room, then went down to his sister's room and knocked. He could hear music and laughter coming from inside, but Mary Jane didn't answer. Knocking again, louder, he shuffled impatiently. Damn it. He was hungry and the idea of having to spend nine million hours to shop and cook made him surly. He wanted to order a meat-lover's pizza instead.

But he had agreed to the plan, so his sister needed to get a move on. Cautiously, in case MJ was indecent, he slowly opened the door, scanning the room.

What he saw about made his eyes bug out of his head. Harley and Mary Jane were dancing. Or rather, Mary Jane was jumping around and fist-pumping. Harley was doing some kind of hip maneuver with her legs bent, a drop-it-down-low move that made Cooper forget how to speak. He'd seen a stripper or two in his day, and many a woman who liked to think she had the moves, but Harley really did. Her hips moved independently of the rest of her and it did really quality things to her ass, her jeans cupping her tightly.

There was some serious rhythm happening and it stunned him stupid.

But Mary Jane saw him, the smile falling off her face as she twirled, doing some weird shoulder move.

"Ah!" she screamed. "What are you doing, Cooper? Get

out!" She came charging at him, and she shoved at his chest. "Get out!"

Harley had also spun around and was giving him a look of pure mortification. He smiled at her and tried to stop his sister from shoving him backward, but Mary Jane shrieked again. "Fine. Okay. Christ." He passed the threshold to her room and let her partially shut the door, but he stuck his boot in it so she couldn't close it all the way. "I knocked."

"So wait for an answer."

"You didn't answer."

"Because I didn't hear you. Duh."

"I texted you, too. Duh." Cooper rolled his eyes right back at her. "Can I talk to Harley, by the way?" Not because he wanted to see her or anything. But because he wanted to see her. Damn. "I'm starving, let's go."

Mary Jane glanced behind her. "She went to the bathroom, I think. She's not here."

And he was born in the fucking cabbage patch. "I just saw her!"

MJ just stared at him.

"Fine. Can you tell her I'm home and ready to go? By the way, is everything going okay? You like her?"

"Yeah, it's fine." Her face was expressionless.

Cooper sighed. "Swell." He tried to push the door open.

"Hey! What are you doing?"

"I would like a hello hug."

Her eyes widened. "That's weird."

It was weird for them, but Cooper felt the need for direct contact with MJ. "Yeah, well, get over it. Give me a hug. I hate that I have to leave all the time. I'm glad to be home." It had never bothered him much to travel every week because he loved his job, but now he had a reason to be sorry he was gone so much.

"Fine." MJ opened the door and stepped out into the hallway, pulling the door shut behind her. She was in black yoga pants and a tight hot-pink T-shirt.

"Do you have a meth lab in there or what?" he teased, still wondering about the freakish need for privacy.

"Please." She rolled her eyes. "Meth is for common criminals."

Not reassuring.

"Let's get this over with." MJ reached up and put her arms around his middle and gave him a quick hug. "Happy?"

"Ecstatic." He rolled his eyes right back at her. "I'll wait for you both downstairs. In five minutes we'd better be pulling out of the driveway or I'm ordering a pizza."

"No!" MJ rushed back into her room and slammed the door shut in his face.

Nice.

HARLEY was mortified Cooper had seen her dancing. It wasn't just sway-to-the-music dancing, it had been down-to-the-ground, booty-grind, open-your-hips kind of dancing. She wasn't even sure what had possessed her to give in to the egging on of a thirteen-year-old, but when Mary Jane had expressed disbelief that she'd been on the dance team in high school, Harley had felt the need to prove she had rhythm.

So now her boss had seen her drop it low, and she was worried that he might fire her for inappropriate dance moves. Or worse, realize that she was capable of total hotness and that he had been duped in Asheville. But neither one of those things seemed to occur to him. He didn't look anything other than tired and a little grouchy when she and Mary Jane found him in the kitchen, coat on, shoes on, keys in hand. He certainly didn't look like he had suddenly been made aware of her extreme sexiness and wanted to take her on the kitchen counter.

But he was a gentleman, so despite his clear surliness he did say, "Hi, Harley. How was your weekend? You settling in okay?"

"Yes, thanks. How about you? It looked like you had a great finish." Yes, she had watched Cooper race. Yes, she had secretly cheered him on.

He shrugged. "I've had worse. But thanks." He gestured toward the door that led to the garage. "After you, ladies. And I'm warning y'all, I'm hungry so I may not have the deepest well of patience. I apologize in advance."

"We'll hurry." Harley followed him into the garage and opened the back door to his SUV.

"What the hell are you doing?" he asked. "Sit in the front."

"I was going to let Mary Jane sit in front." Harley was the help, after all. But dutifully, she got in the front passenger seat and Mary Jane climbed in the back.

Cooper snorted. "She's a kid. You're an adult. She can sit in back. Besides, she didn't call shotgun."

"Shotgun?" Mary Jane asked, pausing in applying lip gloss to look at them both curiously.

"Are you for real?" Cooper asked. "You don't know what shotgun is?"

Mary Jane shook her head.

Cooper gave Harley a look. "Do you know what shotgun is?"

"Of course. I have a twin sister. It was an all-out front seat war my entire childhood." Maybe mentioning Charity was a mistake, but it wasn't like she could spend the next few months pretending she wasn't a twin. It was a huge part of her identity and influence in her upbringing.

Cooper glanced at Mary Jane in the rearview mirror as

he hit the button for the garage door and started the car. "We need to fill in some gaps in your childhood education. Shotgun is—"

"Got it," Mary Jane said, looking down at her phone. "I am reading the definition on the urban slang dictionary. I understand the definition, though I don't get the appeal."

Cooper made a face. "Of course you're looking it up online. So where are we going?"

Harley watched Cooper's mansion appear in front of them as he backed down the drive to the street. It still amazed her in its grandeur. It was like a Tuscan villa plopped down in the suburbs of Charlotte and it never seemed quite like it matched Cooper to her. But she wasn't sure why she felt that way because in the few times she'd been around him, he'd always been surrounded by luxury. It reminded her that she didn't know Cooper Brickman. She just thought she did because she'd been watching him race for years. One night in bed told her truths about a man's character, but not how he lived his life.

"Find the nearest grocery store," Mary Jane commanded her phone.

"I know where the damn grocery store is," Cooper complained. "I just thought maybe you girls had a specific plan."

"I have a list," Mary Jane said. "That's a plan. So go to the nearest grocery store then."

Harley opened up her purse on hearing how grumpy Cooper sounded. She still had snacks in there from her days caring for toddlers. Fruit chews and cereal puffs went a long way. She unearthed a granola bar. "Want this?" she asked him, holding it up for him to see as he drove.

He glanced over and looked like he was about to say no, his head already shaking. But then he rethought it, and said, "Actually yes."

She unwrapped it, pulling the sides down but leaving the

bottom of the plastic for him to hold on to. She passed it over to him.

Cooper made a funny face. "Thanks, Mom."

There it was. The maternal thing. She oozed it. Geez. It was a sickness.

"Sorry. Habit."

But he gave her an indecipherable look. "No, I like it. It's nice."

Harley was nice. It was a compliment, but it was so short of what she wanted to hear, it was a much-needed bucket of cold water.

Shopping with Cooper and Mary Jane was like herding kittens. They went off in all directions and touched everything. Both seemed excited by the endless possibilities the produce department offered, and with a granola bar in him, Cooper had lost the furrow between his eyebrows. He was also putting an insanely large amount of food into their cart.

"Ooh, I love mangoes. And strawberries. And asparagus."

Mary Jane was poking the packages of tofu in the cooler. "What is this?"

"Tofu. It's bean curd."

"Gross."

Cooper was squeezing the avocados. "God, these feel weird."

Amused, Harley told him, "We look with our eyes, not our hands."

He laughed. "Okay, I'll stop fondling the produce."

He could transfer that need to touch to her if he liked. She would be fine with that.

"Oh, Harley, here are the peppers," Mary Jane called. "Your vegetable soul mate."

Cooper pushed the cart toward his sister, raising his eyes at Harley. "Your vegetable soul mate?"

"I love peppers."

"She's going to marry them," his sister told him.

"This is North Carolina, not France," he said. "I doubt you'll be able to get a marriage license for that here."

Oh, Lord. "It's just an expression," Harley assured him. "I wasn't planning to exchange actual vows with a pepper. I'm not that desperate yet."

She meant it as a joke, but Cooper gave her a searching look. "You shouldn't be desperate at all. You're a beautiful woman. But more importantly, you're kind."

Way to embarrass her. And while she did one hundred percent know he meant it as a compliment, it just always seemed like a consolation prize. She wasn't interesting or sexy or adventurous. She was *kind*. Blech. Next he'd tell her she had a good personality.

"Oooh," was Mary Jane's opinion. "Cooper is jelly of the peppers."

Fortunately, that distracted him from the fact that her cheeks were hot and she wasn't sure what to say.

"What the hell does that mean?" Cooper asked.

"'Jelly' is slang for jealous," Harley told him.

"That's just stupid," Cooper said to his sister.

"Don't call me stupid."

"I didn't call you stupid, I said that word is stupid."

Mary Jane stuck her tongue out at him.

"Did you see that?" Cooper asked Harley.

Seriously? Yet Harley had to admit she was enjoying herself. She liked Mary Jane a lot, and Cooper was, well, adorable and sexy and confident. "Do I have to put you both in a time-out?" she asked, giving him a smile. "If you settle down, we'll be out of here sooner."

Mary Jane had wandered off to grab a container of cashew nuts.

Cooper gave Harley a sly smile. "I guess I just need you to keep me in line, don't I?"

They weren't standing all that close to each other, but something about his tone gave Harley pause. It felt like he was flirting with her. But she was clearly just imagining it because that was what she wanted to hear. She responded the way she would to a friend or his sister, making a motion like a whip. "I can't help it. I have the mom voice."

But Cooper's eyes had darkened. "That's not what I meant."

Harley licked her lips. "No?" she asked, nervously.

His gaze was trained on her mouth.

"Are we done?" Mary Jane asked, stepping between them and dumping an armful of random items into the cart.

"Yes," Harley said, looking down, her heart racing. "We're done here."

CHAPTER

EIGHT

COOPER watched his sister taking instruction from
Harley on how to chop peppers as he put away the groceries
they'd bought in the fridge, marveling at how good this felt.
The kitchen felt warm and cozy, olive oil heating in a pan
on the professional-grade stovetop he'd never used. It had
taken some rooting around to find the equipment needed to
cook a meal, with all three of them opening a variety of
cabinets and drawers, but they'd found everything they
needed, most of which he hadn't even known he owned.

Sometimes his house felt like a corporate rental. Decorated by someone else for temporary living. It was amazing
what a thirteen-year-old and a home-cooked meal could do
to change the vibe.

Not to mention Harley.

She took to the domestic role naturally. Which made
sense. She was a nanny, for chrissake. But it was more than
that. There was something about her that made it very easy
to be near her. He felt . . . comfortable. Which didn't sound

right. Content? That wasn't it, not exactly, though he did feel content.

Happy.

That's what it was.

How completely fucking bizarre.

He had flirted with her in the grocery store and it had made her uncomfortable. That hadn't been his plan, but then she had looked so sweetly sensual, teasing him about a time-out. It had given him an erection, without any warning whatsoever. Which was made worse by her little dominatrix whipping motion. She had no idea how sexy she truly was, and that made her all the more appealing.

Which meant he was an asshole. He'd had sex with her sister. He had to keep it in his pants and not make her quit this job and bolt. He needed Harley. Mary Jane needed her.

"OMG, this is hard," Mary Jane said.

"You're doing awesome. I'm going to start some rice to go with it." Harley gave him a smile as she shifted around him into the pantry to get the rice.

It all felt very normal. Like they were a family.

Jesus. He needed a beer. And a lobotomy.

She was his nanny. He *paid* her to live in his house.

But he couldn't help but notice that she was as OCD as he was. When he popped the top off his beer, the cap skittered down the counter. Harley snagged it and tossed it in the trash without missing a beat or even seeming to really notice she did it.

Which was weird because he remembered Charity saying Harley was messy. Maybe she was just being respectful in his house.

Mary Jane was giving all sorts of shrieks and exclamations as Harley helped her lay down her tortilla in the hot skillet. It amused Cooper to see her so excited and so willing to try something new. But he was shoving every loose vegetable into his mouth that was lying around because he was goddamn hungry.

"I get the first quesadilla," he told his sister.

"Why? That's not fair."

"Because I pay the bills."

She made a face. "But I'm a growing child."

That made him snort. "I love that you admit you're still a child only when it's convenient. Most of the time you're trying to convince me you're entitled to the full rights of adulthood."

"We can pull out another pan and make two quesadillas at once," Harley said, already reaching below into the cabinet.

Cooper and MJ looked at each other. "Damn. Harley is reasonable, isn't she?" he asked MJ.

She nodded. "It takes the fun out of fighting with you."

He laughed. "Exactly. But I think Harley is afraid I'll knock you down to get the quesadilla. Which smells awesome, by the way." The pungent scent of onions filled the room. "God, I can't stand waiting."

He knew he wasn't showing a great side to his nanny, but hunger made him an asshole. He couldn't stop himself.

"Patience means you have to wait," Harley teased him, clearly amused. "Touch your nose and count to eight."

Mary Jane laughed. "Touch your nose, Cooper. Do it. You totally need to learn patience."

It was funny, he had to admit. "You touch it for me, Harley," he said, meeting her gaze.

Her laughter died out. She reached out and the pad of her index finger touched the tip of his nose. He hadn't expected her to really do it. But she stared at him with an intensity that went straight to his cock and squeezed. She had the most compelling eyes. They were like a crowded ocean of thoughts and emotions, none of which he had access to.

"One, two . . ." Her voice was a soft murmur.

Nothing about him felt soft. Cooper was debating how much trouble he would get into if he reached up and took her hand and drew that lithe finger into his mouth. A lot. A lot of trouble. Astronomical amounts of trouble.

Mary Jane brought him back to his senses. "So is *Holly* going to be here anytime soon?" she asked in acid tones.

It was annoying, and he didn't like her attitude, but at the same time she had just reminded him of why he could not look at Harley the way he just had been. He did take Harley's finger, but he took it lightly and gave her a friendly squeeze and smile before dropping it down by her side. "I'm sorry for being so cranky. I'm not usually such a bear."

Then he turned to MJ and inspected her quesadilla. "I think you need to flip this," he said, before adding casually, "and not that it's any of your particular business but I'm not seeing Holly anymore."

"Good. She's not right for you."

He helped her use the spatula. "How would you know that? You never even met her."

"I know her type."

"Don't be judgmental. Besides, you don't know what my type is." Hell, he didn't know what his type was, how could she?

"I know more than you think I do."

He wasn't touching that. Cooper took the handle of the skillet and slid the quesadilla out onto a plate. He handed it to MJ. "Let's eat at the table instead of the island." He had the damn monstrosity. They might as well use it.

For a split second, he thought she was going to refuse to accept his changing the subject, but then she just pursed her lips and complied. Harley was finishing with the second quesadilla. Cooper started on a third, reaching over and taking a long swallow of his beer, tension in his shoulders.

"You're doing good with her," Harley said in a low voice. "Just remember you're the one in charge."

That was doubtful, but he nodded. "Thanks."

But despite the uneasiness he felt in his role, he knew Harley was right.

Dinner was an interesting experience, and easier than he would have imagined. MJ talked about her fashion blog, which didn't interest him necessarily, but her enthusiasm did interest him. He could hear the passion and commitment in her voice and he appreciated that. It was how he had sounded about racing at that age. He wondered if there was a way he could do for MJ what his former stepfather had done for him—set her on the path to a successful career.

His sister was always funny. She made faces and used ridiculous hand gestures and slang and he was reminded all over again of how complex and intriguing and brilliant she was. He saw a lot of Bud in her, and he was grateful for that. MJ's dad had been a good man.

After they ate, Cooper stood up and stretched. "That was fine cooking, MJ. I'm full."

"Finally. You ate like seven hundred pounds of food."

"I'm a man. We need fuel."

"If you get chubby you won't fit in your car."

"I'm not getting chubby!" He reached out for Harley's plate to clear the table. "You finished, Harley?"

She nodded.

"MJ, get over here and help me with these dishes," he said, carrying the plates to the sink.

"Leave them for the housekeeper. Isn't that her job?"

Harley's eyes widened, but she didn't say a word. She looked at Cooper pointedly.

But he was already on it, fairly appalled at his sister's attitude. "No, that isn't her job. Rosa is here to dust and vacuum messes we don't intentionally create and I don't have time to maintain. That doesn't mean we can be lazy and just leave dirty dishes lying around for her."

"Mom says only ugly girls have to wash dishes."

Cooper saw red. He was so furious with his mother he actually felt his eye twitch as he paused, trying to control his emotions before he spoke. "You don't agree with that, Mary Jane. I know you don't. And you're smart enough to know that Mom doesn't speak for the rest of this family."

It had obviously been some kind of test because his sister's gaze skittered away from him, her cheeks turning pink. "Yeah. I know that." Then she picked up her plate off the table and took it to the sink without another word.

He found the dish soap. "How about you dry them for me?"

She nodded and they fell into a quiet efficiency as he filled the sink and washed dishes. It wasn't tense and he was grateful for the quiet. Harley was disposing of the vegetable scraps and sponging down the counters. It felt blissfully normal and he was almost past the point of wanting to call his mother and tell her precisely what he thought of her bullshit.

When the last dish was done, MJ said, "Can I go to my room?"

He was surprised she'd even asked for permission. Usually she did a whole lot of what she wanted. It made him feel good, like she respected him. "Sure. I'll see you tomorrow, Skinny Minnie."

MJ slid across the kitchen on her socks and said, "Night!" She added something under her breath that he didn't hear.

He was pretty sure he didn't want to, given the look on Harley's face. "What did she say?" he asked.

"I'm not sure," she said, suddenly dropping her gaze to

114

the countertop and becoming very interested in scrubbing the marble with a sponge.

Since it was damn near ten o'clock and he figured he'd waded through enough of his family muck for one day, he decided to let it go. MJ had probably called him a prick or something. Whatever. He'd been known to cuss at authority a time or two back in the day. Hell, he still did it.

What he really wanted to do was flop on the couch in his basement and watch a movie, a beer in his hand. "I'm going downstairs to watch some TV. Care to join me?"

HARLEY was so grateful Cooper didn't pry that she would have agreed to just about anything. "Sure. Okay." It was a miracle that he hadn't heard his sister call him "Cunny King" because Harley had heard it loud and clear and had promptly wanted to die, for several reasons.

One, because she did not feel qualified as a nanny to address the issue of Mary Jane using that word, or attempting to figure out if she even knew what it meant. Which presumably she did, because Mary Jane looked everything up online, and that made Harley sad. Not that she used the Internet, but that she would gain her knowledge of sexual activity online at such a young age, with no one to explain to her the dynamics of emotional intimacy. Two, because Harley was stupid enough to fall for a man nicknamed the Cunny King, and that if given half the chance, she would do it all over again.

"I didn't even know this house had a basement," she told him truthfully. There were many random doors she never felt comfortable opening, not feeling like it was her place to explore his home. "Where are the stairs?"

He got a beer out of the fridge. "Want one?"

"Sure." Which was probably a horrific idea. But it might ease the tension she was feeling. The dinner had been a success, but she still felt stressed about her ability to successfully mentor Mary Jane. Or compartmentalize her attraction to Cooper.

He opened a door next to the mudroom that she had assumed was a broom closet. "Voilà. The stairs. Ladies first."

While Cooper flicked the lights on, Harley moved past him and down the lushly carpeted stairs. At the bottom, a motion sensor tripped and the lights came ablaze. She was amazed to see that there was a massive rec room, with a huge TV, a bar, a pool table, and arcade games. "Wow. I've been walking over Dave and Buster's and I didn't even know it."

"It feels comfortable down here to me. I like it." Cooper took the beers over to the giant sectional and set them down on the coffee table. He picked up the remote and turned the giant television on.

Harley chose the L of the sectional so she would be a good four feet away from him. "It's very nice. It's like an upscale man cave."

There was a lot of memorabilia on the walls. Standing right back up, she went over and studied the pictures. Him in Victory Lane, champagne exploding in front of him. Him with other Chase contenders. The year he had won the championship, holding his cup at the awards ceremony, grinning for all he was worth.

"Cami did that," he said, sounding embarrassed. "I didn't hang a bunch of pictures of myself. She decorated it down here."

"I think it's fantastic. You should be proud of all you've accomplished."

"Aw, shucks," he said, his tone mocking and silly. "T'weren't nothing, ma'am."

"Ma'am?" Harley came back to the sectional. "I'm too young to be a ma'am, surely." She thought about how bizarre it would be to always have other people doing things for you. What did Cooper really have ownership of, what did he put his heart into? Racing. The rest was just periphery, including her. She needed to remember that. She took a spot even further away from him than before.

"Why are you all the way over there?" he asked. "Do I have onion breath?"

"Not that I noticed." Or had been close enough to him to notice.

"Then come over here. There's only one blanket and I'll share it, but I'm not giving it to you. I'm not feeling that much of a gentleman tonight." He patted the couch next to him. "And I was just teasing. I don't think of you as a ma'am."

An hour later Harley was starting to wonder what he did think of her. They were watching an action movie and she had long ago lost the grasp of the plot. Things just exploded and people raged at each other. But admittedly she wasn't concentrating all that hard because Cooper was altogether so distracting, she couldn't focus on anything other than how close his body was to hers. He didn't seem to think it was odd that they were so close their legs were touching, a fleece blanket spread over them. She tried to tell herself that Cooper was like his sister—a touch lonely and in need of companionship.

It didn't hold water. He could have the company of anyone he wanted at any time. She supposed she was just convenient. Right in front of him.

But that didn't explain why his arm went over the back of the sofa so that she was essentially resting in the crook of his arm. It tripped the memory of him hovering over her, both his biceps surrounding her, while her greedy fingers explored his muscular chest. It *was* fairly ridiculous that a man like Cooper would be lonely. Hell, Holly had been there just the week before. He wasn't lacking for company, naked or otherwise.

It was that thought that had her shifting away from him, drawing her feet up so it would just look like she was trying to get comfortable, not put space between them.

"Are you stiff?" he asked. "Here, stretch out."

Before she could process what he was about to do, Cooper had taken her by the ankles and drawn her legs out straight across his lap. He casually massaged her feet, his eyes still on the movie.

Harley swallowed hard, heat pooling between her thighs and gradually spreading out through her limbs. Her nipples firmed.

Cooper was rubbing her feet. It felt good. It felt intimate. It felt cozy and pleasant. It felt like with a little bit of encouragement he could go from rubbing her feet to rubbing one out for her. Would he do that if she shifted, if she let her legs fall slightly apart, if she gave soft sounds of encouragement and told him how good his touch felt?

To her total embarrassment, she felt her panties growing damp at the thought. She shifted a little.

His elbow was by her knee and when she moved, it ended up jamming her in the thigh. Harley winced.

Cooper glanced over at her, his face alarmed, hand already shifting up to rub her tender flesh. "Shit, I'm sorry, Harley. You okay?"

"I'm fine. That was my fault. I moved." Her nerves had caused her to wiggle, which had caused his hand to move even further into the danger zone. Wonderful. She was inadvertently torturing herself.

He smiled and stopped rubbing her thigh. But he left his hand down in the gap between her legs. That was not a place for a boss's hand to be. It just wasn't. Yet Harley wasn't opening her trap and saying a word. She couldn't. If she did, she just might blurt out the truth. Or climb on his lap and grind her desperate body against his. Either way, she was bound to humiliate herself. Because she liked it. Damn it, she liked him touching her.

But why was he touching her? He knew she was Harley. Not Charity. Plus he didn't look particularly flirtatious or amorous. He just looked comfortable. Relaxed. Like he thought of her as asexual.

It wasn't a pleasant thought. Not when her crotch was hotter than an engine on race day.

The movie went on and on, and Cooper's hand got higher, and Harley got horny. She couldn't help it. It felt like every nerve ending in her body had stood up and was doing the cha-cha. After fifteen minutes she was fairly certain she was going to die. She now understood what every teen boy felt in a dark family room with the object of his lust, because the only thing she could think about was how desperately she wanted his hand to shift higher and tear her jeans off of her.

When she decided she absolutely could not stand it anymore, she dropped her feet to the floor in one smooth motion and asked, "Is there a bathroom down here?"

"Sure. I'll show you."

Why did he have to be a gentleman? And why did his house have to be so big that you couldn't give directions without a map and the use of physical landmarks? There were approximately seventeen doors in the basement. "Thanks."

It was a good thing he was acting as tour guide. He went around a wall and suddenly there was a whole other section of the basement Harley hadn't even seen before. It had a rock-climbing wall and a putting green.

"You know, you and MJ can use whatever you want down here. Well, except for the booze. MJ probably doesn't need to drink." He grinned at her. "But anything else is fair game."

"I've never rock-climbed before." Harley eyed it dubiously.

"Why don't you give it a try?"

"Right now?" Was he serious?

"Sure. Why not?"

That was a good question. Mainly because it meant her butt would be in a sling in front of her boss, who happened to be her onetime lover, only he didn't know that.

"Okay. But you go first." So she could check his butt out before he was subjected to hers. "So I can see how it's done."

It wasn't really sound logic. Because in three minutes Cooper was hooked into a harness that outlined his junk perfectly. It was like someone had taken a marker and circled all the good stuff on an anatomical chart. It emphasized everything he had in a way that had Harley remembering with startling clarity how it felt to have her mouth over his cock. She licked her lips without meaning to. Then he started scrambling up the wall, giving her detailed steps on what he was doing, of which she heard none.

"Are you listening?" He glanced back and down at her.

Busted. She nodded.

"What did I just say?"

"Something about climbing that wall."

Cooper grinned, shaking his head at her. "I knew you weren't listening. You're a terrible liar."

Oh, really? "You'd be surprised," she told him, annoyed that he, like everyone else, thought she was one-dimensional. That she didn't have *layers*.

Cooper kicked off of the wall and dropped to the floor.

He stepped out of the harness. "I can't imagine you'd surprise me. That's something I like about you."

Harley took the harness from his hand and waved him off when he tried to help her. "So everything I've done and said is actually what you would have predicted?"

His grin softened. "Well, no, I suppose not. I wouldn't have predicted what a firm hand you have."

She reached for one of the plastic boulders to grip. "I have a lot of things."

Without warning Cooper reached out and wrapped his hands around her waist. "Your harness is loose."

She should have jerked away. But instead, she found herself leaning slightly into his touch, letting her eyes flutter shut briefly. This had been a mistake. Taking this job. Living in this house. Spending time with Cooper. Because she was still Cinderella huddled by the fire in the kitchen for warmth, and princes only married the help in fairy tales.

Especially when the prince had done the deed with Cinderella's sexy sister.

"I've got it, thanks." She was on her own. Better to remember that at all times.

"SO how you been?" Cooper asked Ryder Jefferson as they sat in the backseat of a car waiting to be driven back to the garage after a fan appearance.

"Tired." Ryder had the dark circles under his eyes to back up his words. "I love having Suz and the baby on the road with me, but he's teething and the kid never sleeps. Ever. I'm not kidding. I didn't know it was physically possible to exist on this little sleep."

"He's training for college frat parties," Cooper told him with a grin. "Though, sorry, man. I can't even imagine." He couldn't. Doing the job and being a parent was a difficult balancing act.

"I'll be dead by then at this rate. I'm going to fall asleep at the wheel."

"Please don't. I plan on being next to you on the track."

"With my luck, I'll hit a pole in the parking lot at Wally World getting diapers at midnight. Least sexy death ever."

"You want your death to be sexy?" Cooper just didn't want his death, period. If it actually happened, he figured the manner didn't matter in the slightest.

"Yeah, well, you know, I'm vain. What can I say? Or maybe I'm delirious from lack of sleep."

"At least my sister sleeps, I'll give her that. It's when she's awake that the trouble starts." Cooper was a little fearful as to what was going to happen in Daytona. It was coming up in just a few days.

"Yeah, uh, she's been known to post a thing or two online," Ryder said, with a pointed glance in his direction. "She's kind of ballsy for a teenager."

"You have no idea." But then he felt disloyal to MJ complaining about her. "She's had too much freedom. And money. I'm trying to rein her in, but it's a process. At least my new nanny is good with her and I think she'll stick around for the long haul." He did. If he didn't scare Harley off with his constant need to touch her. She'd been on the job almost three weeks and Cooper found himself spending every free moment he had at home, seeking her and his sister out. He enjoyed both of their company, and he found himself using every excuse possible to casually touch Harley's arm, her leg, her face.

He couldn't chalk that up purely to gratitude. It was more than that. A hell of a lot more than that. "Though I have to admit, I think I'm starting to have the hots for my nanny. That's not right, is it?"

"Why not? You're not married. She's not married. What's the big deal? You've got a chick living in your house, presumably young and good looking. You're allowed to feel attracted to her."

"But I can't do anything about it." He didn't think. "Besides, I don't think she's into me that way." Which chapped his ass, he had to admit.

Ryder snorted. "So talk her into being into you. What the hell, man? It's not like you ever had a problem getting pussy before."

"This wouldn't be about getting pussy."

Ryder's eyebrows went up and Cooper silently cursed. He'd revealed more than he'd meant to with that statement. But it was true. He liked Harley, as a person. He enjoyed her company. He felt easy and happy around her and any number of gushy and dumb things.

Oh, God. What the hell did that even mean? He felt like he was in totally new territory. But the truth was he was stalking her in his own house. There was no other way to describe it. He listened for her footsteps and followed her. He'd traced her to the kitchen in the morning and to the basement at night, all while pretending like he'd come across her by accident. How pathetic was that?

But Harley didn't seem to mind his presence. She talked to him. Smiled. Laughed. He thought she actually liked him, the real Cooper Brickman, not the guy who grinned for the cameras. Then again, he was paying her. How was she supposed to act around him?

"Really? So if you're not just going for a hookup there's definitely no reason not to go for it."

"I can't. She works for me." What if she turned him down? What if they dated and it ended horribly? He didn't want to lose her as a nanny. MJ was attached. Cooper tossed his hair out of his eyes. "And . . ." Here was the real rub. "I had sex with her identical twin at McCordle's wedding."

He and Ryder had been friends a long time and he needed to tell someone the truth about what he was dealing with. He wanted some solid advice. Because whenever he thought about sex with Charity, he got a hard-on, and how could he have developed a friendship and want maybe more with Harley when he had fond memories of nailing her sister?

"Wait a minute. She has an identical twin you already boned? Did you think you were boning your nanny? Was it like a twin swap? Now that's hot, man."

Harley would never in a million years have slept with him. He hadn't even considered it. "No. I knew which sister I was doing and it wasn't my nanny. I didn't think Harley was the one-night-stand type. Not that I was trying to nail her or anything. But her sister sat on my lap and . . ."

"Enough said." Ryder held out his hand. "I don't need details. But yeah, you're right. You're fucked. Unless they are into the twin tag-team thing."

"*I'm* not into the twin tag-team thing." He might not be known for serious relationships, but he wasn't into group sex.

"Then I guess you should have stopped to think about that before you sacked her sister."

"Seriously?" Cooper gave him an annoyed glare. "That is not helpful."

"Hey. I am sleeping three hours a night and I haven't had sex in three weeks. I'm not brimming with sympathy for the guy who has twin tail at his disposal." He put his finger out. "Not that I'm jealous. I love my beautiful wife and I never want to be single ever again. I'm just saying in the grand scheme of things your problems are lame."

Ryder just might have a point. "So what am I supposed to do?"

"Well, what do you want? That's the real question. Who do you want to bang and who do you want to date?"

There was the rub. "Well. I want them to be the same person. You know?"

"You want twins to become one person?"

"I just want my nanny to be both. The one I bang and the one I date. I mean, her sister was great in bed and all, and I had a good time, but I don't know her."

He did want to date Harley. Duh, as MJ would say. It all suddenly seemed so obvious now. "I feel like I know Harley and I dig her." There. He'd said it out loud and had set himself up for complete and utter humiliation.

"Then what's the problem?"

"I guess there isn't one." Except he didn't think that Harley felt the same way about him, but he wasn't about to admit that to Ryder. He could only be so vulnerable before he felt the need to prove his masculinity by shooting off some fireworks, going hunting, or taking a tree limb down with a chainsaw. None of which he had time for at the moment, so he kept his mouth shut about the possibility that Harley did not see him as potential mate material.

But he wasn't a bad catch. Sure, he had a history of not committing much, but that was because he hadn't been ready. His career had been too demanding. He hadn't met the right woman.

Then he'd stopped on that terrace at the Biltmore and Harley had smiled at him and everything had changed. He hadn't continued to call her just because of Mary Jane. He'd been hoping she would take the position so he could see her. Get to know her better.

The driver climbed back into the front seat and looked back at them. "Y'all ready?"

"Yeah," Cooper said without thinking. "Yes."

He was ready. To do this thing. To grow a friendship

with a woman. Possibly his first genuine friendship with a woman ever. To take it, nurture it, and create a relationship out of it if Harley was interested.

If she wasn't yet, well hell, he'd charm her into it.

Then later, when they'd established something real between them, they would have great sex on a frequent basis.

It all made total sense and he wasn't sure why he hadn't thought of it before.

He was going to make Harley his.

CHAPTER
NINE

CHARITY realized she and Harley had more in common that just genetics. While Charity wasn't a nanny, she was a handler for a rookie driver and it was the same damn thing as babysitting. Her charge for the new season was Roger Wilco. Yes, that was his name. And he was a moron.

Harley had suggested that perhaps she was being a little harsh. After all, he was only nineteen and, generally speaking, the male of the species didn't pull his head out of his ass until at least age twenty-two, but Charity had been working with him for months and it wasn't getting any easier.

"Roger, listen to me. You cannot give this number to women. You can't. Do you understand?" She tapped the smart phone that was his primary means to communicate with his crew, her, his assistant, and the team owner. "Use the private phone you're playing Candy Crush on right now to text girls."

He wasn't even looking at her. His feet were up on the desk between them. "Uh-huh."

"Promise me." She held her finger up and shook it at him, grateful that her job didn't require her to travel to races with him. It was a sorely needed break every Thursday through Sunday. On the road, his assistant had to deal with him. But there in Charlotte, any screwups he made were her responsibility, and already that week he'd lost his expensive racing shoes and been busted sending pictures of his weenie to a forty-year-old female bodybuilder. On his corporate phone.

He made a face at her. "I promise. It was an accident."

"I know it was an accident, but it's very, very bad." Charity felt like she was rubbing a puppy's nose in a puddle it had made on the carpet. "Just don't even send questionable photos of yourself at all. That would really be the best choice to make here."

He frowned, pushing his baseball hat off his head and reseating it. "I feel like you're stifling me. I need to express myself sometimes."

Oh, Lord. "If you really need to send pictures of your junk to a woman, send them to me. That way I at least know it won't go anywhere it shouldn't."

His feet dropped to the floor. "You want to see my junk?"

She would rather see just about anyone else naked, but she had to tread delicately. Charity wanted a cupcake for lunch. And a drink. It was the only way she was going to be able to fortify herself for an afternoon return to Roger. "That's not the point. It's my job to make sure you are retaining professionalism."

He grinned. "I like your brand of professionalism. You're kind of young, but we could have some fun."

She was actually almost ten years older than him and he was a string bean, but she didn't waste her breath pointing out the obvious. "Knock it off. I am not playing around here, Wilco. Straighten up or I'm putting you in a time-out."

"Oh. Kinky."

Unfortunately, a head popped into the doorway right then. "Hey, Roger, have you seen Jeff?"

Charity turned around. Shit. It was Cooper Brickman. The last thing in the world she needed was a seasoned driver witnessing her inability to handle the teen texter. Especially a driver who had made out with her sister. As her. Oh, God. He was looking at her, and thinking he had kissed her.

That was so awkward. Charity almost never saw him, and as the months had gone on, she'd assumed she never would.

His eyes went round. "Charity. Wow. Hi. What are you doing here?"

Her palms got sweaty under his scrutiny. Why was he looking at her like he wanted to lick hot fudge off of her body? Harley must have slipped him some tongue. "Working. I haven't seen Jeff. Roger, have you seen Jeff?"

She wished she had seen the big boss. She was still harboring a huge crush on him, but he'd been scarce around the offices. He obviously had VIP things to do that didn't involve talking to a lowly handler he clearly wasn't attracted to.

"No."

"I didn't know you worked here. What kind of work are you doing for Wilco?" Cooper had walked into the room and he had his hands on his hips. He looked put out, like her employment personally pissed him off. "You never said you worked here."

Which made Charity wonder what Harley had said when she had been posing as her. Or hadn't said.

"She's wiping my ass," Roger said.

That was truly about the only thing she hadn't done.

"I'm Mr. Wilco's handler. He's being naughty today and I'm giving him a time-out."

His brow furrowed. "Well, I guess you and Harley have a lot in common then."

"She giving you time-outs?" Roger asked.

Cooper scoffed. "Charity's twin is my sister's nanny. I guess they're both good with children. Yes, that means you, rookie."

Though Charity had it on good authority that Harley made more money than she did. Not that she was bitter or anything. She was happy for Harley, but she was starting to wonder if it was time to move on herself. "Tell my sister hi. I hardly get to see her anymore."

He frowned like she'd said something wrong. "That's all you want to say?"

She wanted to add that she was annoyed that Harley got to go to Daytona and she had to see pictures of Roger's penis, but she kept that to herself. "Yes. I miss her. Harley and I may look the same, but we're way different people. She's super sweet and keeps me somewhat sane."

"Can't say the same for you," Roger said under his breath.

Charity turned and glared at him. "I've had just about enough out of you today, mister." She had learned in her two years on the job that some guys she needed to be charming with, others a disciplinarian. Roger needed a firm hand, the product of too much, too soon in life. "You'll do what I tell you to and you'll like it."

When she turned back to Cooper, she gave him a bright smile. He couldn't get her fired, she didn't think, and she was seriously done for the day with Roger's teen antics.

That furrow in Cooper's brow had deepened. He stared at her for a second, and she looked at him expectantly. Finally, he shook his head, looking a little miffed. "Nice to see you again, Charity."

"You, too, Cooper." She gave him a generic smile, making a mental note to press Harley for a few more details on that kiss.

Cooper gave a wave and left, and Charity was left alone with Roger and the thankless task of ensuring he kept it in his pants.

"Pull out your calendar on your phone and mark down that I won't be here on Monday or Tuesday in two weeks," she told him. "I have a bachelorette party to go to on Sunday night and a wedding on Monday."

"Where's the bachelorette party at?"

"No."

"What do you mean, no?"

"No. I'm not telling you that, are you kidding me?" She'd have to be stark raving mad to give him access to her friend Shawn's big girl's night. The whole concept of a bachelorette party after the elopement seemed a little off to Charity, but hey, it was a party. She was perfectly happy to throw on a miniskirt and cowboy boots and celebrate love. But with Shawn's new husband, Rhett, having many, many sisters who were all in the age bracket Roger seemed to prefer, she was keeping the location a state secret.

"You're mean."

"Get over it."

Jeff Sterling knocked on the door frame. "Roger, I need to see you in my office."

Charity straightened up and gave Jeff a smile. The owner of the team that Cooper and Roger drove for, inherited from his stepfather, Bud Rawlings, Jeff was in his forties, fit, efficient, and quiet. But something about him really appealed to Charity. She saw the way he stayed calm in a crisis and how he spoke to all his staff, and she really admired him. Yet he never seemed to glance twice at her even though she had it on good authority, from his stepsister Mary Jane Rawlings and her blog, that he was single.

At Ty and Imogen's wedding, she'd made her best play for him as Harley, and while he had been friendly and conversational, he had not been flirty. Whenever she saw him at work, as herself, he always seemed faintly displeased with her and she had no idea why.

"Cooper Brickman was looking for you, Mr. Sterling."

"Hm?" He glanced in her direction like he hadn't realized she was in the room. Why was it the one man she wanted to think she was sexy didn't seem to notice she actually existed?

"I said Cooper Brickman was looking for you."

He eyed her. "Thanks, Charity. Do you spend a lot of time with Cooper Brickman?"

Um . . . She popped back out of her chair and gave him another sunny smile, not liking that look on his face. "No, of course not. I work with Roger. Cooper just stuck his head in looking for you."

But that explanation didn't seem to satisfy him. "Roger, give Charity and me a minute, please."

Fudge. That didn't sound good.

"What do you mean?" Roger asked.

"Wait for me in my office." Jeff gave him such a pointed look that even Roger, slow on the uptake as he was, knew when to hop to.

Roger dropped his feet to the floor and stood up, giving Charity a smirk that conveyed he knew she was in trouble. Though how she could be in trouble she had no idea.

"Can I help you, sir?" she asked, starting to sweat, but determined not to show him how nervous she was.

"How long have you worked here, Charity?" Jeff's stance looked casual enough, his hand in his pocket, his voice normal and even. But he was a businessman with huge demands on his time. Charity knew he wasn't just making small talk.

"Two years." Her heart rate kicked up a notch and her palms went damp. Was he going to fire her? Had Roger complained about her heavy-handedness?

"I don't think it's wise for you to be spending time with Mr. Brickman socially."

She was so startled she had no idea what to say. "But . . ."

"I know that doesn't feel fair because you don't work directly for him, but there are just some types of relationships that aren't appropriate for the office."

Charity could feel the blood draining from her face. "There is no relationship of any kind. He popped his head in the office just now and that was the first time I've seen him since Mr. McCordle's wedding."

Jeff nodded. "Ah, yes. At the wedding. You know, I talked to your twin that night."

Her. He'd talked to her. Charity still didn't understand what was happening so she just stood there, still smiling, no fucking clue what to say to that. "Oh?" When she was nervous, she joked, so she added, "She's the beauty. I'm the brains."

His eyebrows went up. "So Harley is working for Brickman now? You know Mary Jane is my ex-stepfather's daughter. I care about her."

Okay. "Harley is really good with kids. Mary Jane is in good hands."

"And you don't care that Harley's living with Cooper?"

"No. I think it's a good opportunity for her." What the hell were they even talking about?

But Jeff shook his head and made a sound in the back of his throat. "Okay, then. Well, just do yourself a favor and keep your distance."

"Sure." That should be easy enough since she never saw Cooper, but Charity felt like she had missed something seriously important here. Like Jeff knew something she so clearly did not.

"Good. Right." Jeff turned on his heel and left.

Gone. The biggest boss of all the big bosses. He had clearly been trying to tell her something and she had no idea what. Charity dropped her head on the desk and thunked her forehead hard on the metal. She was still lying there five minutes later when Roger returned.

"You want to borrow my helmet?" Roger asked. "Oh, wait, I'm not sure what I did with it actually. Do you have it?"

"No, I don't have it! You're supposed to." The day officially sucked.

Roger was smirking at her. "Hey, can I meet your sister? She sounds hot."

Funny. "Go to hell."

"That's not very professional."

"Look who's talking, Boy Wonder Weiner."

Let him fire her. She'd go tame jungle cats. It would be easier.

EATING dinner together with his sister and Harley was a ritual Cooper was really starting to like. He hadn't had the greatest day what with running into Charity at the office, of all places. It had caught him off guard and she'd just stared at him like he was an inconvenience. Talk about being spanked. Was he really such a forgettable lover? He'd thought they'd had a hell of a time.

Then he'd come home to her twin sister. If that wasn't the definition of fucked up, he didn't know what was. Not that he was coming home to *her*, but it was starting to feel that way. He even heard himself saying things like, "How are you girls today?" Like he had ownership of them.

"I'm so excited to go to Daytona!" Mary Jane said, twirling around the kitchen in her socks and showing more enthusiasm than he'd seen in a long time. "I've packed all the things."

"All the things?" He looked to Harley for translation. "What does that mean?"

Harley was straining pasta, her hair pulled back in a ponytail. "She just means a lot. It's an expression. Wear all the things. Pack all the things."

"I don't get it." He reached into the strainer and stole a string of pasta and popped it into his mouth. "I'm going to run up and pack real quick."

"We're going to eat in five minutes," Harley told him, steam rising in front of her.

He gave her a smile when he really wanted to reach over and kiss her. Like, he really, really wanted to kiss her. But instead he stole another piece of pasta. "I'm quick. Except when I need to be slow."

Her eyes widened. But all she said was, "Five minutes? I'll time you."

"I can't ever resist a challenge." Cooper took off for the steps, already mentally cataloging what he needed to throw in a bag. He traveled so much he had a system. His toiletries always stayed packed and he just switched out jeans, socks, boxer briefs, and a few shirts. Easy.

Except when he got to his bedroom, the overwhelming scent of incense hit him. Damn it. Rosa had been praying for his soul again. She did it every time he had a woman spend the night or every time she found some indicator of sexual activity, like a condom wrapper in the master bath. It always made his eyes water but he never said anything in reprimand. It couldn't be a bad thing to have someone praying for his soul, right?

She always burned the incense and left him a prayer card with Mary on it on his nightstand. He had started tucking them into the edges of the full-length mirror in his walk-in closet. He had covered two of the four sides of the mirror now, but honestly he couldn't imagine why she had left him one today. It had been weeks since Holly had stayed over and he was living like a monk, pure of body, if not pure of thought. It wasn't like Rosa knew he was having fantasies about keeping Harley in his bed for about six days straight.

For a split second, the thought that his housekeeper could read his mind made his nuts draw up, but then he dismissed it as impossible.

So he went into his closet and grabbed his travel bag. That was when he realized why Rosa was burning incense. Charity's bra was missing. He'd brought it home from Asheville in his bag then tossed it on the floor, not sure what to do with it. The bra had remained there for three months, behind some luggage. Obviously his housekeeper had found it when she vacuumed the carpet.

At least that eliminated the problem of what to do with the bra. Now he didn't have to worry about why he found it necessary to keep it. Nor did he have to glance at it longingly when he stepped into the closet, like a teenager with pilfered lingerie. It wasn't doing anything for his ego, that was for damn sure. He packed quickly and took his bag back downstairs, holding it up for Harley to see.

"Done."

"That was six minutes."

But she gave him a smile that was so damn sexy Cooper felt his dick harden. She didn't mean to be sexy. She just was. Which made it even sexier.

It was killing him.

"That's all you're taking?" MJ asked. "That's insane."

"Where is your bag?" he asked.

"*Bags.* In my room. They're too heavy for me to carry down the stairs."

"Wonderful." He accepted the plate of food that Harley was holding out for him. "How is it that a girl as tiny as you needs two suitcases? I could roll your jeans to the size of a carrot."

"I need to be prepared."

She was their mother's daughter in some ways, that was for sure. "How about you, Harley?"

"By the back door." She pointed to a small black carry-on bag.

"Now that's what I'm talking about." Again, he felt the urge to kiss her. It just seemed like he should. Like they should be together. They were living together. Sort of. It felt real in many ways. It seemed like a natural correlation that he should be entitled to touch her.

He wondered what she would do if he actually leaned over and put his mouth on hers.

Quit. That's what she would do.

He needed to work this thing slowly, seductively. He couldn't just attack her out of left field. Or make assumptions. Women hated when men made assumptions. It was all about the slow approach.

"Have I told you today, Harley, how much I appreciate you?" he asked, as they sat down at the kitchen table. "Because I do."

Her eyes widened and she gave a nervous laugh. "Thanks."

"Gross," was MJ's opinion.

Cooper suddenly wished that Harley were anything but his sister's nanny. Why did every single encounter with her have to be while a tween was spouting her opinions around them? When he and Harley had watched that movie together and he'd helped her rock-climb, he'd enjoyed how relaxing it was. He wanted that, all the time. The right to massage her feet.

But if she weren't MJ's nanny, she wouldn't give him the time of day anyway.

"I'm glad y'all are coming with me. I get lonely on the road." Then he realized immediately that his words were an invitation for MJ to make a snarky remark about Holly or other women, so he turned and pointed his finger at her. Her mouth was already open. "Nope. Uh-uh. I don't want to hear it."

She froze, clearly busted. But then she shrugged. "I don't know what you're talking about."

"The hell you don't." What were the odds MJ would fall asleep on the plane?

His sister wiggled on her seat and sucked down a soda.

Slim and none. Those were the odds.

CHAPTER
TEN

HARLEY couldn't believe she was sitting in a private jet. Talk about feeling like Cinderella. Yes, she was still just the hired help, but it was hard to remember that with Cooper. He treated her like an equal. In fact, he deferred to her opinion almost entirely when it came to Mary Jane and the household issues. She was falling into a comfortable pattern in his house of homeschooling, enrichment activities, cooking, and relaxing with Cooper in the evenings after Mary Jane went to her room to do whatever she did online. It was like they were together, and that was a dangerous thing to be lulled into feeling.

It was the strangest unnatural relationship ever, if you broke it down. They were platonic, employer/employee, yet they ate together, hung out, shared thoughts, and hit the grocery store together. She had no idea what to do about it, other than brazenly pretend there was nothing remotely odd about what they were doing.

Mary Jane was lying on the couch in the plane on her

back, headphones in her ears, as they flew south. Cooper had been working, handling business calls and e-mails, while Harley had read a book. But now he seemed done, and he stood up and moved to the seat next to her. She was aware of his knee brushing against hers, and the fact that he was looking at her, reading over her arm.

She read the same sentence three times, totally distracted by Cooper. He smelled good, his cologne the same one he'd worn that night at the Biltmore. Her fingers ached to shift to his leg, to stroke him to arousal. She wanted to tilt her head and nibble on his ear, rub her lips over his beard shadow. It was a challenge not to change her breathing. She felt very aware of the rise and fall of her chest, the rush of air through her nostrils, the way his jeans rustled against hers. Her body was responding to his presence, clearly an imprint of their night together wreaking havoc on her pheromones.

It took every ounce of self-control she possessed to sit still and not ask him what the hell he wanted. He had every right to sit wherever he wanted on his own private jet.

Finally he spoke. "Are you actually reading? You haven't turned the page in five minutes."

Harley felt her cheeks flush. "I was daydreaming. What are you doing?"

"I'm bored." He gave her a smile. "Play with me?"

Now there was a question that went straight to her no-nos. But obviously that wasn't what he meant. He didn't want to *play* with her. Though if she wasn't mistaken, there was some good old-fashioned lust in his eyes as he showed her his iPad.

She had to be wrong. Cooper didn't want to have sex with her.

Which was confirmed when she glanced down at his tablet. "Words with Friends? You want me to play Words with Friends with you?"

"Please?"

Like she could say no. "I've never done it before. I usually say no to game requests."

"But you like me better than all of those other people, right?"

Yes. She did like him. At first, it had been purely a physical crush on a man she didn't know. On his public image. Now the crush was on the real Cooper. The man who had been so tender in bed with her. Who cared about his kid sister. Who massaged her feet.

But she couldn't let him know that. "You're overselling this."

Cooper laughed. "Should I mention how highly intelligent I think you are?"

"Please don't embarrass both of us. I'll play with you."

"Awesome." He pointed to where she could create her login. "So did you pack your sunscreen? And a bikini?"

Like she intended to ever let him see her in a bikini. "Yes, I did."

"Is it teeny-weeny? A yellow bikini?"

Harley narrowed her eyes at him. What kind of a game was he playing? "Why?"

"I'm just making conversation."

She could think of better uses for his tongue. "I look terrible in yellow."

"I doubt it. But actually, I picture you in red."

She found it hard to believe he was picturing her at all. "I don't imagine you'll have time to go to the beach with us."

He shook his head. "No. Never bothered me much before, but I don't know. It would be nice to be able to just do what I want, to relax a little."

"Now I feel guilty that you're paying me to go to the beach." She meant it as a joke, but there was truth to it.

"You won't feel so guilty when MJ complains about the

sand for two hours straight. She clearly hates the beach, yet she loves the water. Why she doesn't just go to the pool is beyond me."

"When did you take her to the beach?"

"We were down there at my condo right after the season ended. Took nanny number one. She quit on the flight back. It was like she couldn't even wait to get back to give her notice. She had to make sure she'd never be forced to go to my house ever again."

For some random reason, Harley was jealous of the unknown nanny. Here she'd been feeling a little special going to Daytona with Cooper and Mary Jane, yet she wasn't the first. "That's tacky," Harley said, not bothering to cover her disdain. "You don't quit a nanny position in front of the child you're in charge of."

Cooper smiled. "So you're not going to ditch out on me?"

Harley knew almost nothing could make her quit this job. It had only been a few weeks and she was already attached to Mary Jane. And Cooper. She was attached to Cooper. It was foolish. Dangerous.

"No. Not at all."

"Are you going to wear my gear?"

"What? You mean, like a Cooper Brickman T-shirt?" Good God, he'd better be joking. She couldn't imagine anything more grasping. "I confess, I don't have one."

He laughed and she was pretty sure that indicated he was joking. He didn't really want her to wear his face on her breasts. But then he said, "Or a Cooper Brickman bikini."

Harley snorted. She couldn't prevent it from slipping out. "First of all, if those exist, I'm terrified. Second of all, you'd better be joking. I don't even wear makeup. I'm definitely not going to wear something that attention-grabbing."

"You don't need makeup," he said. "You're very beautiful naturally."

That voice. She knew that voice. It was the voice he'd used at the wedding right before she'd found herself naked with his tongue sliding over her clitoris. She swallowed hard, shifting her leg away from his, palms suddenly damp. He was flirting with her. There was no denying it. He was just flat-out flirting with her.

"I wasn't fishing for a compliment."

"I know. But I felt like giving one." He squeezed her knee. "Just say thanks, Harley."

"Thanks, Harley."

He laughed again. "Smart-ass. I didn't see that coming."

"I'm a twin. I know how to dish it out and to take it."

The minute the words were out of her mouth, she realized it was stupid to mention her sister. Instantly the smile disappeared.

"Guess I can see that." His expression was shuttered as he glanced at her, then down at the tablet in his hand.

She knew he was thinking about Charity, but she had no idea what he was thinking. Not that it mattered. In fact, maybe it was a good thing that he thought he'd slept with Charity because it kept him from crossing that line with her, because Harley knew that if he crossed she'd be a goner. Now that she'd seen Cooper in his home, watched him studiously attempt to parent Mary Jane, witnessed his kindness and lack of pretentiousness, she knew it wouldn't take much for her crush to free-fall into flat-out love.

Yet she still heard herself say, "Though Charity is more relentless than me when she dishes it out. I feel bad and give up, but she goes for the kill."

And she threw her twin under the bus. No matter that it was true. She knew precisely why she was doing it—to dissuade Cooper from further pursuing her sister. Not that he had. He'd never shown the slightest interest in contacting Charity.

Which suddenly made her wonder if he hadn't found the sex nearly as exciting as she had. His expression was impassive.

"I can see that." Cooper reached out and tucked her hair behind her ear.

Harley felt her eyes widen and her body freeze.

Then suddenly Cooper's head jerked. "Hey!" He turned in the opposite direction. "What the hell do you think you're doing?"

Harley leaned around him to peer at Mary Jane, who was sitting up now looking mulish. "It was an accident," she said.

"Hitting me in the head with a travel pillow was an accident?"

"Yes. I'm sorry."

Harley wasn't buying it and neither was Cooper, obviously, but he just said, "Well, now the pillow is mine." He picked it up off the floor where it had fallen and stuffed it behind his head.

"That's rude," Mary Jane said, drawing her legs up to her chest.

"So is hitting someone with a pillow."

It was her natural instinct to soothe both their feelings, but Harley knew they needed to find their own dynamic together. It was hard to see them eye each other with irritation, though. Plus, she felt somehow it was her fault that Cooper's attention to her was making Mary Jane jealous, which she didn't want.

So Harley was about to say something when Mary Jane stood up and tried to yank the pillow back from Cooper. The look he gave her was so murderous she giggled. Then he grinned.

And suddenly he had his sister back on the couch and was tickling her.

"Quit!" she was shrieking. But even as she clawed and smacked at Cooper, she looked like she was enjoying herself, her blond hair sliding into her eyes. "Harley, help me!"

If she were a normal nanny who didn't harbor a secret fascination with her employer, she would reprimand them lightly and break it up. But because she was a lustful Cinderella who really wanted to bang Prince Charming repeatedly until she could no longer walk, and then possibly marry him, she stood up with a stern look on her face.

"Now, Mary Jane . . ."

And when Cooper paused to glance at her in triumph that she was apparently on his side, she went straight for the abs. She knew what his body felt like and where he was sensitive. With unerring accuracy she wiggled her fingers across his flank and had him squawking in protest.

"Damn, no fair," he roared, doubling over, trying to prevent her from tickling him.

"Yes!" Mary Jane yelled with glee. "Get him!"

So she did. She had him gasping for air and smacking at her for a full sixty seconds before he grabbed her wrists and managed to overpower her.

"Oh, you're in trouble," he told her, pulling her arms straight out from her sides so she felt like a scarecrow.

"Hey, let go."

"I'm just protecting myself," he told her.

Giggling herself, Harley took a step back, trying to pull her arms out of his grip. "I promise I won't tickle you."

"Like I believe you."

She supposed he really didn't have any reason to believe her. After all, she'd lied to him about something huge. She wondered what he would say if he ever found out the truth. It wouldn't be pretty, she could guarantee that.

"I pinky-swear."

"Your pinky is not up."

"Because you're holding my arms too tight."

Cooper had moved in close to her. Too close. His expression was playful, yet intense. Harley took a step backward. She couldn't let him look too deeply into her eyes or he would see that she was attracted to him. See that she wanted him in the most base and primal way possible.

Or maybe he already saw it. Because his eyes narrowed before he murmured, "Sorry," and brought her arms down to her sides. "I guess I'll have to trust you, Harley."

It felt like he was asking her something else, or maybe that was just her own guilt. "I won't tickle you."

"But I will," Mary Jane said.

Cooper was tugged backward by his sister and the moment passed.

Or maybe there had been no moment. Maybe it was just her imagination.

Then he winked at her, so Mary Jane couldn't see.

Harley went back to her seat to read and convince herself that her panties weren't damp with desire.

It didn't work.

"CAN I ask what the hell you're doing?" Ty McCordle said to Cooper as they stood next to the stairs that would lead them up onto the podium.

"What do you mean? I'm standing here waiting to be introduced, just like you." Cooper was keyed up, more so than usual. He was distracted; he knew he was. By Mary Jane, by his previous season's poor standing. By the nagging concern that maybe he'd lost the edge with his driving.

By Harley. He was very distracted by Harley. She was fifty feet away talking to his sister, her access pass clipped to her sundress. He'd never seen her wear a dress, not since the wedding, and to see it exposing the tops of her breasts and her clavicle made him want to suck her flesh there. She was wearing cowboy boots, which brought all manner of inappropriate visuals to mind. Harley against a wall, sundress up, boot wrapped around his leg. Harley naked except for the boots.

Worst of all, he figured even though he'd never see Harley naked, his visual was probably damn accurate because he'd seen her identical twin naked. Which was just messed up. Yet helpful in stirring a boner, nonetheless.

Yeah. He was distracted.

"Why do you have your nanny here?" Ty asked.

"Because she's watching my sister. That's what a nanny does."

"Dude. Keep telling yourself that's the only reason she's here." Shaking his head, Ty gave him a look of disbelief. "No one brings their nanny to driver's intro. You're playing house, bro, aren't you?"

Maybe. What the fuck was it to Ty? "I wanted my sister here, but I don't trust that kid without a keeper. So that's why Harley's here. No big deal. It's not like I'm going to call her up on stage." He'd never done that. Ever. Having a woman stand next to you at driver's intro was like a promise ring. It meant an engagement was likely coming at some point. So he'd never done it and had never really thought twice about it, never been jealous of any of the other drivers.

Until now.

"I think you're playing with fire."

"I think you're as bad as the girls with your gossip." The announcer called his name then and Cooper gave Ty a grin. "See you on the track in my rearview mirror."

Ty grinned. "You wish."

Cooper put a smile on his face, jogged up the steps, and started waving. Unlike some of the guys, he enjoyed this part of the business. He loved the roar of the crowd, the interviews, the spotlight. Nothing gave him a greater sense of awe and appreciation than seeing fans wearing his number. It had been a great career, one that he was grateful every day for.

Yet today something was flat. Missing. Daytona was the big one, the race everyone knew, but Cooper just felt restless. He couldn't help it. Looking out into the crowd, he searched for MJ and Harley. His gaze landed on them and MJ gave him an exaggerated thumbs-up, the little shit. But he was glad she was there.

Harley looked solemn.

But then she winked at him.

She fucking winked.

Right on.

Cooper grinned back, the day suddenly all right.

UNTIL he hit the track, that is. It was a hotter day than usual in Florida in February and the track was sticking, car running loose. Sweat was rolling down Cooper's neck and forehead and he was watching the heat gauge carefully, instinct telling him the car was going to overheat.

"You're going to have to pit," his crew chief told him over his headset on lap ninety.

"No way," was his response. "I don't need tires for another twenty and you know there will be a caution." It was a gamble, but the way the sun was rising in heat waves off the track, interfering with visibility, he knew someone would tap another car and there'd be a flag. Or there would be debris. There was always something and he was willing to take the risk.

"You pay me to be smarter than you," Aaron told him. "I say pit."

Cooper laughed. "I appreciate your advice, but no." The

field was running clean and he was sitting in sixth place. He wasn't stopping now.

Which probably would have been a good call except for the 56 car floating up the track without warning and hitting the wall hard. Cooper was running so close to him there was no way to avoid the collision when the 56 spun out. He hit the back end of Monroe's car hard and went into the zone, years of training and experience allowing him to shut out everything but the need to regain control of his car and the situation. He could hear Aaron's voice guiding him to avoid further traffic and he obeyed easily, automatically, until within seconds he was stopped on the track, smoke rising from his engine.

"You alright?" Aaron asked.

"Fine. Car isn't looking so good, though, is it? Everyone else out there okay?"

There was the crackle of the radio for a brief second while Aaron listened to the other drivers and crew chief chatter and Cooper worried about his fellow drivers, who were his competition, his co-workers, and his friends.

"All clear. Everyone is fine. Head down into the apron and out of there. You're going to need to hit the garage from the looks of it."

"No doubt." A few minutes later, Cooper was climbing out of his car in the garage, ready to confer with his crew.

But before he could even gather his thoughts, Aaron was over his radio again. "Uh, Coop, bit of an issue of a personal nature."

"If you have diarrhea I don't want to hear about it. No time for the shits on race day." Annoyed, Cooper pulled his helmet and gloves off and wiped the sweat from his forehead.

But then his engineer waved him over. "Jeff Sterling is coming down to talk to you."

"Jeff? Why the fuck would Jeff want to talk to me? I have a car to get back on the track."

What had started out as a promising race was turning into a total bumblefuck. In all his years of racing he'd never had a quote-unquote "personal issue" pop up in the middle of a race. Suddenly a horrible thought occurred to him. His mother. Had something happened to his mother?

Wouldn't they wait until postrace to tell him if she had died or something of that nature?

He was about to go for his cell phone, race be damned, when Jeff entered the garage, wearing a suit and looking concerned. "Sterling, what is going on?" Cooper asked him, a pit in his gut.

"Harley McLain came to me. It seems Mary Jane is missing. She gave Harley the slip at the beach."

Okay, that was better than his mother being dead. And not surprising. MJ was known for wanting to do her own thing. Cooper was able to swallow his heart again. But he was worried. This was not a weekend for MJ to be running around on her own. There were all sorts of fans, drunk and otherwise, in town for the race. There was no telling where his sister was either, and that made him nervous. There weren't many places to go on the beach.

"Damn it." Cooper rubbed his forehead. "Did y'all call the cops?"

"I just did. Harley is hysterical. She won't leave the beach."

Cooper glanced back at his car, which his crew was working on. They were barely into the season. If he could get his car back out there he needed to, just to preserve whatever points he could by finishing the race. But how could he drive knowing his sister was missing?

"Fuck." He felt the sudden urge to throw his helmet all the way across the garage.

"I'll go over there, Brickman, you don't need to worry about it. I can handle it and we'll find her. I promise you."

"I know. But I can't go back out there until I know she's safe. How long will it take to get to the beach they're at?"

"Twenty minutes."

"Shit. Shit." He raked his hand through his hair and unzipped the front of his jumpsuit.

There was nothing for it. He had to go.

CHAPTER
ELEVEN

HARLEY was pretty sure she was going to have a heart attack and drop dead on the beach. In a bikini of all things. One minute she and Mary Jane had been lounging on the beach in a couple of chairs, then the next she had suddenly realized Mary Jane hadn't returned from the restroom.

Every Liam Neeson movie about abduction and sex slavery was running through her head and she was convinced that Mary Jane was tied up in the back of a windowless van on her way to the black market. She had looked everywhere on the beach and Cooper's sister was nowhere. She'd asked the ice cream stand workers and everyone in sight if they'd seen her to no avail. She had even asked a random man to go into the men's room and make sure Mary Jane wasn't being assaulted in there while she wandered around helplessly.

Finally, after a frantic twenty minutes she had tried to call Cami, Cooper's assistant, to see if there was a way to contact him during the race. Cami had given her Jeff Sterling's number and she had called him. He had said he would meet her there but in the meantime she should call the police. Harley was so distraught it had been helpful to hear a rational and calm voice in her ear, reassuring her that Mary Jane frequently disappeared and that he was sure she was perfectly fine.

She had continued to pace the beach after she had hung up with Jeff and called the cops. They had told her they would be out as soon as possible, but given that another twenty minutes had ticked by, she wasn't sure how seriously they were taking her call. Maybe she should have name-dropped and told them Mary Jane was Cooper Brickman's sister. It was sad but true that celebrity status garnered more attention.

It was with both relief and fear that she saw not only Jeff coming across the beach, wearing a suit, but Cooper with him in jeans and a T-shirt. Harley power-walked over to meet them.

"I'm so sorry, Cooper, I'm so sorry." And she promptly burst into tears.

"It's okay, it's not your fault." Cooper reached out and pulled her into his arms.

Harley collapsed against his chest, sobbing, realizing it was utterly ludicrous that he was comforting her when she was the one who had lost his sister, but appreciating the strong body to lean against nonetheless.

"She said she was going to the restroom. I thought it was fine for her to do that by herself."

"Harley, it's okay. Mary Jane is fine. She just answered my incredibly threatening text message."

She peeled her damp cheeks off his T-shirt and looked up at him. "What? She's okay? You're sure?"

He nodded. "It seems she decided to hang out with a group of middle school boys. They're over by the clock tower. We're on our way to go collect her thoughtless ass and take her home."

Relief had Harley's breath whooshing out of her lungs. "Oh, thank God." Suddenly she felt light-headed and she bent over, resting her palms on her knees, trying to fight off the black spots in front of her eyes and the nausea in her stomach. "I'm going to puke. Or faint."

Mary Jane was safe. She wasn't being tortured while Harley scurried around the beach, dodging sand pails.

But then another thought occurred to her. She stood straight up, her vision going black from the sudden movement. "Why aren't you on the track? Oh, my God, you left the race, didn't you?"

The serious look on his face confirmed that he had. "It's okay, Harley. I wanted to make sure Mary Jane was alright. Now let's go get her." He rubbed her arms before turning to Jeff. "Can you deal with the police while I retrieve MJ?"

"Sure, no problem." Jeff smiled at her. "You did the right thing, Harley."

Sure she had. She'd just caused Cooper to forfeit his standing in the race and any points he might have accrued. "Please tell me you weren't running in first place when you quit the field," she said to her boss.

He laughed. "Not even close. I had a bit of a dustup with Monroe and was in the garage making repairs. Jeff is right. You did the right thing. Come on."

The clock tower was just past the beach. Just past where Harley had gone in her search for Mary Jane. It figured. It just figured.

They spotted Mary Jane at the same time she spotted them. She leaped off the ledge she'd been sitting on, looking very cozy with a floppy-haired pubescent boy, and gave them a nervous wave.

"Oh, hey."

Oh, hey? Harley wanted to both hug her and shake her. Harley was so upset that she didn't even wait for Cooper to take the lead. She stopped in front of her charge and said, "Say good-bye to your friend. We're leaving *now*."

Mary Jane's eyes widened at her tone. "Fine." She turned back to the boy, who looked both terrified and in awe. "I guess I'll see you around."

"Aren't you Cooper Brickman?" he asked.

"I'm her brother, that's who I am." Cooper glared at Mary Jane. "You heard Harley. Get moving."

Mary Jane mouthed *Text me* to the boy, then stomped off with a glum look on her face, cell phone in her hand. "Fine. I'm going."

"I need a drink," Cooper muttered as they followed behind her. "Maybe it will prevent me from strangling her."

"I'm not sure whether to squeeze her in relief or scream at her."

"Exactly. I say we do both." Cooper shook his head. "And I also would like to cover her up with a fleece jumpsuit. My God. She's wearing next to nothing."

Now that he mentioned it, so was Harley. Fear receding, she was suddenly aware of the fact that she was also in nothing but a red bikini walking beside Cooper. "We are at the beach."

He glanced over at her. He seemed to likewise suddenly realize what she was wearing. Or wasn't wearing. His gaze dropped to her breasts and his eyes darkened. "You need to reapply your sunscreen." His finger brushed across her collarbone. "You're getting pink."

Harley shivered, despite the heat. "We're leaving anyway."

Mary Jane had reached where they had been sitting, their bags still tucked under their lounge chairs. She pulled hers out and started rifling through it. "Aren't you supposed to be at work, Cooper?"

It was the exact wrong thing to say.

Cooper exploded. "Yes! Yes, I am supposed to be at work! But when you go missing for forty minutes and don't answer Harley, she rightfully worries about you and calls me. So I left in the middle of a goddamn race because you're too selfish to understand that what you do affects other people. Harley was frantic. I was frantic. What the hell were you thinking?"

Mary Jane's expression was mulish and she glanced around, obviously self-conscious of the fact that other beachgoers could clearly hear her brother's angry reprimand. Harley put her hand on Cooper's arm to attempt to calm him down, but honestly she didn't blame him. She never wanted to feel that level of fear again. She had been absolutely convinced Mary Jane had been chloroformed.

"It wasn't a big deal. I was just hanging out."

"You snuck away. Admit it."

"Maybe we should talk about this in the car," Harley said, pulling on her cover-up and quickly packing up her sunscreen and paperback. "Do you think you have time to get back to the track?"

Cooper stood there, hands on hips, scowling. "It's not like I can just jump back in the car."

"It's a five-hour race." Guilt kicked in again. If she had been able to handle the situation on her own, Cooper wouldn't have left the track.

"And I'm sixty laps down at this point."

"I'm sorry." Harley shook out her flip-flops and stepped into them.

"Don't apologize. It's not your fault. It's Mary Jane's."

Harley pursed her lips. She wanted to tell him that she herself did bear some responsibility. She was there to ensure Mary Jane was safe, and she hadn't done that. He would be well within his rights to dismiss her without a reference. It wasn't like he hadn't warned her that Mary Jane was capable of going rogue.

But she didn't want to discuss it in front of his sister.

So she just followed both of them, sick to her stomach all over again. This had been a harmless wander-off, but what if it wasn't next time?

She would be watching Mary Jane like a suspicious hawk with a magnifying glass from now on. But that didn't mean Cooper would ever fully trust her again, and that sucked.

It just sucked.

COOPER wasn't kidding about that drink. Every muscle in his body was tense as their solemn little trio went into his condo after Jeff dropped them off at the front entrance of the high-rise. The longer he thought about what had happened, the more pissed off he became. The only thing that had saved him from completely losing his shit on his sister was the presence of Jeff and an occasional look of concern from Harley. He knew if he yelled she would get upset because somehow ludicrously she thought this was her fault.

It said wonderful things about her that she had been so concerned about his sister's safety and that she worried that in any way she had been remiss in her duties. His feeling was the kid was as slippery as an eel and looked deceptively sweet. There was no way Harley could have foreseen she would make a run for it. She didn't have the experience with her to see the signs. Cooper didn't have the experience himself, how could he expect Harley to have MJ's number completely?

He knew he needed time to calm down so once they were in the condo, he flatly told Mary Jane, "Go to your room. Don't come out until I say you can."

"What?" She shot him a look of pure indignation. "What is this, prison?"

"It's the nicest prison you'll ever be in." He was a little tired of the attitude. No, he was actually a lot tired of the attitude. He didn't remember being such a dick when he was thirteen. If he had backtalked his gran like that she would have slapped him silly.

"Argh!" she yelled, stomping off as much as you can in flip-flops and a bathing suit.

Despite the rubber shoes, MJ managed it damn dramatically, he had to give her credit.

"I want a beer the size of my head," he told Harley, heading into the kitchen. "Can I get you anything? Earplugs, maybe? A raise?"

"I wouldn't mind some sweet tea."

"With whiskey in it?"

She laughed. "No, I'm good. Technically, I'm still on the clock."

He snorted. "Screw that. I say do a shot after the day we've had."

"It was a rough one, I have to admit." Harley rubbed her arms with her hands, padding into the kitchen after him, her feet bare. "Besides, it's cold in here, so maybe I will have just a splash of whiskey."

"The housekeeper keeps the A/C on arctic. I leave notes that she ignores." Cooper wondered what Harley thought about his rather bizarre lifestyle. People he paid had more control over his day-to-day existence than he did. "I can turn it down now, though. Or is it up? I've always wondered about that."

"Well, you're turning the temperature up. But turning the A/C down. So both are accurate."

"So I'm always right? Excellent." He winked at her. It took him a second to remember where the thermostat actually was. He was just too transient to be able to log in minor details like that. But it was right in the entryway and he quickly adjusted it before heading back. He didn't want Harley to retreat to her room. He wanted her to understand he didn't blame her in any way.

He also just wanted her company. He'd gotten used to being able to relax with her in the evenings. And he definitely needed to relax after the debacle of a day they'd had. But she hadn't bolted. She had poked around in the cabinets and found two highball glasses and was filling them with ice.

The whiskey was in the cupboard above the fridge. That he knew. He got it down and poured himself a full glass. In hers he splashed a finger of whiskey, then fished around in the back of the fridge for a can of iced tea. It wasn't necessarily classy, but it was what it was.

Harley took a sip and shuddered. "Oh, dear Lord. I'm not much of a liquor drinker."

He knocked his own back like he was a dying man in the desert. It burned, but in a good way. "Let's chill out on the balcony for a few."

It had a good view of the water and given the time of day the temperature outside was probably perfect. He left the door open to kill some of the A/C and to listen for the sound of the front door if MJ decided to escape from her pampered prison.

"It's beautiful out here," Harley said.

"It is." Then because he'd been thinking about how beautiful she was for damn near every minute for the last three weeks, he spoke before he could turn on the filter between his brain and his mouth. "Not as beautiful as you, though."

Her eyes widened. "Cooper . . ."

"What?" He brushed his knee against hers. She looked

like a hot fudge sundae in her bikini, even with that wrap thing on over it. "It's true."

"Thank you, but . . ."

"But what?" Now he found himself brushing his fingers over her bare knee, enjoying the way she shivered. "I find you very attractive, Harley."

"I work for you."

"I am very aware of that. I am also aware of the fact that every minute since I've found myself thinking about you. What I don't know is if you find me attractive."

"Are you kidding?" She looked shocked. "Of course I do!"

Well. Fuck yeah. His cock swelled in response to her vehement conviction. "Then what's the issue?"

"The issue is that I work for you."

How did he phrase this without scaring her off? "That would be a problem if I just wanted something casual. But I don't want to just mess around with you. I want to have a relationship."

He hadn't been planning to blurt that out either, but looking at her, staring into her beautiful and warm eyes, he couldn't resist. She needed to know he wasn't the dude who banged the help then either let them go or ignored them. He needed her to see that he thought she was amazing. He thought she was maybe The One. In fact, he was pretty damn sure she was. Thirty-five years, a lot of women, and no one, not one single person, had ever made him feel as calm, protective, and content as Harley did.

"I admire you. I like you, as a person. I like you a whole hell of a lot. I want to take this to its natural conclusion." He traced a pattern on her knee with his thumb. He wanted to touch her, everywhere. To own the right to be the man who put his arm around her, to whisper in her ear, to touch the small of her back and kiss the corners of her mouth. He wanted that so bad he ached for it. Was willing to throw himself out there for rejection just on the off chance he'd get it.

"What? A relationship? With *me*?"

Cooper took her hand and squeezed it. "Yes. You. I think you're honestly the most amazing woman I've ever met. Please just give me a chance. Truth be told, I think we're already having a relationship, aren't we? A friendship at the very least."

"But . . . but . . ."

She was just about sputtering. Cooper knew how to fix that. He slid his fingers into the softness of her blond hair and drew her head toward him. Then he dropped his lips over hers in a soft kiss. When he pulled back she was quiet, blinking at him. "But nothing, Harley."

Then a horrible thought occurred to him and he finished off the rest of his whiskey to brace himself. There was no way around it. If they were going to have a relationship it needed to start out honest, and he had a big old naked skeleton in his closet.

"I do need to tell you something, though."

"I need to tell you something, too."

"Me first." Because his sucked, and he wanted it out before he dropped his balls down onto the beach and lost his nerve. "I, uh, had sex with your sister."

She blinked at him. "You what?"

"I had sex with Charity. At the wedding. But don't worry about it. It didn't mean anything." Then because her lip was starting to tremble and he was starting to panic, he added what he thought she would want to hear, even though it was a total lie. "It wasn't even good sex. It was terrible, actually. Awful." So much for being honest. "A complete mistake."

Her highball slipped out of her hands and shattered on the concrete floor of the balcony. "Oh, my God."

Harley leaped to her feet, shoved past him, and retreated into his condo. He heard the definitive slam of her bedroom door.

Shit. That hadn't gone so well. Not that he could have hoped for any better, frankly. But he'd had a running start. He was almost certain Harley had been contemplating dating him until he'd told her about Charity.

He stood up and promptly cut his foot on a piece of glass.

Perfect ending to a perfectly miserable day.

THE return trip to Charlotte the next morning was a thousand times more awkward than the trip down. Harley kept her earbuds in the entire time, while trying to pretend that Cooper wasn't continuously giving her smoldering looks at frequent intervals. He kept trying to corner her, but she didn't want to talk to him. She couldn't.

His words on the balcony kept ringing in her ears over and over, the humiliation poignant enough to give her hot cheeks and a sick stomach every single time she thought about it. Even now on the private jet Cooper had rented, she winced as she aimlessly flipped through the pages of a magazine.

She sucked in bed. She was a bad lay.

And not only was she a terrible lover, she was too stupid to know it. The whole time she'd been thinking that she and Cooper had shared a night of mutual pleasure and passion, and he only reflected back on it with a wince. Fabulous. Just fucking fabulous.

In the past twelve sleepless hours she had dissected everything about that night trying to determine where she'd gone wrong and how she could have misread Cooper's response to her. Was she not flexible enough? Admittedly, she was terrible at yoga. Should she have showered first? Did she have a hooked vagina or something and no one had the heart to tell her? Had she scraped him with her teeth? The number of potential horrors was astonishingly high and she had run through every single one. Then started back at number one and run through them again.

It wasn't particularly productive.

Nor was it a great idea to be contemplating texting every man she'd ever slept with and asking him to rate her bedroom skills on a scale of one to ten, one being he'd had root canals more pleasurable, ten being he'd pick her over a porn star. Fortunately, she was on the plane and in full view of Cooper, so she resisted the urge. Her grandmother had always said if you don't want to hear the answer, don't ask the question. It definitely applied to this situation.

The most horrific part of the whole thing was that she had been stunned to hear that Cooper actually liked her. Wanted to date her. He'd said she was amazing. It had been like everything she could have ever wanted handed to her in a pretty package with a beautiful bow on top. Then she had dropped it and watched it get promptly run over by a semi-truck. And set on fire. She'd been prepared to tell Cooper the truth. That she was the one he had slept with. That she had lied, allowed him to think she was her sister. He would have been angry, but she had been prepared to deal with that. There was no way around it. She couldn't engage in a relationship without being honest.

Clearly, he felt the same way, which told her everything she needed to know about his character. Everything she had already seen, truthfully, but it was a further reminder. He was a good guy who cared about doing what was right. Having him care about her? Want to be with her? It was something really special and for the briefest, most fleeting of moments she had felt giddy at the very concept.

Only to hear that on the sexual scale she was about as seductive as a slug.

So here they were, trapped in a tin can together, Cooper moving restlessly in his seat, Harley so tense she had a softball-size knot in her shoulder, Mary Jane pouting as her brother continually snapped at her.

It was a whole lot of not fun.

Her knee-jerk reaction was that she clearly needed to quit her job.

But she didn't think she could do that to Mary Jane. Everyone always left her, from her father dying, to her mother taking off at random intervals, to the two previous nannies ditching after just a few weeks. Harley couldn't do that to her as well. Mary Jane acted with bravado and nonchalance, but she was still a little girl and she had shown Harley moments of great vulnerability.

Abandoning her was out of the question, so Harley was going to have to figure out how to deal with Cooper. Or not deal with Cooper.

He chose that very moment to sit down next to her, dropping down with long-legged sexiness, filling her space with his scent and presence. He tossed his hair out of his eyes. "We need to talk."

Actually, she'd be perfectly content to never do that again. She couldn't even look him in the eye. "This isn't the time," she said, voice low and tight.

"You're not going to quit, are you?" he murmured.

So much for this not being the time or place. Harley forced herself to turn and look at him.

His eyes were pleading, his head leaning toward her. "Please don't. No matter what you think of me, please don't quit. You never have to see me if you can't stand the sight of me."

This was a perfectly horrific irony. She wanted nothing more than to spend every day with him. The fantasy Cooper had been outdone by the real Cooper and she had been steadily and easily falling hard for him. At the moment all she wanted was to close the distance between them and kiss him. But he would probably end up gagging from disgust, she was so clearly unskilled.

"I'm not going to quit," she whispered. "Mary Jane is important to me."

"But I'm not?"

He looked so earnest, so sincere, that Harley felt everything inside her melt like hot butter. She gripped the armrests with sweaty palms and wondered if she had the courage to confess that she was the dud he'd slept with. "You are."

"But I fucked it up." It wasn't a question.

Harley shook her head. She opened her mouth, but nothing came out. She didn't know how to tell him.

Cooper sighed when the pause drew out. "Fine. I won't bother you anymore."

There was nothing satisfying about that at all.

COOPER arrived home in a foul mood. So that was that. He'd finally met a woman he wanted to settle down into a relationship with, and in the most ridiculous of all scenarios possible, he'd banged her identical twin already. It wasn't even like he could chalk this up to misguided youth. He was thirty-fucking-five.

But it wasn't like he walked around with a sexual crystal ball. How the hell had he known he was going to fall head over ass for Harley? With the knowledge he'd had at the time, he hadn't made a faulty decision when he'd slept with

Charity. He just regretted it now more profoundly than about anything that he'd ever done. Harley obviously had seen through his desperate and unconvincing attempt to convince her the sex had sucked. She wasn't even willing to discuss it with him.

He was grateful she wasn't going to quit as MJ's nanny, but it was cold comfort.

Rosa was in his bedroom when he got home, and that irritated him all over again. It reeked like church in his inner sanctuary and he didn't even know what church smelled like. But he was convinced this was the smell and he didn't need to be reminded of his sins, thank you very much. He was well aware of them.

"Rosa, stop burning that shit in here," he said sternly. He was way too lenient with his staff. Hadn't he just been reflecting on the fact that their preferences dictated his life, not his own personal likes and dislikes? "It makes my eyes water."

She made the sign of the cross in front of him. Rosa was short and curvy and she cleaned in jeans and an astonishing diversity of cardigans with embellishments. He'd never known there were so many colors of yarn in existence until she'd started working for him. He really did like her. She was like a Hispanic grandmother to him and MJ. But at the moment he couldn't deal with the incense.

"Then stop taking the nanny's intimate apparel. It's not right."

"What are you talking about? I've never taken Harley's . . . intimate apparel." That particular phrasing made him want to laugh. It was like he was six and in Sears shopping for bras with his gran. It had never ceased to amaze and intrigue him, that particular department with its bins and bins of lacy cups, while simultaneously making him feel like a first-class creeper. He felt exactly the same way at the moment discussing Harley's underwear with Rosa.

"That bra I found in your closet. It's Harley's. Don't think I don't know."

She was giving him some kind of evil eye.

"No, it wasn't. It was someone else's." He wasn't going to say who, but definitely someone else's.

"But I do the wash, and so I saw that Harley has the matching panties. It's a set." She gestured to her breasts and to her crotch.

Cooper could have done without the visual aid. He didn't need Rosa's body parts pointed out to him. It was so distracting and scarring that it took him a second to process what she was saying. That didn't make sense. "There are lots of types of red lingerie. How do you know it matches?"

"It has a little pearl heart in the middle on both and the fabric is the same." She waved her hand to dismiss his protests. "They match."

That was weird. Did identical twins share underwear? That seemed a little hard to believe. "Well, it's not hers. Trust me. It's just a coincidence."

Her eyebrow went up. She made the sign of the cross again.

"Stop doing that."

"I'm allowed to practice my faith."

"Not in my bedroom." Enough was enough.

She started muttering to herself in Spanish and threw her hands up in the air. But she started toward the door. Cooper felt guilty immediately. "Rosa. Thanks for caring about my soul."

She stopped and nodded, a smile splitting her face. "Open your eyes, Cooper Brickman, and your heart. You're a good man and you deserve love. Not harlots."

He was fairly certain he'd never slept with a harlot, and that one woman shouldn't be morally judging another. But he appreciated her sentiment all the same. "Thanks."

Then he went into his closet and instantly lost all positive feelings when he discovered a two-foot statue of the Virgin Mary nestled among his dress shirts. It looked like it belonged in someone's garden. Mary was looking up at him solemnly, her hands clasped in prayer over her turquoise robes.

"I never touched Harley's bra," he told her. "I've been framed."

She didn't look like she believed him.

CHAPTER
TWELVE

IT was a long week that sucked. Hard. Cooper was in the kitchen, ready to leave for the weekend and a Saturday race. He desperately wanted to escape the tension in his house, yet at the same time he was dragging his feet, not wanting more time to slide by without any communication with Harley. She was being polite to him, nothing more. All her conversation focused on his sister, and she had bailed on dinner on Monday and Tuesday, claiming a headache both nights.

Sinus weather, she'd said.

It wasn't her sinuses and they both knew it.

She couldn't look at him without picturing him in bed with her twin.

"What time will you be home on Sunday?" Harley asked Wednesday night, scooping cookie dough onto a baking sheet. She made cookies. How could he not love her? "I have a bachelorette party to go to."

A bachelorette party. Hello. He had to admit, the thought

of Harley at one of those girls-gone-wild nights was a hell of a turn-on. He suddenly had an image of Harley cutting loose with her girlfriends in a tight tank top and a short skirt. He would really like to see that. There was most likely more to Harley than met the eye and he wished he could see any or all of it. "On a Sunday night? Who is getting hitched?"

"Shawn Hamby married Rhett Ford a couple of weeks back and they're having a reception on Monday, bachelorette party on Sunday. I know, it's weird because they're already married, but the bride was overruled by his family."

Ah, the marriage-after-a-minute MJ had been talking about. "Sounds fun. Where's it at?"

"The Silver Buckle. It starts at nine."

That bar had a mechanical bull. Damn, but what he would give to see her wrapping her thighs around a bull. He cleared his throat. "I'll be home by then. If not, then Rosa can stay with MJ for a couple hours. It's all good."

"I don't need a babysitter," MJ protested.

He and MJ had been as polite with each other as he and Harley. He felt like his relationship with his sister had taken a step backward and it was contributing to his misery. "I would feel better if Rosa were here," he said simply, not wanting to argue with her.

"That sounds good," Harley said. "Shawn and I have been friends for a few years. I would hate to miss it."

He had a thought and it was a bad one to have. He could crash the party. It was a free country. He could happen to be at that bar, right? He was bound to know a person or two.

Harley would be pissed, though. But maybe under those circumstances she would loosen up and he could talk to her, press his case. He wasn't ready to throw in the towel yet. He looked at her and he just ached to hold her. He'd had one brief taste of her lips and it had been the ultimate tease. One potato chip before someone yanked the bag out of his hands. God, he cared about her so much. He wanted to hold her and kiss her and love her and build a life with her.

Maybe Rosa had a candle for that.

"I'm sure you'll have fun. But watch out for Eve. She'll draw you into trouble." Like a fetish club. Damn. He'd forgotten about that. But he suddenly remembered and it was clear Harley did, too.

"I can handle Eve."

"Well, you certainly handle us." He meant it as a compliment, and hell, it was the truth, but it didn't sound quite right.

Harley's expression was solemn, searching. He missed her warm, bashful smile, occasional sass sneaking in. He wanted to coax that smile out of her again, see it directed at him with a genuine light and sweetness. But mostly now when she even looked at him, she stared at him like he was a Grade A fuck-up.

Which he was. But he was an inadvertent fuck-up. Didn't that count for something?

"You handle yourself just fine."

Okay, now that sounded even worse than what he'd said. Cooper wanted to laugh. But the look of horror on Harley's face had him coughing to hide it.

"I mean, have a safe flight and a good race."

Cooper picked up his bag. "Alright, well, have fun if I don't see you before then."

"Thanks. I hope everything goes well for you down there. This is going to be your season. I can feel it."

How was he supposed to think rationally when she said nice things like that? Women weren't nice to him, not really. They were usually angling, trying to please. But that wasn't the same as being nice.

No one ever called him out either. Harley already had, multiple times. She had offered her honest opinion on how he was failing his sister, and he appreciated that she had MJ's best interests in mind.

She was the perfect woman for him. He just knew it.

Yeah. He was so going to the Silver Buckle Sunday night.

IT was her one night to finally have some fun and Cooper was ruining it. Absolutely freaking ruining it.

Harley sat at the sticky table at the Buckle with Shawn and Eve and jammed her straw into her drink over and over, thoroughly agitated. "I seriously cannot believe he's here. Why is he here?" She had specifically mentioned where she was going to be so he didn't accidentally decide on a whim to come to the same place. She didn't want to see him. She had avoided him all week after their awkward encounter in Daytona when she had learned she blew in bed and her subsequent complete lame-ass inability to tell him the truth.

"He told me he was here for the salsa," Eve said, shrugging.

"The salsa?" What the hell. "He could have ordered the salsa and had it waiting for him at the house if he really wanted this particular salsa. He could have flown the damn salsa to Florida and back. He's the kind of guy you say could buy a second boat when the first one gets wet, that's how much money he has." She'd seen it firsthand. A few bucks were not a concern for Cooper.

He was playing some kind of game. He had to have known Charity was going to be here at this bachelorette party with her. Was he trying to make her jealous by hitting on her sister? That made no sense because he'd already told her the sex had been terrible.

Egotistical as it was, when she'd first seen him, she had thought he was there to pursue her and her vagina had fluttered. Hard-core, girl-bits-on-fire, call-of-the-wild shit. She wanted him. Despite the fact that if he knew she was the woman he'd had sex with, he wouldn't want her. It was torture. Like complete and utter agony. "I hate feeling this way."

"What way?" Shawn asked.

"At the mercy of my hormones. It's about as useful as an ashtray on a motorcycle." Because she was distracted, and damn it, she was jealous. So if that was his plan, it was sure as shit working. Cooper had waved to her and given her a big old smile, but then he had grabbed a beer and made his way to the dance floor, where he had a steady stream of admirers shimmying around him.

"Maybe you just need to get laid."

Yeah, well. She had at the wedding and look how that had turned out.

"By who? I'm not hiring a male prostitute." She sucked hard on her rum runner, feeling particularly bitter. "But I'll shut up now because this is your party and this is a happy occasion."

"That was convincing," Eve said with a grin.

Rhett and Nolan's sisters had come up to the table and they were all talking. Harley silently stewed. Now Cooper was dancing with her sister. Seriously? Charity was laughing, her head flung back as he murmured something to her. What the hell? Granted, she had never told her sister what had really gone down. Charity did know they'd kissed and as her twin she should know not to flirt with the guy Harley had secretly slept with as her. Which sounded so ludicrous even in her own head that she took another hard sip of her drink.

Without warning, Rhett's sisters grabbed Harley by the hand and dragged her onto the dance floor. She tried to resist, but she was so distracted, she was no match for middle-aged married women on the loose from their husbands and children. Trying to blend behind their undulating bodies, Harley halfheartedly danced as she used the cover of the wives to watch Cooper.

His hand was on Charity's back and was heading south down the I-77 of her ass crack.

Wait a minute.

Why would he be doing that?

He had said he wanted to be with *her*, Harley. Was this retaliation for turning him down?

Whatever it was, there was no mistaking it when he kissed her sister.

If she had been holding her drink she would have dropped it. Or thrown it in his face. And you know what? Charity's, too. Her twin was letting a man kiss her knowing full well Harley had already kissed him.

Just stick a fork in her. She was so done.

COOPER had a buzz and a hard-on. He was damn confused and thinking that showing up at the Buckle had been a bad idea. Like one of the worst he'd ever had. Not to mention that he had impulsively invited his former stepfather's former stepson, Jeff Sterling. He wasn't sure what that made them relation-wise. Former half stepbrothers? Did such a thing exist? Though maybe, because the marriages had all been at different times, the step label didn't even apply. But be that as it may, Cooper usually liked Jeff's company. Plus he thought it looked less sketchy to show up at the bar with a wingman.

Except that Jeff had spent the first twenty minutes asking about his nanny, and staring over at Harley, where she was sitting with her friends.

He did not want his former half stepbrother hitting on

Harley. Because damn it, he had a feeling that Jeff was precisely the kind of guy Harley would go for. Steady, intelligent, thoughtful. Jeff said he'd met her at the wedding. Which made Cooper wonder if "met" was a cover for "made out" or more. The thought of Jeff's mouth on Harley's at any point in the past, present, or future made him see red. And green.

"I think I'll go see if Harley wants a drink," Jeff said, standing up from his stool.

What a dick.

Feeling surly, Cooper just nodded and ordered another beer for himself. Didn't Jeff know that he was treading on Cooper's territory here? Where was the damn guy code these days?

Which was completely irrational, he knew, because he had never once mentioned to Jeff that he had even the slightest interest in Harley. Their relationship was private. He hadn't ever felt the need to discuss or share it with anyone past Ryder, and that had been out of pure desperation. He'd needed someone to tell him to go for it, which he had, and look where that had gotten him.

"I'm hitting the dance floor." Maybe grinding with a random stranger would improve his mood. Which was perhaps the most pathetic thought he'd ever had in his entire life.

When he got out on the sticky floor and tried to find his groove, he was startled to see that Charity was out there, dancing in a way that left little to the imagination. Wearing a tiny, short denim skirt, pink cowboy boots, and a shirt with fringe dangling off her chest. He hadn't even realized she was there, which if he hadn't been totally preoccupied with his own personal misery and unrealistic quest to get Harley to talk to him, he would have realized made total sense. Of course Charity would be there. She was Shawn's friend, too.

But now he really regretted his impulsive decision to crash the party. Obviously Charity had not told Harley about their night together, so she couldn't be happy with him for spilling it. He wasn't sure how to act or what to say or who may or may not slap him at some point during the course of the night. It was hard to process even for a sober man, and he was pretty damn sure he was no longer sober.

Before he could exit stage left, Charity offered him a smile. She didn't look like she wanted to rip his balls off. "Hey, Cooper!"

"Hey," he said to her, giving her a smile, relieved that at least one twin didn't look at him like he was pond scum. "Y'all having fun?"

"A blast!" She continued to gyrate her hips. "How about you? Funny bumping into you here."

"Yeah. Total coincidence." That he had orchestrated carefully and thought about repeatedly for the last three days. "I bet you're glad to be Roger-free for a night."

"Oh, God, you have no idea." She made a face. "Having him here would be like setting a cat loose in a catnip factory."

"He's nineteen and making bank. He's going to get a little wild before he reins himself in." Or he would wind up like Cooper. Thirty-five and single with a string of failed pseudo-relationships behind him.

Yeah. Not where he wanted his thoughts to go.

"I'm not cut out to be the reins." Charity gave him a grin and shook her fringe. "It's not really my style to hold back."

Was she flirting with him? Reminding him of their night together? When he looked at her, he saw Harley. Why couldn't she be her? It made him melancholy and confused. God, he was drunk. "I can respect that."

The song changed to a slower tempo and he felt compelled to put an arm around her. Because it was the polite thing to do. To dance with her. Not weird and inappropriate and fucked up in the least. Plus if he tilted his head and squinted, it was almost like she was Harley.

Charity laughed and because he wanted nothing more than for Harley to find him funny, he felt overwhelmed by that realization. He was in so much trouble. Harley was off-limits. She'd made it clear how she felt about him. Hell, she was talking to Jeff at that very moment, probably smiling and laughing for that asshole. Harley thought Cooper was a douchebag. Harley was too nice for him. He didn't deserve her.

Charity was his type of woman. Charity didn't think he was a shitty brother and a moron. Charity laughed and smiled at him like Harley would laugh for Jeff. Charity had already tumbled into bed with him. Maybe he should have fallen in love with her instead of Harley. Maybe he still could and it would be like he really *was* with Harley.

So with that logic soundly backing his drunken motives, Cooper bent his head and kissed Charity.

It felt . . . flat. Like something was missing. It wasn't an awkward kiss. But it just didn't feel like much of anything.

And he had the overwhelming feeling that he had never kissed this woman before in the whole of his life.

So what the hell did that mean?

CHARITY was caught off guard by Cooper Brickman laying one on her. One second they'd been dancing two feet apart, then two inches apart, then suddenly he was dropping a kiss on her. She was so shocked it took a few seconds to respond, as in slap the shit out of him, but by then he was pulling back, taking his beer breath with him.

Glancing around, she wondered if anyone had noticed. She was all for a little fun and spontaneity, but it wasn't standard procedure for her to make out with men she didn't know on the dance floor. Especially a man who had made out with her sister. God, what a jackass. Fortunately, no one in their immediate vicinity seemed to be paying them any sort of attention. But then she saw a familiar face across the room, watching them with a fair amount of disdain.

Jeff Sterling.

Seriously? How it was possible that he was there to witness a kiss she hadn't initiated or wanted? She dropped her arms from Cooper's neck and tried to laugh, but it sounded brittle. "I wonder what Jeff Sterling is doing here. I don't usually run in the same social circles as he does." She was not even going to acknowledge that Cooper had just kissed her.

"Oh, he came with me." Cooper put his hand on the small of her back and started to lead her off the dance floor, but she hustled forward so his hand was no longer touching her.

"It looks like he's with your sister," Cooper added.

Jeff was. He had crossed from the bar to sit down next to Harley, clearly setting a drink in front of her. The only time Jeff had talked to Harley was when he had really been talking to her, Charity. It made her instantly jealous of her twin, a feeling she detested. "That's weird," she told Cooper. Awful. Shitty. Chock-full of suck.

"Why?" he asked.

"Because I just wouldn't think they would gravitate towards each other." But even as she said it, she knew that her conclusion was a dumb one.

"Actually, I bet they have a lot in common, including temperament." Cooper sounded thoughtful and unhappy as he was staring at her sister and Jeff. "I want a shot of whiskey," he said, sounding annoyed. "Care to join me?"

"I can't do a shot because I have a wedding reception to

go to tomorrow, but I will get another beer." That probably even wasn't a good idea, but she was doing it anyway. She was stuck with Cooper while Harley had Jeff chatting her up and plying her with alcohol? So not fair.

This crush on Jeff had brought her nothing but annoyance and low self-esteem.

She was so not having fun.

Worst bachelorette party ever.

INITIALLY as Harley sat at the table and watched Charity and Cooper on the dance floor, she was grateful for Jeff Sterling talking with her and serving as an occasional distraction. But then it occurred to her, as the nonalcoholic drink she had requested and her buzz both started to disappear, that Jeff was being abnormally attentive. She didn't know him at all other than calling him out of desperation when Mary Jane went missing, and at first she'd thought he was just being friendly since she was Cooper's nanny and was sitting alone at a bar.

Even when he asked, "So what are your days off from work?" it didn't click.

"Monday and Tuesday."

It wasn't until his next question that she realized that Jeff was actually showing some kind of actual interest in her.

"Could I take you to dinner some time?"

Harley stopped staring at Cooper on the dance floor and turned to stare at Jeff. Seriously? No men paid attention to her in oh, two years, and suddenly she had both Cooper and Jeff wanting to date her? What the hell. Jeff was giving her an encouraging smile. She suddenly realized his arm was on the back of her chair. So she was a total idiot who couldn't pick up on a man's signals. And while Jeff was exactly the kind of man she should be turning cartwheels to go out with, she felt a little deflated by the idea. A lot deflated. Flattered, yes, but not particularly interested. But at the same time, she would have to be a total idiot to turn down a date with a successful and kind businessman to moon over the man who was never going to want to have sex with her ever again once he learned the truth. Which at this point should be never.

"Sure," she heard herself saying. But even as she said it, she suddenly realized that Charity liked Jeff. Or at least thought he was attractive. She couldn't go out with him. But she'd just said yes.

Of course, on the other hand, hadn't Charity just kissed Cooper knowing full well how Harley felt about him?

Screw Charity. If Jeff wanted to take her out she had every right to say yes since Charity had already violated the girl code. Sister code. Twin code. Every code there possibly could be.

"Excellent. Do you like Asian food? There's a new fusion place that opened up downtown that I would like to try."

That sounded like a real thing. Like cute clothes and a pricey menu. "Sounds wonderful." Or awful. But she was fueled by righteous indignation and jealousy, always a magical combination.

"Is tomorrow too soon?" He gave her a smile. "Am I coming off as overeager?"

Frankly, she couldn't imagine why he would be eager at all. She'd been about as interesting as watching sawdust settle for the last twenty minutes. "Tomorrow I have a wedding reception to go to, and I anticipate Tuesday will be recovery time. So how does next week sound?" Because now she was in, and she was having to go out on this date. With a nice guy. She mentally kicked herself for even thinking it was a hardship.

"That would be great. How about eight? And where should I pick you up?"

Harley wished she didn't have to drive everyone home in a few hours, because she really regretted having cut herself off from the alcohol. This called for a drink. A stiff one. "Well, you know I live at Cooper's." Far, far away from his bedroom. "I don't think it's really okay for you to pick me up, do you?"

"Sure. You know Coop and I are related in a manner of speaking, so I'm sure he's fine with it."

Oh, somehow she doubted Cooper was going to be fine with it. If she weren't currently so pissed off at him for kissing her sister after he had told her how he felt about her, she would feel bad to be having another man pick her up at Cooper's. But she shouldn't feel bad. He was the one groping Charity right in front of her in the rudest of all rude moves. That was seriously rude. It was downright awful rude. It was like saying she didn't matter at all, that she was completely and quickly replaceable. And had she mentioned it was rude?

Anger started to spread, like an ugly and itchy rash, throughout her body. You know what? Cooper and Charity could have each other and their bad sex.

And who cared if the bad sex had actually been her? Cooper thought it was Charity, so probably their sex would suck, too. At least that's what she was telling herself.

"I'm glad Mary Jane has someone around now to guide her. She's a special girl and I know Bud would be happy with how she's turning out, and the fact that someone like you is there for her."

Right. Jeff. He was talking to her. Complimenting her. It made her feel shitty for all sorts of reasons. She didn't deserve his praise. "I did lose her in Daytona."

But Jeff just smiled. "Not your fault. Don't beat yourself up over it. She has her mom's ability to disappear without warning."

Harley gave a wan smile, not really feeling any better about it. "It shaved a decade off my life I think."

"The next time you bring her to a race, let me know. You and Mary Jane can sit in my box with me."

Oy. That sounded awkward. Intimate. "Excellent."

If only it had ended there, the night might have turned out completely differently.

Instead, Jeff excused himself after getting her number and Harley went over to watch Eve and Shawn duke it out on the mechanical bull.

And Charity told her that Cooper had asked her out.

"He asked you out?" Harley freaked. She couldn't help it. Of course she knew that something was going down between Charity and Cooper since she had seen them lip-locked, his hand on Charity's ass, but hearing it out loud, like it was more than just a dance floor grope, had her thoughts catapulting into a future where her sister and Cooper became a couple, married, and had babies with stupid hybrid names like Chooper and Cority.

What. The. Hell.

So she was that forgettable? Literally after four days of pursuing her he just gave up and defaulted back to her sister? What a prick. She officially totally and completely hated Cooper Brickman. She was going to start a club. The Cooper Is a Cock Club.

"Yeah. I so didn't see that coming." Charity shrugged her shoulders. "And considering he made out with you, I think that's just downright shitty. It's a good thing neither one of us is actually interested in him, because he pretty much has bought a ticket to DoucheCon in my opinion."

"Did it ever occur to you that I *am* interested in Cooper?" she asked Charity.

Her twin looked astonished. "You are? Well, shit."

It should have made her feel better that Charity looked so surprised, but she was not in a mood to be mollified. So she just said, "Well, shit is right."

Charity started to speak, but Harley very childishly walked away, afraid of what she might say if she stayed. She knew it wasn't her sister's fault that Cooper was fickle and clearly going for the lowest sexual denominator. He'd rather have bad sex than no sex at all. It did not say good things about him, and she was feeling hurt and vulnerable and stupid for being duped by his character. Or clear lack thereof.

All of it was just too much to handle in one week, and when they left the Buckle later after she had spent an hour stewing and staying far away from her sister and Cooper, she was still furious. So furious that she felt like punching Rhett when he spoke to her from the backseat as she drove.

"So Harley, you're quiet up there. Did you have fun?"

"It was fine." Or shitty, however you wanted to look at it.

Charity snorted.

"Wrong question, hon," Shawn told Rhett.

Great. Even Shawn had realized she was in a mood. She felt like a jerk for being a brat on Shawn's big night.

"I'm sorry, Harley. Didn't mean to poke a sore spot," Rhett said.

Then before she could apologize to the car as a whole, and Shawn in particular, Charity exploded at her from the passenger seat. "I didn't know you were crushing on him. If you would actually share something with me once in a while, I wouldn't have kissed him. You know, it's really very hurtful that you won't let me in, Harley. I tell you *everything*."

"Wait, so this is my fault?" Harley asked in shock, taking a turn a little hard and running them over the curb.

"Maybe I should drive," Rhett suggested. "Were you drinking, Harley?"

"No. I cut myself off three hours ago because that's what I do," she said. "I am the driver and the wallflower while Charity gets drunk and dances half naked with the guy she totally knew I was into!" Okay, that wasn't fair, and she knew it. Charity hadn't known anything. She had intentionally withheld information from her sister. But then again, hadn't she just admitted she'd kissed him?

"Uh!" Charity gasped. "Don't you dare throw the slut flag at me. I was not hitting on him and I didn't know you liked him. For your information, I was actually shocked that he kissed me and embarrassed because it just so happens the guy I like was there. Flirting with *you*. Which I'd like to point out, you knew."

"Paybacks are a bitch," Harley said, which was totally unlike her and very irrational, but seeing her sister with Cooper? That shit *hurt*.

Shawn leaned forward before Charity could respond and inserted her head between theirs. "Harley, if Charity didn't know, then I don't see how you can be upset with her. And Charity, if you want Harley to share, maybe you should let her speak from time to time. Y'all know you love each other and would never do anything to hurt each other intentionally. Chicks before dicks, right?"

"Absolutely," Charity said as they pulled into Eve's apartment complex to drop her off. "I did not kiss him, Harley. He just caught me off guard."

"So you really didn't kiss him back?" She really did want to believe Charity.

"Of course not! I mean, I didn't know you were actually interested, but even so, I know you made out with him, so why would *I* make out with him? Jesus, give me some credit. You're my sister."

Harley felt instantly like a jerk. Why was she lashing out at Charity? It was ridiculous. It wasn't her fault. It was Cooper's. Okay, and maybe her own. The deception was all hers. "I'm sorry. I know you didn't know. I don't know what is wrong with me."

"It's okay. It's been a weird night."

"I love you," Harley said, giving Charity a hug as they sat in park, Eve clambering out of the backseat.

"I love you, too." Charity wiped at her cheeks, where tears had started to trickle.

The sight of that made Harley start up, too, so they were both crying and miserable. "So what did Cooper say to you?"

Charity gestured to Shawn and Rhett making out in the backseat. "I'll tell you in a minute."

"Okay." Though she was pretty certain it wasn't good. The truth was she was stunned that Cooper hadn't actually made some reference to his and Charity's night together. That was a scary thought she'd been too consumed with jealousy to have earlier. What a total disaster that would have been if both Cooper and Charity had figured out on the dance floor at the Buckle that Harley was a lying sack. That would have been bad. Like really bad.

She needed to come clean with her sister. There was nothing for it.

The minute Shawn and Rhett tumbled out of the car to go screw each other's brains out, Harley put the car in park and shot Charity a glance. "Okay, I have something to tell you. Don't be pissed at me."

Charity gave her a long look. "Given that opener I can't promise anything."

"So here's the thing. I did sleep with Cooper at the wedding." She bit her fingernail nervously and waited for Charity to ream her.

"You did *what*? You had sex with Cooper Brickman as me? Are you crazy?" Charity flopped back in her seat. "Oh, my God," she moaned. "That's why he was so weird when I ran into him at the office one day."

Uh-oh. "He was weird? In what way?"

"He was all sort of creeper, undressing-me-with-his-eyes, we-share-a-secret dude. I had no idea why he was acting like that. Now I do." Charity smacked her on the leg. "How could you let me wander around not knowing something like that? Do you know how disastrous it would have been if he'd actually said something? Or tried to grope me?"

"I'm sorry! I didn't think it through. I was just . . . I don't know. Embarrassed. I knew it was wrong not to tell him the truth and I knew you would call me out on it, as you should have. Are." Harley put her hands on her cheeks to try to cool them down. The car felt like an oven despite it being February. She'd never fainted before, but this felt like a precursor to passing out.

"Does Jeff know? I will kill you if Jeff knows."

That startled her out of her impending fever and subsequent faint that seemed actually possible. "How would Jeff know? No one knows. I left Cooper's room before morning and no one saw me."

"You have to tell Cooper the truth," Charity said sternly. "I cannot look at that man knowing that he thinks he's seen me naked. It's horrifying."

"There's one slight problem."

"There is no problem bigger than the one you're going to have if you don't fess up, Harley Harlot. You, of all people? I can't believe this."

That annoyed her enough that she made a face at her

twin. "What difference does it make at this point?" But then she answered her own question because she hadn't even told Charity the whole truth. "But wait, there's more."

"But wait, there's more? Seriously? It's like a bad comedy sketch." Charity shifted her purse on her lap. "I suspect I'm not buzzed enough for this."

"Cooper said he wants to date me. Like for real, have a relationship."

"Really? Then why the fuck was he trying to tonsil-tango with me on the dance floor?" Charity looked absolutely indignant.

"I'm not sure, exactly. But he told me he has feelings last week. So I started to tell him the truth, but then he told me that he slept with you."

"Which was you."

Yeah, that. "Correct. But then when I was about to admit it was me, he said the sex with you/me didn't mean anything and that it was absolutely terrible. Horrible. All kinds of awful." Even now, saying the words out loud made her wince.

Charity's eyebrows shot up. "Say what? Oh no, he didn't."

"He did." Harley groaned.

"I am not lousy in bed!"

She rolled her eyes at her sister. "It wasn't you, remember?"

"Oh. Right. But that was still rude."

Whatever. She couldn't be too concerned about her sister's ego at the moment, given hers had been trampled on. "So then how could I tell him the truth? Oh, and by the way, I'm actually the one who is miserable in bed? Awkward. Beyond awkward. All kinds of awful."

"You're not miserable in bed. That's ridiculous."

"How do you know? You've never slept with me."

Charity rolled her eyes right back. "You would know if you were bad in bed. Men are not kind or subtle. Did you think it was good sex?"

"Yes! It was great sex. I had multiple orgasms. When does that ever happen?"

"Apparently not often enough. Did he come?"

"Yes." Unless he had faked it. Then she realized there was literally no way for a man to fake it. "He did."

"Then how bad for him could it have been?" Charity waved her hand. "The truth is very simple. He was obviously trying to protect your feelings. He didn't want you to think that you would have to compare yourself to me."

That stymied her for a minute. "No. That can't be it." Could it?

"Either that or he was just trying to be truthful, yet keep your anger to a minimum. Men don't like to be screamed at or cried to."

"You have a point."

"You do realize that you've been basically torturing Cooper. The poor guy has been falling for you while thinking he nailed me. That is just wrong, sister."

"I didn't know he was falling for me! I thought he liked sexy and sassy. I didn't think he thought of me as anything other than helpful."

"Yeah, helpful with his libido." Charity shook her head. "Oh, honey, you've never had a particularly sensitive guy-dar. You never know when someone is into you. So clearly we made some erroneous assumptions here, didn't we?"

Harley chewed her lip. "So the guy I have been crushing on from afar and slept with thinking he would never be interested in me is now interested in me, only he just kissed you for no apparent reason."

"I think he was jealous of you talking to Jeff."

"Who asked me out because clearly he thinks I'm the person he talked to at the wedding."

"Shit," was Charity's opinion. "I also think he was feeling rejected by you."

"Huh." As they both pondered this irony, Harley's phone buzzed in her lap.

"Oh, my God. It's Cooper."

"What does he want?"

"He says they're still at the bar and we should come back. He is clearly drunk." Harley felt annoyed all over again. "He must want to make further moves on you."

"Then why is he texting you, not me?"

"Does he have your number?"

"No. But he could get it from someone else. He clearly wants to see you, Harley." They were still sitting in the car in the apartment complex parking lot.

"You think so?" Harley felt deflated. She had no idea what to do, but she did know she didn't want to go home to Cooper's house and lie alone in her bed all night, wide awake, pondering all the ways she had blown it.

"We *could* go back," Charity said.

"Why? So we can drive each other insane with jealousy? I don't want to see Cooper grabbing your ass anymore. I've had enough tonight."

"I don't want to see Jeff fawning over you either, trust me." Charity shook her head. "But you have to tell Cooper the truth. For everyone's sake. Might as well get it over with."

Ack. "You're right. I know you're right." The thought just made her want to hurl. He was going to hate her.

"We should switch clothes, go as each other, and then unmask. They'll both be so shocked they won't be angry."

"Are you insane? That is a terrible idea!" It would be

like an episode of *Catfish*. Oh, my God. She'd be out of a job and Cooper would never speak to her ever again.

"About as smart as you sleeping with Cooper as me."

Fair enough. "You don't want to do that. Not if you are truly interested in Jeff. But you need to fess up, too. You did chat him up as me."

"Why? Jeff isn't interested in me. He likes you."

"Jeff is attracted to my appearance and who he *thinks* I am. But once he spends time with you he will totally fall for you. He already did."

It wasn't a line to talk Charity into coming clean as well. Harley definitely believed it was true. Charity had just as much substance as she did. Men just generally chose to ignore the possibility because Charity was gorgeous and larger than life. Jeff Sterling was a reasonable guy. He would see the merits of her twin and fall for her. After all, he was talking to her, Harley, after having spent time talking to Charity as Harley. It all made sense, really. In the most bizarre way imaginable.

"Jeff is going to be pissed we lied."

"This was your idea. Don't talk me out of it."

"Fine." Charity grabbed Harley's phone out of her lap and started typing, speaking out loud as she did. "On our way. Winky face."

When Harley took her phone back and saw that Cooper had responded with a simple "Good," her anxiety increased. She had a feeling that before the night ended someone was going to be madder than a wet hen.

She wasn't sure which would be worse—if it was Cooper or it was her.

CHAPTER
THIRTEEN

"I'M calling you a cab," Jeff said.

Cooper glared at his friend and pseudo-stepbrother. "I'm not ready to go home."

"Oh, I think you were ready a good hour ago, bro."

Why was it that some guys never made idiots out of themselves? Jeff was one of those, and at the moment Cooper resented the hell out of him. Granted, it had been his own stupid idea to show up at the Buckle and he'd pretty much walked in with a busted heart and a dry mouth, which was a lousy combination. Then had seen Jeff making a move on Harley. His Harley. The woman he was pretty damn sure he was in love with.

Only he had ruined it. Not once, but twice, by kissing Charity on the dance floor.

But something kept niggling at the back of his whiskey-soaked brain that maybe it was a good thing he'd kissed Charity, because she was the woman he'd remembered from the dance floor at the wedding. Annoyed with him. Cold. Sarcastically polite.

Not the woman who had come apart for him in bed.

Not the woman who had stared up at him from the pillow with guileless eyes and soft, breathless sighs. Not the eyes that were remarkably similar to the way Harley looked at him sometimes when they were cooking in the kitchen, or discussing his sister. Kind, caring eyes.

One and one wasn't adding up to two here. Or maybe it was. Twins.

"Don't you think twins are a mind fuck?" Cooper asked Jeff. "I mean, they look the same but they don't."

"Don't strain your brain tonight, my friend."

"No, I'm serious. Like, for example, Charity works at your office. You've seen her. Now you've been talking to Harley. They carry themselves different."

At times he found himself totally confused as to which sister was which. Harley had a habit of tilting her head so she looked up at him from under her eyelashes, and he could have sworn for a minute when Charity was looking at him in bed, it was Harley. But then again, Harley would never sit on his lap or make out with him in public, he was sure of that.

Given how identical their features were, it would be easy for most people to confuse them, especially if they shared similar gestures and tics. Or especially if they wanted to fool someone. How hard would it be?

He was getting a really goddamn bad feeling about a few things.

"It really is," Jeff said, leaning against the bar. "There is something that actually makes me uncomfortable about it, but I can't put my finger on it, exactly."

Cooper knew what it was. He had found himself attracted to both of them, and that seemed wrong. Creepy. He shouldn't want to nail both of them, yet he had. Did? He no longer wanted to nail Charity, that was for damn certain. But now he was starting to wonder if, in fact, he ever had. It was crazy.

They wouldn't swap spots with each other. Would they? No. Of course not.

"It makes me uncomfortable, too," he said to Jeff. "Because for some reason, it makes me feel like a pervert."

Jeff grinned at him. "And that's a new feeling? Bullshit."

"Suck it." Cooper finished off the last of his drink. He wasn't sure how to explain what was going on in his head to Jeff. "So you and my nanny, huh? Don't mess with her head. She's a nice girl and MJ really likes her. I don't want to upset the balance of my household."

Jeff's eyebrows rose. "So hooking up with your nanny's twin doesn't have that same potential to disrupt MJ?"

Well, shit. "She didn't know about that!" And wait a minute. "How do you know about that?"

"I saw you leave with her. It wasn't like a dozen people couldn't have looked over and seen it just like I did. People only wander off into the bushes together at a wedding for one reason, Brickman."

Then it was a miracle MJ didn't know. "It's got nothing to do with my sister." His whiskey brain was a little foggy and he didn't like that somewhere in the back of his mind those warning bells were getting louder.

"And there's the difference here. I want to date Harley, not hook up."

That sounded like a criticism, and it pissed Cooper off. "Quit saying 'hook up.' You make it sound like we're twenty and we're sneaking into the bathroom at a frat house party."

"You ever do that?" Jeff asked him.

"No. I didn't go to college, you know that."

"I might have done that once or twice at Princeton." Jeff

grinned, like the memory was a good one. "I'm not judging, don't get your dick in a twist."

"Well, hell, I definitely don't want that." Cooper wanted to adjust himself just at the idea of that.

"But look, I'm older than you. I was married once in my early thirties and you know how that turned out. Hitting the wall at Talladega would be less jarring. I had fun playing the field for a while, but now I'm tired. I just want to date a nice woman."

Like Harley.

Cooper heard the implication, loud and clear. Harley was a nice woman who deserved a nice guy who would treat her right.

He stared at Jeff, something again niggling at him that the situation was not quite as it should be. "Yeah, I get that. But I've got to be honest with you, bro. I have feelings for Harley myself."

Jeff pushed off the bar. "Excuse me? You can't sample both twins. I'm trying to stake a legitimate claim here. That is not fucking fair."

It wasn't like Jeff to swear or sound so pissed off. "I saw her first, Sterling."

"Yeah, and you fucked her sister, who I was about to ask out. I've been seeing her at work and thinking I would like to ask her out, and you stroll in and snag her at the wedding. So back off. You can't have both."

The challenge in Jeff's voice made Cooper stand up straighter, posture automatically defensive. "Hey. How the hell was I supposed to know you liked Charity? And if you liked Charity, why are you moving in on Harley now? You can't just swap them out like a couple of ink cartridges." That pissed him off, actually.

"That's exactly what you did."

"I did not!"

Had he? That's not what he'd meant to do.

"Yes, you did. Now quit playing around and quit the field. I am looking for something serious, not a play date in the sand box."

"What the fuck does that even mean?" Annoyed, Cooper shoved the remains of his whiskey away from him and reached for the water he'd ordered. "Did you ever tell Charity you were interested in her?"

That gave Jeff pause. "No."

"Well, then why are you pissed that she slept with me if she didn't know? Maybe she would have preferred you to me."

Now Jeff looked stymied. "You think?"

Cooper wanted to roll his eyes but refrained. "Why not? It's not like she was ever really into me. She always acted like I annoy her." Except in bed.

Which again reminded him something was just not right.

Suddenly he remembered Rosa matching the bra to panties Harley owned.

Hold the phone.

Speaking of phones. He pulled his out. "Something is not right here." He texted Harley and asked her to come back to the bar. He didn't think she would, given the time, but now that the idea had caught hold, he didn't want to sit on ferreting out the truth.

To his surprise she responded in the positive. With a wink.

"Jeff, when you talked to Harley at the wedding reception, did she seem any different than when you spoke to her tonight?"

Jeff frowned at him. "I don't know. Maybe. A little. Yes. She was flirtier at the wedding. Sassier."

Fuck a duck. "I think they twin-swapped on us. I didn't sleep with Charity. I slept with Harley."

Cooper distinctly recalled going up to the table and thinking it was Harley, only to have her tell him he was wrong. He hadn't been wrong. He hadn't been wrong at all.

"*What?* Holy fucking shit."

His thought exactly.

HARLEY walked into the Buckle with what was probably a completely misguided optimism that maybe Cooper would forgive her.

Especially when her eyes landed on him, sitting at the bar, his eyes fixed on her. She felt the heft of his lustful appreciation from across the room, and immediately her body responded to the intent in his eyes. But then he glanced behind her, at Charity, and his expression changed, looked thoughtful. For a second it gave her pause, but then he was undressing her with his eyes again and her panties went damp and all rationale went out the door.

"Jeff is so cute," Charity murmured from behind her.

Harley hadn't even noticed Jeff, which made her feel like a total jerk. But she couldn't help it. Jeff just didn't do anything for her. He was a nice man, but he reminded her of their father—stable, sweet. Just a touch boring. The male equivalent of herself. She imagined together the two of them would have exactly nothing interesting to say.

Which was exactly what had happened when they'd been talking earlier, in her opinion. She couldn't fathom why he actually thought he was interested in her.

"He's smiling at you," Harley told her, though it looked a little lascivious. Jeff Sterling, generally speaking, didn't look like a wolf about to pounce, yet he did.

Something was off. Why had Cooper texted her really? Was he going to plead his case again or was he just hoping to get a green light from Charity for another roll in the hay?

"I'm really nervous," she told Charity, glancing back at her twin for support. There was a tension in the air she didn't understand, a crackling.

"Me, too. Jeff looks . . . smoldering."

As they approached the guys at the bar, Cooper gave her a dirty-boy grin, his legs spreading apart as he leaned back onto the bar with both elbows. "Thanks for coming back."

He looked deceptively casual, but there was tension in his posture, despite the way he leaned back. Harley realized that over the few weeks she'd been sharing a house and meals with Cooper, she'd really gotten to learn his body language. Something was wrong here. He wasn't just drunk. His actions were purposeful.

"Hey, Charity," he said, leaning around her to acknowledge her sister. "Or should I say One Night Harley."

Oh, yeah, he knew something.

"Excuse me?" Charity asked.

"So tell me this. When did you all change dresses at the wedding? Just curious. It was obviously after the bouquet toss but before the last dance."

Charity pursed her lips.

Harley felt her cheeks start to burn. But there was nothing for it. She took another step forward. "Maybe we should talk about this someplace other than a public bar."

His eyes narrowed and his grin stayed deceptively in place. But he was angry. Very, very angry. "You're always telling me now isn't the time. Well, when is the goddamn time to tell the truth?"

She swallowed hard. "If we just go outside . . ."

Cooper stood up and leaned over her, so close to her ear

his breath was hot on her flesh. "Just tell me . . . who did I have sex with?"

His fingers traced along her jaw, over her bottom lip. A shiver rolled up her spine. "Hmm? Who was it, Harley? Whose lips did I kiss, whose body did I touch?"

She closed her eyes, his body so near to hers triggering an automatic response. Her nipples tightened and she ached to kiss him, to feel his arms around her. The only way to ever have that again was to tell the truth.

"It was me," she murmured.

There was a pause, where she felt his entire body tense. Then he cursed and reared back from her. "Fuck. Fuck, fuck, fuck." His fist hit the bar, making the glassware bounce.

Harley jumped, mouth hot, nerves taut. She knew she had about sixty seconds to convince him she wasn't a horrible human being and that he shouldn't hate her. "I didn't mean to trick you."

"No? You just thought it would be fun? That I'd never find out?" He raked his hands through his hair. "I have been feeling like the biggest dick asshole cocksucking jerk for the last month wondering how I could be falling in love with you when I had sex with your sister. And the whole goddamn time it was *you*."

Which made it better, when you thought about it. Harley rushed to explain. "I didn't think we'd wind up having sex that night! I talked to you, as me, and all you wanted to do was talk about your sister, and I had this huge crush on you already from watching you drive and I wanted once, just once, to be seen as sexy. It was like a . . . fantasy. Like Cinderella gets her night with the prince." God, that sounded so bad. Like she'd just been using him. Which she had.

Harley flushed, arms tightly crossed over her chest. She wanted to reach for him, but he looked so . . . volatile.

A glance over showed Charity and Jeff deep in conversation, his head tilted down toward her, his jaw clenched. Charity was talking a mile a minute, making hand gestures. That looked promising. Not.

"But why couldn't you just be you? Why not just tell me you wanted to hook up?"

Please. Like he would have responded positively to her, the woman he saw as a mother figure, throwing it out there that she wanted to have sex. He would have been horrified. "You wouldn't have! You saw me as maternal. You called me that. Then you saw my sister and you basically started drooling. And we look the *same*." That still baffled her. "I just wanted to feel sexy. But clearly I failed since you told me that the sex was terrible. The worst. Awful." At the thought of that, tears came to her eyes. She couldn't help it. That night had been amazing to her, but to him . . . nothing. Worse than nothing. Shitty.

"Don't do that." He kicked the stool so hard it slid out away from him and hit the ground with a crash.

"Whoa," the bartender called from a few feet away. "Chill out."

It was so late in the night there were only a few patrons left in the bar, but they all turned to stare. Harley sniffled, unable to stop herself, despite the fact that crying would only make him even more angry.

"I said that because I felt terrible for sleeping with your sister! The sex didn't suck. The opposite, in fact." Cooper picked up the stool and slammed it back into place. "Christ, Harley!"

Now her lip was trembling and she couldn't seem to stop it. She almost reached up and held it to stop the pathetic tremor. She so desperately wanted to believe Cooper had enjoyed their night together, but more than likely he was just trying to flatter her. "You're just saying that."

He shook his head and made a sound of exasperation. "Harley McLain. I don't know whether to strangle you or kiss you."

"How about both?" She deserved to be yelled at, she could own that.

His jaw dropped. "I hope you don't mean that literally or I'm forbidding you to ever go to a fetish club again."

She started. "What? No! I didn't mean literally. I just meant, yes, I did a bad thing."

"A bad thing? You let me think I was having sex with your sister. That's sort of like a big fucking deal. Not just a bad thing or a little white lie. That was a whopper of a lie."

She couldn't stop herself from reaching out and touching his arm. She just wanted some form of contact. "I'm sorry. I never thought for two seconds that you would be interested in me for real. I never even thought I'd be working for you."

"You lied to me. Repeatedly."

She nodded, feeling miserable. "I was going to tell you the truth, but then you said the sex was awful and I was too humiliated to tell you. I . . . I didn't expect to fall for the real you, along with the one I fantasized about, but I did. I really, really did."

"I'm very angry with you," he said, frowning down at her hand on his arm. The tone of his voice was stubborn, but not emphatic.

Hope took root. He wasn't walking away. In fact, he'd stopped clenching his fists. Maybe, just maybe, he would stop, reflect. Forgive her. She wasn't sure she deserved it, but she was optimistic by nature, and she wanted Cooper to look at her again with that adoration in his eyes. Look at her like she was special, important.

"I know. You should be. I'm sorry, Cooper. I'm so, so

sorry." Harley took advantage of his hesitation to shift closer to him, easing her body between his legs, shifting her hands to his chest. "I made the mistake of thinking of you as a celebrity, not a person, and that was really unfair of me. That's why I left without leaving a number. I knew the deception was wrong, knew it couldn't continue. I never even thought you'd want to sleep with me."

He didn't say anything, just looked down at her, his eyes dark, searching.

This was her one shot at making this happen. Sure, he might forgive her and they would go on as friends, or more likely employer-employee, but if she wanted to be with Cooper, to explore their relationship, this was her only chance, she knew that instinctively. So despite the fact that her heart was thumping painfully and her palms were sweating, she dragged out every bit of courage she possessed and went up on her tiptoes.

"What are you doing?" he muttered roughly.

"I'm going to kiss you, if that's okay."

"I'm not sure."

That wasn't a no.

"So let's just try it and see how you feel about it." Harley was tired of letting life just happen. She was driving this car for once and she wasn't about to let Cooper slip through her fingers because of her own stupidity.

So she reached up and kissed him, a soft, gentle, but passionate kiss that she hoped conveyed to him that she thought he was an amazing man and if given half a chance she would fall madly in love with him and work the rest of her life to make him happy.

It was a lot to ask of a kiss.

But she tried and for a few agonizing seconds when he didn't respond, she thought she had failed.

Then he hauled her against his chest and kissed her back. Hard.

Harley sighed and gave him everything she had.

AS he held Harley, Cooper was so furious he couldn't speak. Yet at the same time he was so relieved he wanted to shake his head and laugh. But given that his mouth was busy with hers and his arms full of her sweet, warm body, he did neither.

He just kissed her.

It had been Harley. The whole goddamn time. It had been Harley whose eyes had locked with his when he was buried inside her. Harley who had demanded he make her come.

All this time he'd been falling for Harley, feeling like a supreme asshole for having nailed her twin, and it had been her he'd nailed.

So it was with a whole lot of mixed emotions and whiskey that he kissed her, gathering her up tightly in his arms and holding her against him. It felt like she might disappear again on him, like this, too, might prove to be a con. If it was, he was damned well going to enjoy it while it was happening.

She had opened her mouth for him, and he slid his tongue between her lips to tangle with hers, the soft sighs of encouragement she gave him setting fire to his insides. It felt so damn good to hold her, to smell her skin, to feel her petite fingers curling into the fabric of his shirt, like she needed to hold on or collapse. The kiss went on and on, and it felt alive, the most intimate kiss he'd ever experienced, a mix of desire and frustration and exhilaration all at once.

Harley broke off the kiss, then disarmed him by rubbing her lips softly across his jaw and murmuring in his ear. "Take me home, Cooper. Please. Take me to your room."

His cock, already half hard, pressed against her thigh. God, he wanted her so badly. But he hesitated, not sure she understood what she'd be getting. This wasn't going to be suave and choreographed. It was going to be raw. Emotional. He'd thought he'd lost her entirely.

Now here she was, telling him it was all okay.

But it was only okay because she'd lied.

And he wasn't sure that was okay.

He had shit to work out in his head. This might be premature.

But her hands were wandering down over his erection and her lips were gently tugging his earlobe, and how the fucking hell was he supposed to resist any of that? He was a man, not a machine.

"Harley . . ."

"Yes?"

"Maybe we shouldn't . . ."

"I need to," she said, her expression earnest. "Let me show you *me*. And I need to know that you want me. Take me home and show me."

No. He definitely couldn't resist that offer.

"This is going to be angry sex," he told her, wanting it clear this would be no tender lovemaking. His emotion was running too high. "Because I'm still frustrated with you."

Her eyes widened and she looked a little frightened. "Angry sex?" She swallowed.

He thought she would ask for an explanation, for reassurance that didn't mean he was going to smack her around or something. Which, of course, he wasn't. He just meant there would be a lot of yanking of clothes, pushing against walls, pounding hard. But Harley just nodded.

"Whatever it takes, Cooper. I trust you with everything." She kissed him softly. "My body. My heart. My soul."

Something cracked in him. He swore it did. It was like

being kicked by a mule. Or having your car roll over a few times. His chest just cracked and he couldn't have resisted her if she had told him she had lied about everything ever in the history of all words that she'd ever spoken.

But he knew she hadn't. Harley wasn't deceptive by nature and her gaze was open and honest, and he felt the weight of her words, her trust handed to him. It was something special, immense. Sexy.

"I will take you home, Harley." He swept his lips over hers. "But I can't promise I'll be able to control myself."

"I don't need you to control yourself. I just need you to take me."

Cooper couldn't help himself. He hauled her up completely, lifting Harley off the ground. She made a small sound of surprise, but then she wrapped her legs around his thighs and gave him a seductive smile.

It was disarming, seeing Harley looking at him like that. Everything he could ever want, all in one woman, and even though he was still a bundle of mixed emotions of anger and frustration, he was knocked on his ass by how much he wanted her. He held her against him, hands on her backside, mouth brushing over hers.

"Let's go home."

CHAPTER
FOURTEEN

"*CARE* to explain to me what exactly is going on here?" Jeff asked.

No, she really didn't. Charity made a face and crossed her arms over her chest. Cooper looked like he wanted to tear Harley apart with his teeth, and it was both a little terrifying and a little sexy. Jeff was looking at her like he had indigestion and a healthy dose of disgust for her. Not nearly as promising.

She wasn't exactly sure what to say. "Well. Funny thing. You remember Ty and Imogen's wedding?"

"Yes." If it was possible, his frown actually deepened. "I don't need to hear about your hookup with Brickman, okay? So if that's where this is going, just spare me."

Fabulous. Wonderful. Jeff knew that she had slept with Cooper. Which she hadn't, of course, but clearly for the last three months, that was precisely what he'd thought. Charity wanted to smack her sister upside the head. "I didn't hook up with Cooper at the wedding."

"I saw you leave with him," Jeff said. "Look, it's not a big deal. We're all adults here. I just don't want details."

Would she be reaching to think that was because it actually bothered him to think of her with another man? Probably.

Jeff was so goddamn cute, it just wasn't fair. She'd never thought she was the type to be into the silver fox, but from the first time she'd laid eyes on Jeff, there was something about him that tickled her insides. She felt girly and giddy and stupid around him. But in a good way.

"I'm serious. I did not sleep with Cooper. My sister did." There it was. Let him freak out accordingly.

"Harley?" His eyebrows shot up. "She wouldn't do that."

Excuse me? She had expected disbelief but not because Harley wouldn't do that. "Oh, but I would? I'm the type who hooks up with a random guy at a wedding? Thanks." The more she thought about it, the more pissed she got. "You don't know me. You've said half a dozen words to me in two years, so don't be judging me. And you know what?" At some point her finger had come out. She couldn't help it. "It's none of your business who my sister or I sleep with. I could screw Bozo the clown in the back of the circus tent and you are not entitled to an opinion about that."

Her rant wasn't having the effect of shaming him like she intended. His frown had evened out and he seemed on the verge of cracking a smile. "Are you finished?"

"Maybe."

"You're right. I have no business judging anyone or having any opinion on who you or Harley sleeps with."

Typical Jeff. So fucking reasonable. He made it nearly impossible to hold on to her anger.

"But I am confused. I am positive that I saw you leave with Cooper. You had on a blue dress with a strapless sweetheart neckline. Harley had on a sweater over her dress."

He noticed her neckline? She wasn't sure what that meant, exactly. "This is going to sound very bizarre, but we switched dresses." Charity dropped her arms and brazened her way through it. "Harley wanted to be seen as sexier for one night. I wanted to be taken seriously for a change. That was me you sat and talked to for half an hour."

His eyebrows went up and he stared at her. "You switched dresses? Seriously?"

She nodded.

"Do you do that often? Pretend to be each other?"

"No. We haven't done it since high school. But Harley wanted a crack at Cooper and was afraid to do it as herself." She glanced over at her sister, who was being held tightly by her boss, their lips locked. "I think he's forgiving her for the deception."

"Looks that way." His jaw was tense and he stared at them before clearing his throat and looking back at her.

"I'm sorry, Jeff. I hope you realize there was nothing malicious about what we did. It was stupid and impulsive, I'll give you that, but it was not malicious." Sadly, it shouldn't matter to him anyway. It wasn't like he had an emotional investment in either of them.

But then she remembered that he had actually asked her sister out. "Don't be mad at Harley. Please. She thought that Cooper thought sex with her sucked and she was feeling hurt that he was hurt and was hitting on me, despite the sex sucking, so she figured the right thing to do was say yes to you, a nice guy, instead of being hurt all over again by Cooper, who is her boss, and the guy she slept with."

When she paused for a breath, Jeff shook his head. "I have no idea what you just said. But I asked Harley out because I thought she was the one I spoke to at the wedding. And I spoke to that woman at the wedding, who was

207

you, because I was secretly hoping that she, Harley, would intrigue me the way you, Charity, have."

Now she was the one thoroughly confused. "What?" she said, staring at him blankly.

"I've been attracted to you for two years."

"You have?" He was lying. He so had to be lying. He never talked to her. He looked at her like she was a nuisance. Her voice squeaked a little. "No, you haven't."

But then he reached out and took her hands in both of his.

Oh, Lord, he was touching her. The first time ever he was touching her and she had no clue what was actually happening. He was the only man who made her feel like a thirteen-year-old at a middle school dance.

"Yes. I have. But I didn't think it was appropriate given you work for the company. I also didn't get any particular vibe that you were interested in me. You seem to always have all the young studs sniffing around. I didn't think you'd be interested in an old guy like me."

Was he for real? He had been interested in her the whole time she'd worked for Sterling Motors? She wanted to fist-pump. Do a cartwheel. Kiss him.

"I don't like boys," she told him. "I like men." She rocked on her heels a little, bringing her chest closer to his. "I've had the most ridiculous crush on you since the first minute I saw you. I like your voice. I like that you're always so calm and in control. I like that you clearly care about your employees and your family."

"Well. This changes things a bit, doesn't it?"

She nodded. She certainly hoped it did.

"So, uh, I'm going to assume that your sister will not be upset if I cancel the plans I made with her."

"No, she won't be." Charity looked down at her hands where Jeff had laced his fingers through hers. He had rough hands, callused with age and a lifetime spent working on cars and doing manual labor. She knew he had completed an Ironman competition a few years back and spent some time at his stripped-down cabin by the lake. It was an intriguing combination, the manly man who was wealthy as sin and as completely comfortable in a suit networking as he was splitting wood.

It was intimidating, she had to admit. She was a confident woman, but Jeff was a whole other league that she wasn't sure she could compete in. Whereas with another man, she might have, okay, definitely would have taken the lead, with Jeff she didn't. She wanted him to take that final step forward and seal the deal. "Are you upset?" she asked.

He shook his head. "No. Because clearly she wasn't who I thought she was."

"I have slept with random men," Charity blurted, because she didn't want him to think she was one, judging her sister, or two, free of a past. "And I don't feel the need to apologize for it."

Jeff laughed. "Charity. I wasn't upset because you had a hookup, I was upset because I felt like I'd missed an opportunity. Your sex life is your own business." He gave her a wry smile. "I'm almost fifty years old. You can bet I have had a hookup or two in my time."

"Okay. Good." Then she realized how ridiculous that sounded and cracked her own grin. "Jeff, what are we doing? I can call you Jeff, right?"

"I certainly don't want to be Mr. Sterling right now. Yes, call me Jeff." He lifted her right hand and brushed his lips over the back of her knuckles.

Charity shivered. It was the simplest of touches, but she felt it deep between her thighs. "All right then, Jeff. What are we doing?"

"We're going to take you safely home. I'm going to give

you a slow kiss good night. Then as soon as you will allow me to, I'm taking you out to dinner so we can do this right."

There was a concept. It was so sexy, the way he was looking at her. The way he waited and asked, "How does that sound to you?"

It sounded divine. "I think I can get behind that plan."

"Wonderful." He leaned down and his lips barely touched hers.

It was an erotic tease, just a hint of his taste, his feel. "You don't care anymore that I work for you?"

"The only thing I care about right now is your eyes and how beautiful they are."

And excuse her while she collapsed on the floor in a puddle of girly goo.

Best night ever.

COOPER had called a cab for obvious reasons, and Harley was glad he had. For one thing, he had clearly had more than his fair share of whiskey and was about three drinks past a potential DUI. But it had the added benefit of allowing him to touch her in the cab on the way back to his house.

And for her to touch him.

She kissed him hard almost immediately when they tumbled into the cab, throwing her leg over his in an aggressive move that surprised her. But she rolled with it. Cooper inspired her to be bold, and she was so relieved that he hadn't kicked her to the curb, she wanted to show him all manner of appreciation. She also desperately needed to see him enjoying her, to eradicate the niggling doubt that he hadn't been into the sex with her.

"Holy hell," he said. "You feel so good." He pulled her

up onto his lap, his hands sneaking under her sweater to stroke across her lower back.

It was surreal, to be there with him, as herself, everything out in the open, including her feelings, her crush. Now her genuine feelings of attraction and admiration that she wasn't even sure how to label. Was a little afraid to label. But she wanted to touch him everywhere, to hold him, in case the moment passed and she woke up.

Harley realized she was staring at him, her fingers tracing his bottom lip when his grip tightened.

"Kiss me, Harley."

So she did. Gripping the front of his shirt, she reached up and touched her lips to his. She kissed him greedily, leaning against him, legs moving restlessly as she tried to climb higher on him, to give her lips better access. He tasted like beer and sexy male and she wanted to eat him alive.

Yet every time they kissed, it started out rough, wild, desperate, and every time, somewhere in the middle of his tongue taking hers, they shifted from greedy domination to a worshipful tenderness. Maybe hard-core wasn't in her nature. Or maybe it was something between the two of them.

Maybe it was love.

The thought had her pulling back again, breath shallow, palms flat across his chest. She broke away to breathe, putting a bit of space between them as she panted. The words were on the tip of her tongue, but she kissed him again to stop herself. Too soon. It was too soon. Instead, she ran her hand over the length of his erection.

"You sure you want to do that?" he asked. "I offer no guarantees of what will happen if you let the tiger out of his cage."

She laughed softly, brushing her lips over his chin, enjoying the feel of his beard rough on her lips. "I'm just petting the tiger, not unleashing it. We're still in a cab."

"Longest drive of my entire life," he said. "And if I wasn't convinced my junk would end up on TMZ I'd say take it out anyway."

"You drive in a circle for hours every weekend," she reminded him, comfortable on his lap, amazed that it could feel so natural, so normal to be with Cooper like this. "I think you can wait ten more minutes."

He gave her a naughty grin, his hand firmly cupping her backside. "I've never anticipated a finish like this one."

Harley shivered, his words causing a tugging sensation deep inside her womb. God, she wanted him so badly. "Me either. Though I can't say this was how I expected this night to end."

Cooper bit her bottom lip gently. "This night isn't going to end until morning. I have a thing or two to say to you but for now I'm going to let my cock do all the talking."

Shifting restlessly on his lap, she whispered, "Is this the angry sex part you were talking about?"

"Not even close."

Oh, my. "I don't think I have any experience with that then. My mind is drawing a blank."

"Don't worry. I'll show you."

"I don't usually make men angry." There was a thick taste of desire in her mouth, the need to touch him further, show him that she cared. "I'm sorry, Cooper."

"I know. If I didn't believe you, I wouldn't be here with you. And for the record, I owe you an apology for kissing your sister on the dance floor tonight. That was pure petty jealousy on my part and a total dick move."

Hey. Yeah. Good point. Harley felt a little less guilty. "I forgive you. And I think that makes us even." Which was a stretch, but if you didn't ask . . .

"Um. I don't think so." Cooper murmured in her ear. "But I'll take the rest out of your ass. Then we'll be even."

All right then. It was safe to say that her feelings for Cooper were above and beyond what she had experienced in the past when that actually made her damp with desire.

"We're home," he said, glancing out the window.

The cab came to a stop. Cooper's house was dark, but Harley knew Rosa had spent the night with Mary Jane. She hesitated, wondering how tomorrow morning would work. She didn't want Cooper to have regrets.

"Are you sure you want to do this?" she whispered. Suddenly she was nervous. This felt so . . . huge. Monumental. She felt vulnerable and exposed as herself.

She liked him more than was wise.

He hadn't mentioned a relationship again. Was that off the table now that she had lied to him? Was this just about sex?

Not that it mattered. She wasn't going to stop him either way. She couldn't. It would be impossible to walk away from him.

His eyes widened. "I swear to God if you blue-ball me right now I will probably die. Do you want that on your conscience?"

"No, of course not. I just want to make sure you're sure."

If he couldn't look at her tomorrow, she would have to leave. She couldn't stand the idea of being a regret to him.

Loving him, but not knowing how he felt, was damn, damn hard.

So she sat there and waited, knowing that no matter what he said, she would always look back and be glad she had taken the risk, that she had put herself out there.

But if he didn't say something in the next thirty seconds she was pretty damn sure she was going to go running out of this cab screaming.

CHAPTER
FIFTEEN

COOPER studied Harley, not sure what she was trying to say. He was well aware the cab was stopped and the driver was looking at them over his shoulder expectantly, waiting for them to exit. The night had been a roller coaster. The kind that flipped you upside down and rattled your teeth. If he had to walk into his house and go to bed alone, without any understanding of what was going on in Harley's beautiful head, he was not going to be a happy man.

But he realized that for all her moments of sassy bravado, Harley was, and always had been, a woman who kept her thoughts to herself. That didn't mean he didn't know her, because he felt strongly like he did. So he paused and thought about what he knew about her and what she was trying to say to him. It occurred to him that she was feeling insecure about his stupid insistence that the sex with her, who he had thought was Charity, was awful. That was what lying got him.

Of course, she had lied as well, so they were about even, if he was keeping score. But he wasn't.

This was about stepping into his house with the only woman he'd ever met who made him feel like he could picture waking up next to her every morning for the rest of his life. And he hadn't even woken up next to her yet.

He didn't want to screw that up.

He cupped her cheek with his hand and kissed her softly, feeling her tremble a little beneath his touch. That alone humbled him, erased his anger. "Harley."

"Yes?"

"I'm sure. I've never been so damn sure of anything. Now let's go in the house before this driver starts video-recording us on his cell phone." For all he knew, six pictures had already been taken over the guy's shoulder. Not that it mattered. He hadn't exactly defined discretion at the Buckle. He'd made out with Harley in full view of half a dozen people. Tonight had not been one of his finer moments, on the whole.

Shoving the car door open, he stepped out, then held his hand out to Harley to help her. Once she was standing on the front stoop, the overhang shielding her a little from the biting cold wind, Cooper leaned down to talk to the cab-driver, a guy in his fifties who was staring at them with wide-eyed curiosity. It was obvious he had recognized Cooper or the house, or both. It usually wasn't a secret which driver lived in which house.

So he pulled out his wallet and held up three times what the actual fare was, giving the guy a charming smile. "Thanks for the safe ride, man. Had a bit too much to drink tonight."

"Sure, no problem. My pleasure. You're Cooper Brickman, aren't you?"

He nodded. "Yep. Crashed a bachelorette party tonight."

"That the bride?" The driver looked past Cooper to Harley standing there. "Damn."

"No! It's not the bride. This is my girlfriend." He wasn't sure he had the right to say that, but he did it anyway, testing the word on his tongue. It felt good. Right.

"Oh, okay." He laughed, his nose twitching as he did. "Sorry. Didn't mean anything by that."

"No problem. Thanks, bro." Cooper handed him the money and gave him a fist bump. "Keep the change."

"Thanks a lot, Mr. Brickman. Thanks, I really appreciate it." His eyes were huge as he fisted the cash. "And have a good night."

Cooper grinned. "I'm pretty sure I will."

The driver laughed, eyes darting past him to Harley. "No doubt."

The cab had barely pulled away when Harley was tugging him on the hand. "Get in the house, Cooper. It's freezing."

Shoving his key in the lock, he gave her a smile. "And here I thought you were just eager to get me naked and have your way with me."

Then she surprised him, as she frequently did, by slipping past the door he held open for her, her hand reaching out with unfailing accuracy and landing on his cock. She gave him a long rub and a sassy smile. "That goes without saying."

"Oh, I'd prefer you say it." He closed the door softly, well aware of the echo in the silent house. As Harley walked over the marble floor he glanced upstairs, waiting for MJ's head to pop up suddenly and without warning. "But hold that thought."

He took her hand, kicked off his shoes, and tugged her

up the stairs. She followed him obediently, without a word, without a sound, and there it was again. That kick in the nuts, the crack to the ribs, that overwhelming realization that she trusted him. He wasn't sure he'd ever truly be granted total trust. Nor had he ever really asked for it.

It made him feel insanely romantic. Like he just had to go for the grand gesture, the thing that would cement her opinion that he was the guy for her. So when they got to the top of the stairs he swept her up into his arms. She gave a startled sound, but she looked at him with so much raw emotion he was really damn pleased with himself.

She felt perfect in his arms and he was fucking Romeo. Without the melodramatics. Or the dying-at-the-end crap.

"I can walk," she whispered.

"But why should you when I can carry you?"

"You make a strong case. Though I wonder if I shouldn't always let you have your way."

She wasn't heavy in his arms, but he enjoyed the scent of her flesh, the feel of her curves pressed up against him. Her ass tucked along his hip. "I'm the one in the driver's seat, sweetheart."

The look she gave him was one only Harley was capable of. It was seductive and sweet all at once. "We're not on the track."

"True." He kicked the door to his bedroom open with his foot. "Would you like to be in charge then?"

She shook her head. "I don't want either of us to be in charge. I want to be partners."

Again, she disarmed him. Had a way of making him understand what was real, how this should work. But that didn't mean he wasn't going to press his case. He stepped inside and nudged the door closed behind them. After a second he realized it would be wise to lock it, so he did.

"Think of yourself as the crew chief. You can spot for me and call out hazards, but ultimately the decision is mine whether to go low or high."

That seemed to amuse her. "We'll see. And don't talk to me in driving analogies. I'm no pit lizard. I don't think it's cute."

The sass was back.

Cooper was so turned on he wasn't sure he could take another step.

But he was sure he was about to thoroughly enjoy himself.

"Yes, ma'am."

"And don't call me ma'am."

Now she was just pushing it. Fighting the urge to grin, Cooper walked over to his bed and dropped Harley down onto it. "When did you get so bossy? *Ma'am.*"

"I'm not bossy." Wiggling backward on the bed, Harley unzipped her coat and peeled her arms out of the sleeves.

Cooper almost never wore a coat. He was just in a sweatshirt, but he took a cue from her and lifted it off over his head. Things were about to get a whole lot warmer in there and he didn't need layers. "You have your moments, sweetheart, I hate to break it to you."

She made a noise, but she didn't outright disagree.

He walked to his nightstand and turned the lamp on. He didn't want to make love to Harley in the dark. He wanted to see what he was touching. He wanted to see her expression as she shattered beneath him.

"I've never been in your room before." She looked around in curiosity. "It's weird that I live here, but not *here*."

He was hoping to change that, but now wasn't the time to bring that up. "It's like the rest of the house—big."

"It's very tasteful. But it doesn't look like you to me." Harley shook her head. "I'm sorry. That was rude."

But Cooper was curious. He climbed onto the bed with Harley and pulled her down alongside him so he could look into her eyes. "No. It's fine. What do you think I look like? Or what do you think would make sense for my bedroom?"

"I know you like things clean, tidy. But maybe not so . . . cold."

"Maybe it just needs you to warm it up." Cooper laced her fingers through his. "You being here in the house? It's made me very happy."

"I'm very happy here," she murmured.

"So even though I'm still upset that you lied to me, I can't resist you, Harley, you know that, don't you?"

She shook her head.

That was pure insanity. How could she not know what she did to him? Cooper brushed his lips over each corner of her mouth and the divot in the middle of her chin. "I. Can't. Resist. You." He punctuated each word with a kiss.

"I've never been irresistible," she whispered.

"I find that hard to believe." But before she could answer or protest, Cooper covered her mouth with his, enjoying the way she relaxed and sighed. They were lying on their sides, facing each other, and he lazily stroked her back, liking that she was so close to him, that he had the right to touch her without guilt or recrimination.

Because she was Harley and she was his.

He loved that. He loved her.

It was a scary-ass thought to have, but as he tasted her, he knew it was true. He loved her.

Moving down her chin, to her neck, he explored and tasted her, running his tongue along her collarbone, pushing her sweater down with his chin to give him more access to her flesh. He had tasted her before, at the Biltmore, but this was different. He hadn't known her then. This was slow, exploratory. This was him learning the contours of the body of the woman he admired more than any other. He listened to her reactions, to the soft sigh she gave when he brushed her nipple, when his hand strayed low on her hip. To the way her chest heaved when his thumb stroked across the front of her jeans.

He kissed her again and again until her body was shifting restlessly and she was making the most delectable sounds of desperation and desire. It was a sweet torture for him, his own body tense, erection throbbing and hard, mouth hot with saliva. But he wanted to draw this out as long as possible. Hell, all night.

But Harley was getting impatient enough to spur him on. She tugged at his T-shirt, yanking it up so that she could brush her fingers across his chest.

"You have a nice chest," she said.

"So do you." He cupped her breast and gave her a smile.

She laughed. "Thanks. Would you like to see it?"

"Yes. Lie on your back," he urged, wanting to be the one to take her shirt up inch by inch, wanting to be the one to expose her to his view. He didn't want her to just tug off her top in a quick motion.

She complied and he bent over her waist, lifting her shirt just an inch, just enough to allow him to press his lips on her belly and dip his tongue into her belly button. Harley sighed.

"Why is it for a man who goes fast every weekend, you're going so damn slow right now?"

He chuckled. She sounded so put out. "What's the rush, McLain? We have all night."

"It's two in the morning already."

"So?" He popped the button on her jeans with his teeth. He enjoyed the way her breath caught.

But then she said, "I have to get up with your sister. She's online by eight every morning."

He did not want to discuss his sister at the moment. "Shh. Don't worry about it."

"But . . ."

He hadn't intended to strip her jeans off so soon, but she left him no choice. He wanted her eyes rolling back in her head again. So he yanked the denim down to her knees and pressed a kiss against the front of her panties. Her response was to give a low groan that was so throaty and arousing, he had to pause and listen, absorb the sound, appreciate it. Holy shit, she sounded turned on. That spurred him on to tug aside the lace of her panties and slip his finger into her wet heat. And wet she was. Damn. He felt his nostrils flare and his cock harden as he stroked her, her pleasure obvious from the way her eyes rolled back and her breath caught.

Shifting upward, he kissed her again, wanting to capture those low moans. Her hand landed on him, and her rhythm quickly matched his, while their mouths melted together with an ease, yet a ferocity that was new to Cooper. He'd never thought he'd held back with a woman before, never thought that he had any more to give than what he had been giving, but kissing Harley, he realized there had always been a reserve, a control. With her, there was no keeping a part of himself remote.

He wanted her, all of her. He wanted to give, all of him.

Focusing entirely on pleasing her, he angled his finger deeper inside her and listened for her reactions to his touch so he could adjust accordingly. With his other hand he cupped her breast and angled his body so that his legs forced hers further apart. "Does that feel good?" he asked.

"It's good." But her breathing revealed it was way more than just good.

He caressed her clitoris with his thumb, enjoying the way she started to rock onto his touch, her fingers gripping his biceps tightly for support. There were a whole lot of things he wanted to say to her, but for some reason there was a lump in his throat and his chest felt tight. He couldn't force any words out, wasn't even sure how to formulate what he was thinking. Instead, he let his fingers do the talking. He found a rhythm and kept it steady as her breathing grew ragged. When she gripped his wrist tightly, her eyes widened as the orgasm swept over her.

Cooper watched her, in awe. She was beautiful in her pleasure. She was beautiful in the way she gave herself, her trust, to him. He felt humbled and grateful that she was here, with him. He didn't deserve her. Part of him felt that was why she had lied about who she was. She had known he didn't deserve her, that he wasn't the guy the nice girl stayed with. That he was good for some fun, but that he didn't have staying power.

He wanted to prove to Harley that he had staying power. That he could commit to her, to a future between them. That her pleasure, her comfort, her happiness, was a priority to him.

Cooper kissed her softly. "How was that? Good?"

She nodded. "I didn't think I was going to come. I'm sorry."

He laughed. "Oh, I knew you were going to come. That's kind of the point, honey."

But Harley didn't smile. She just looked at him with her heart in her eyes and it took his breath away. It robbed him of speech, thought, action. No woman had ever looked at him like that.

So without thinking it through, without caution or fear, he told her, "I'm falling in love with you. I've been falling in love with you since the day I met you."

Her mouth formed a perfect O. "You are?" she whispered.

He nodded. "I am." It felt right, easy to tell her how he felt.

Her fingers came up to brush his hair back. "I've been falling in love with you, too. You're an amazing man. I feel very, very lucky right now."

"I'm the lucky one," he told her honestly.

Then because his emotion felt like a big old hot air balloon about to levitate him out of bed, he dealt with it the only way he knew how. He tore off his shirt and his jeans, wanting to feel his skin against hers. Pulling her into his arms, he rolled onto his back, so that he could feel her weight pressing down on him. Her sweater was bunched half up, so he divested her of it, tossing it onto the floor. It felt glorious to have her warm flesh on his.

With his foot, he caught her jeans that were still around her knees and shoved them down to her ankles as he kissed her. She was making those sounds he loved, and her hips were rocking against his cock. The heat radiating off her inner thighs excited him, made him want to feel her wetness again, squeezed around him. He also wanted to see her taking pleasure from him, in charge of her own desire.

"Ride me, baby," he urged her, popping the back of her bra.

Her eyes and her hair were wild. She rolled off him and shoved her panties down while he did the same with his briefs. Half in shadow, she took the time to take off her socks, too, and roll them together, which made him smile in the midst of his desperate need to take her. When he went for a condom, he yanked the pull on the drawer of the nightstand so hard the whole thing flew out and landed on the floor.

"Fuck." Leaning over, he left it there, just digging in the exposed drawer for the condoms he knew were in an unopened box.

"You don't need it, Cooper. I'm on birth control."

He froze, hand still outstretched. Looking over his

shoulder at her he wanted to groan. Damn, she looked so sexy, so tempting. She was sitting up, hair tumbling forward over her shoulder, lips swollen, nipples high and taut. She was leaning on one arm, and he couldn't see the apex of her thighs because of the way she was sitting, but he knew the sweet wetness that awaited him beneath her soft blond curls.

"But . . ." he said, well aware he was sputtering. He didn't go bareback with women. He just didn't.

Then again, it had been a decade since he'd been exclusively with one woman for an extended period of time, and damn it to hell, that's what he was doing here, whether Harley liked it or not. So why couldn't he forgo the condom?

"Are you sure?" he asked. Then before she could answer, he wanted to assure her. "You can trust me, Harley. I would never do anything to hurt you. Anything."

The corner of her mouth turned up in a smile. "I know. Come here."

She didn't have to ask him twice. Cooper abandoned the condom project and reached for Harley.

CHAPTER
SIXTEEN

WHEN Cooper threw her on her back with more enthusiasm than care, Harley had the wind knocked out of her. But then again, she'd been having the wind knocked out of her since the minute she had first laid eyes on him at that wedding. She hadn't planned to tell him to hell with the condom but she hadn't wanted to wait for him to get one, and it had felt right. Like she was telling him there would be nothing between them from here on forward. No lies, no secrets. No past.

Just here. Just now. Just tomorrow.

So when Cooper rested her ankle on his shoulder and pushed inside her, she was as open to him as it was possible to be. His groan came from deep in his throat and he paused inside her, staring down at her. Harley felt tears prick at the back of her eyes. Oh, God. She was going to cry. She was having sex with the man she loved for the first time, sort of, and she was going to ruin it by blubbering.

But it was impossible not to feel emotional. She had

never thought that she would have this—a man looking at her like he thought she was the be-all, end-all. Like he was in awe of her. Her. The ordinary, nonsexy Harley McLain, lover of the twinset, sunscreen, and yoga pants.

His right hand stroked her ankle and he kissed the bone there with a soft brush of his lips. "What's wrong, baby? Is it too much? Should I pull back?"

She shook her head. "I just . . . I didn't think . . . I never thought that you—that we—" Her tongue failed her.

But he squeezed her ankle and started to move inside her. "I know. I know. We've started something good here, Harley, and I don't plan on letting it go."

Did that mean that he wanted a relationship with her? She hoped so. She wanted that, more than anything. But as he pushed deep inside her, gripping her ankle tightly, she decided now wasn't the time to worry about it. Though she couldn't prevent herself from repeating, "I'm sorry I lied."

"Water under the bridge, baby. Let's just move forward." He paused again and gave her a frustrated yet amused glare. "Now can we cut out the chatter and get down to brass tacks here? I'd like to think you can enjoy my dick inside you. Just saying."

Yep. She was ruining it. She pursed her lips and stopped herself from pronouncing another apology. He didn't want that. He just wanted to let their bodies do the talking. She could do that. She could give him what he wanted. So she stuffed down her insecurities, her doubts, her nagging little voices of self-recrimination and hesitation that Cooper could want her, and she concentrated on him. On his eyes.

They spoke to her as he found a slow and steady rhythm inside her. She relaxed, reassured by the emotion she saw in his soft gaze, and the way his thumb gently stroked her foot and on down her calf. It was hard to trust that he was enjoying it, her, when he had so many options available to him. But she'd be an idiot not to believe that the look he had on his face was genuine. While he was certainly charming, Cooper wasn't a particularly good liar. Unlike her, apparently. It was a hidden talent she hadn't realized she possessed.

Damn it. The guilt was back.

Harley didn't understand how she could let her thoughts crowd out the pleasure she was feeling.

Cooper knew it. He put her foot back on the bed and pulled out entirely.

The loss of him inside her had her reaching out for him and protesting. "What are you doing?"

"I can see the little wheels in your head actually turning." He kissed her raised knee. "What the hell are you thinking about?"

"I'm worrying," she admitted. "That I'm not good in bed. That you can't possibly mean to be here, with me."

"You are truly insane." He bent over and kissed her. "I'm not exactly a guy who is talked into things, you know. If I'm here, it's because I want to be here. It's because I want *you*."

Cooper lay down next to her and pulled her against his chest.

Great. She had officially interrupted sex with her bullshit. "It was easier to do this when I was pretending to be Charity."

"Why?" he asked, puzzled. "Do you doubt that I find you attractive?"

"Yes. No." Now she really wanted to cry. She couldn't believe she was doing this. "I'm so—"

Cooper cut her off. "Knock it off. You're starting to piss me off."

Now she was pissing him off. That went beyond just ruining sex. That was potentially ruining a relationship before it even got started. That took mad skill, really. To muck it up before it really even began. To bring sex and confessions of tender feelings to a screeching halt. Not everyone was capable of such a feat. Gold star for Harley.

When it was on her lips to apologize again, she bit the bottom one with her teeth, hard, to prevent herself.

"Exactly," he said. "No more being sorry. I know and appreciate that you are, but you can't be dragging that into the bedroom with us. I find you sexy. I have always found you sexy. I have deposited at the spank bank more than once thinking about you."

Oh, my. Harley had to smile at his ridiculous phrasing. "Really?"

"Really." He stared down at her. "Now I'm starting to think you do just want angry sex. Is that what you want, Harley? Do you want me to fuck you hard and prove that I can't stay away, that I can't resist you? That I want you so much I'll be selfish about it and pound you until you're slamming into the headboard and all day tomorrow you'll walk around well aware of your sore pussy? Is that what you want?"

While he spoke, Harley was mesmerized, shocked by the intensity of his expression, aroused by his words. No one had ever spoken to her like that, and she felt her body respond, her nipples tight and high, her inner thighs hot and wet, an ache low in her abdomen. She could hear her own breathing, that eager pant of anticipation, as goose bumps rose on her skin.

"Yes, please," she told him.

He gave a low groan and shoved her further up on the bed. He raised her hands above her head and held them together with his own rough enveloping grip. "Brace yourself."

Harley wasn't sure if that was literal or figurative, but before she could make a decision he was inside her with a hard thrust. "Oh!" She started to moan, but he captured her breath with his mouth at the same time his cock pushed in and out possessively, taking her hard. She couldn't raise her hips to meet him. He had her held down by the force of his body pounding her, and she just lay there, stunned, open to him everywhere. His tongue slid over hers and she didn't care about showing finesse or sophistication. Nor did she doubt he wanted her.

She just let him take her, while her inner muscles squeezed on him in a delicious reflex. It didn't seem possible that she could orgasm with this kind of speed, this intensity, but without warning it was there, hard and tight and wet, the wave of pleasure forcing her to yank her mouth from his and let out a cry of ecstasy.

He forced her to look at him again, using her chin to turn her face back to his while she rode out the climax. Their eyes locked and Harley felt a connection that was so intimate, so raw, so unexpected, the tears were back in her eyes, but for the right reasons. As her orgasm slowed, so did his thrusts.

"I want you," he said. "I need you."

There was something so romantic about the way he spoke to her, so low, so unpracticed, that Harley felt her heart swell. Raising her leg to wrap around his, drawing their bodies closer together, she moistened her lips. "You have me, Cooper. You have me."

He kissed her, hard. Then his eyes shuttered and he came inside her with quick, hot pulses.

It felt good, to have him connected to her that way, to

have him grit his teeth and lose control. They were both breathing hard, dew on their warm skin, and Cooper collapsed on top of her. When he pulled the bedcovers over them, their bodies still entwined, Harley felt that for the first time ever, she'd found her place.

Here, with him.

CHAPTER
SEVENTEEN

"MORNING, sunshine," Cooper said, his voice hoarse, lips brushing over her hair at her temple.

Harley had wandered away from him while she slept, but now she shifted so she could snuggle right up against his chest. She needed to touch, to confirm that this was real. She was dating Cooper Brickman. She was sleeping with Cooper Brickman. She was with a man who loved her.

Crazy. It was just crazy.

Beautiful. Wonderful. Amazing. Orgasm-inducing.

"Good morning. Do I even want to know what time it is?"

"It's only nine." He yawned. "I think we slept a total of three hours. But sleep is overrated." His hand strayed down her back and rested on her hip. "We can sleep when we're old."

"What is on your schedule for today?"

"Hell if I know. Cami will be bugging me soon enough with details. There's a lot of details."

Idly, Harley scratched her nails lightly over his chest, enjoying how hard his body was. She wasn't sure how to be the woman in Cooper's life. It seemed bizarre that everything had changed, yet nothing had changed. She would go and help Mary Jane with her schoolwork. Cooper would go to work. They would eat dinner together, like they did every weeknight. Yet this weeknight their relationship had completely changed.

"Are we going to tell Mary Jane? Or do we keep it a secret for now?"

"I think we can ease her into the idea. I don't think she needs to know you're sleeping in my bed, but we should introduce her to the fact that there will be a you and me."

Knowing Mary Jane, she was probably already on to them. Harley wasn't in her room, and Mary Jane had most likely gotten up already. She would question where Harley had been. "I agree. But she's smart. It will be a challenge to smoke it past her. What if she gets really angry?"

Her finger had gone up to her mouth and she was chewing on her nail without even realizing she was doing it. Cooper pulled it out of her mouth and laced her fingers through his. "No worrying, remember? We're not going to let my sister put a Tootsie Roll in the punch bowl. She'll be fine."

That might be wishful thinking on his part. "I hope you're right."

"I'm always right. Haven't you figured that out by now?" He gave her ass a smack. "Now I'm going to either make love to you again or get out of bed and be a responsible adult. Which do you think I'm going to choose?"

Except right at that moment the door to Cooper's bedroom opened and Rosa came in with a laundry basket. "Ah!" she shrieked when she spotted them. Her eyes widened and she let go of the basket long enough to make a hasty sign of the cross.

Harley wanted to crawl completely under Cooper's posh covers. And die. At least all her important parts were covered, but it was a small consolation.

"Morning," Cooper said to his housekeeper. "I had a late night, so late start today."

"I see." Those two words held a world of censure. "I'll come back later." She turned but as she left she pulled something out of her pocket and left it on Cooper's bureau.

He started laughing the second the door shut.

"What did she leave?" Harley asked, her cheeks hot from embarrassment. She was a grown woman and could sleep with whoever she damn well pleased, but she didn't particularly want anyone to be a party to it.

"Probably a prayer card. She is perpetually trying to save my soul. I appreciate the effort." He gave her a charming smile. "Now what can I offer you in exchange for you making coffee for me?"

She wasn't sure why the coffeemaker stymied him as much as it did, but she thought it was cute. "I'll do it for no reason other than the fact that I think you're adorable."

He made a face. "Adorable? I'd rather be manly and strong. Can't I just buy you some jewelry and have you think I'm the hottest thing since Flaming Hot Cheetos?"

Harley laughed and pushed herself up on his chest to stare down at him, her nipples teasing over his skin. "Do you ever see me wearing jewelry? Save your money, please."

For a second, he looked surprised. Like he couldn't comprehend a woman turning down a gift of precious stones. But then he grinned. "I suppose you're right. Dang, you're a cheap date. Now I know I really am the luckiest man in the world."

Which brought her to another point. "Don't you find it a bit awkward that you're paying me to be Mary Jane's nanny when we're seeing each other now?"

"It wasn't weird until you just brought it up." He gave her a smirk. "Should I stop paying you? Would that make you feel better?"

That made her laugh. She really was borrowing trouble. It was a gift she had. "Don't even try it. I'll sue you for wages earned."

"Tough words." He tweaked her nipple and shifted out from under her. "Have your people call my people. I need some goddamn coffee."

"You're a caffeine addict, you know."

"Duh." Cooper gave her a sleepy, sexy smile as he maneuvered out of bed. When he stood up, he stretched his arms over his head, giving Harley a delectable view.

There was nothing between him and the good Lord but a smile, and she was heartily grateful.

"Like what you see?" he asked.

"Duh," she parroted back.

He laughed and Harley wondered how it was possible to be so truly and thoroughly happy.

COOPER tucked into his eggs and took a sip of his second cup of coffee. He couldn't stop smiling at Harley across the kitchen table. She looked beautiful. Sexy. Unintentionally seductive. The way she tilted her head, licked her lips, looked at him from under her eyelashes, all turned him on. Made him grateful that despite their rocky and bizarre start, they had worked their stuff out and were together.

It had been years since he'd felt this giddy.

The only downside was that everyone else seemed to

notice it as well. Rosa had given him the evil eye several times as she had passed through the kitchen for no apparent reason. Cami had remarked on it over the phone before sniffing that he was late coming in to the office.

But the worst was MJ. She was eyeing him over her orange juice with a hearty dose of suspicion.

"What's wrong with you?" she asked. "You look like you have some creepy secret."

"Creepy" wasn't the word he'd use for it, but it was a secret that he was itching to tell. When a man fell in love, he didn't exactly want to stay quiet about it. "I don't know what you're talking about."

"Did you get Serge back for me?" she asked.

"Who the hell is Serge?" he asked, caught off guard.

"My llama!"

Right. The llama. "I told you six months of good behavior. It's only been one."

"Then what?"

He suddenly had a fabulous idea. "You and Harley are coming to Phoenix with me. There's a charity fund-raiser going on after the race. Y'all can be my dates."

Harley coughed and her eyes widened.

MJ gave a whoop of excitement. "Holla! It's black tie, isn't it? I can't wait to buy a new dress. This is awesome-sauce."

But his brand-new secret girlfriend didn't seem to share the same enthusiasm. In fact, she said, "I forgot I need to take care of something. Excuse me."

Then she abandoned her breakfast and rushed out of the room. He could hear her running up the marble steps a minute later.

"Huh. Wonder what that was about," he said.

Before he could reflect further, his phone buzzed on the table between him and his sister. They could both see that it was Holly calling him. Odd. He hadn't heard from her in weeks.

"I thought you were done with her," MJ said, scornfully. "Please don't tell me she was at the Buckle last night. How pathetic would that be?"

He didn't even want to know what MJ knew about the goings-on at the Buckle. "She wasn't there. And why does Holly bother you so much anyway?"

"I told you. She's all wrong for you."

"Who is the right kind of woman?" He knew. But did his sister?

"Do you really want to know?"

"Yes, I would really like to know."

"Someone like Harley."

Amen. She was preaching to the choir. "I couldn't agree more."

"But don't wreck my nanny. She's no use to me with a busted heart."

And with that, his Machiavellian sister made him, a grown-ass man, feel completely like he had to defend himself. "I'm not going to wreck your nanny, for chrissake. You make me sound like I have a string of destroyed women in my past."

"Just sayin'."

"And she's just upstairs. I'm sure she wouldn't appreciate this conversation."

Mary Jane shrugged. "Not that she would be interested in you. She's too smart to get involved with a guy like you."

He wasn't going to ask. He wasn't going to ask. "What kind of guy is that?" Damn it. He asked.

"A player."

Nice. Cooper ran his hand through his hair. He refused to defend himself to a thirteen-year-old. "For your information, Harley *is* involved with me. That's why I'm wearing a shit-eating grin. She has agreed to be my girl."

Mary Jane dropped her toast. "Are you serious? But my sources say you were seen kissing Charity, Harley's twin, last night."

He was going to have to strangle these mysterious sources. "Your sources are wrong. Harley and I are an item. Put that on your blog."

But his sister looked worried. "This is a totally stupid idea. It's not fair to Harley, Coop."

That irritated him. What exactly did she think he was going to do to Harley? "I don't believe I asked for your permission in who I date."

"You're a jerk," was her opinion as she shoved her chair back. "You could have any stupid girl you want, why do you have to pick Harley?"

"Because she's the most amazing woman I've met."

But she just shook her head. "I'm not going to Phoenix to watch you trying to touch her butt all the time. I'm staying home."

He was so offended, he just shrugged. "Suit yourself. Rosa will have you on lockdown then."

"Ugh!" She yelled in frustration, then ran out of the kitchen.

Cooper looked down at his breakfast and wondered what the hell had just happened.

Rosa came in right then and stood in front of him, arms crossed over her chest.

He sighed. "Yes?" he asked when she didn't say anything.

"I cannot work here if you are going to be doing the thing with the nanny. It's not right and I quit."

"What thing is that?" he asked, out of spite because he

was pretty damn sick of everyone telling him he was misbehaving when for once he was just trying to enjoy the love of a good woman.

"Sex," she hissed. "It's not good for the child."

"The child isn't in the room when it's happening." He knew he was being an asshole to Rosa, but enough was enough. "Look. I care about Harley, alright? I plan on being with her as long as she's willing to put up with me. This isn't some wham-bam, thank you ma'am. So I think you should just accept that sometimes people have sex and go about the job I hired you to do. I respect and admire you and I don't want to lose you. But how I live my personal life is my own business."

Her response was entirely in Spanish. Then she went the way of Harley and MJ.

So he had no idea if he even still had a housekeeper, let alone a sister or a girlfriend.

Cooper took a sip of his coffee. It was cold.

HARLEY hadn't meant to run away like a complete and total coward, but the idea of going to a black tie event at the track with the swanky people had her butt cheeks forming a fist. The most comfortable she'd been at Ty and Imogen's wedding was when she had been out on the terrace by herself.

Plus then she'd felt the unmistakable sensation of warm fluid between her legs, dampening her panties, from the aftereffects of not using a condom. It had just been too much, sitting there with Mary Jane, who was clearly suspicious, Rosa passing through in silent judgment.

She wasn't sure how to navigate these waters. Cooper, on the other hand, looked perfectly at ease. But then he always did. She was the only one who was perpetually a hot mess. The only time she had any confidence was when she was with kids, and this upset the balance of even that.

After taking a five-minute shower, she changed into clean panties and jeans and a sweatshirt. When she stepped out of her en suite bathroom into her bedroom she jumped. Mary Jane was lolling on her bed.

"I see you made your bed today," she said pointedly.

"Are you done with your breakfast already?" Harley asked, avoiding that obvious dig.

"I'm not hungry. Neither are you, apparently."

"Upset stomach."

"Are you having sex with my brother?" she asked, baldly.

Oh, God. "Mary Jane. I don't think this is a conversation we should be having."

"So, in other words, yes."

She wasn't going to lie to her. Mary Jane had had enough people brushing her off in her life. "Cooper and I have gotten closer, that's true."

It caught Harley completely off guard when Mary Jane's lip trembled and tears came to her eyes. "No, don't do this, Harley! He's going to dump you and then you're going to leave and I don't want you to leave."

While it was not reassuring to hear that Mary Jane assumed Cooper would get tired of her and ditch her, it was nice to know that his sister would miss her. "Hey." Harley climbed onto the bed with her and pulled her into her arms for a hug. "I'm not going to leave. No matter what happens, okay? You need to trust me."

"You're *mine*, not his."

The words were muffled against Harley's sweatshirt, but they still made her heart squeeze. She cared a great deal about Mary Jane. She'd fallen in love with her as well and she knew how much she meant to Cooper. It was scary to think that if what happened between them went south, Mary Jane would be impacted. No pressure or anything.

But it was important to let Mary Jane know she mattered. Her feelings would be taken into consideration. "My friendship with you is totally separate from my relationship with Cooper. If it doesn't work out with us, he would never ask me to stop being here with you. He's a good man, sweetie, and he wants you to be happy. So do I."

Mary Jane pulled back. "I'm just scared."

Harley gave a choked laugh. "Oh, trust me, so am I. I don't know what tomorrow is going to bring, but I've spent thirty years playing it safe and I don't want to play it safe anymore." She petted Mary Jane's long blond hair. "Remember when you told me I shouldn't be going for stable and sturdy? That I needed to feel a tingle when I was with a man? Well, I feel that with Cooper."

Mary Jane gave a hearty sigh. "I find that makes me want to throw up in my mouth, but I can't argue with love. Who can argue with love?"

"Many have tried. It usually just gets you in the end, though."

"I told Cooper I wasn't going to Phoenix. That was dumb. Will you tell him I changed my mind?"

"Sure." That made Harley feel better. Mary Jane didn't look like she was about to stage a coup or plan a full-scale runaway. If she was willing to go to Phoenix, then Harley might feel a little less terrified about the prospect herself.

There was a knock on the door.

"Come in."

Cooper's head popped in. He looked sheepish and a little nervous. "You girls okay?"

"Everything's fine," she told him. "Right, Mary Jane?"

"Yeah, I guess. I'm going to Phoenix and don't give me crap about it, Cooper."

Poor Cooper looked so bewildered as he came into the room. "Why are you so belligerent about it? I offered for you to go."

"Fine. I'm going. And I'm warning you, I've got my eye on you." She put two fingers up in front of her eyes then turned and pointed them at her brother. "No pit lizards. No Budweiser girls. No stop-offs at Hooters when you're with the 'guys.'" She used air quotes on "guys."

Harley was amused. It was nice to have Mary Jane in her corner telling Cooper all the things she would never voice out loud. Though she as usual found it oddly disturbing that Mary Jane sounded like a forty-year-old cynic.

"I haven't been to Hooters since I was twenty-five. Maybe twenty-four. If women hit on me, I will dissuade them the way I always do. No one needs to be worried I will stray." Cooper shifted his gaze from his sister to her. "I promise I would never betray you like that."

When she looked at him, she never doubted it. Not for one minute. "I know."

So it seemed that Cinderella got her prince after all.

Her phone buzzed in her pocket. It was a text from Charity.

I'm in love.

What a coincidence. So was she.

Harley grinned at the object of that affection. "So when are we leaving?"

CHAPTER
EIGHTEEN

COOPER finally got it. He understood now what put that swagger in a guy's step and that pride in his voice when he walked his woman into a room and introduced her to his friends, peers, co-workers. He could feel how nervous Harley was next to him, her palm damp in his, but he didn't feel any nerves at all. He was thrilled to finally be walking into an event with a woman who he thought was all that and then some.

MJ wasn't nervous either. She was leading the way into the lounge where the fund-raiser was being held. The room was dim with some kind of red backlighting. There were tufted velvet sofas and leather club chairs scattered around in seating groups, while waiters moved around with trays of cocktails. The downside of his schedule was that he'd been forced to leave Harley on Wednesday—Valentine's Day, as a matter of fact—and travel ahead without her. She and his sister had just arrived on Friday on the first commercial flight Cami had been able to secure after she'd gone to Rhett and Shawn's wedding reception, and they had barely seen each other in the ensuing twenty-four hours. He knew it had contributed to her nerves, but he was hoping she would be fine once he introduced her to some of his friends.

"You look beautiful, baby," he said, squeezing her hand and leaning over to brush a kiss at her temple. "Like an absolute angel."

She had wanted to wear a simple black cocktail dress. He had talked her into wearing a fitted yellow dress that showed off her curves and made her stand out. He thought she looked amazing. She kept pressing her hand down over her stomach.

"I feel sick," she said. "I don't think I can do this."

"Of course you can. Look, here's Ty and Imogen." His sister had disappeared, probably off to eavesdrop on conversations. "Hey," he said in greeting, raising his free hand to wave at the approaching couple. "How was the honeymoon?"

"I'm still on it," Ty said, raising his eyebrows up and down and smacking his wife's backside.

She jumped. "Oh, Lord. I don't think I will ever get used to your chosen form of affection."

"You love it."

"I didn't say I don't enjoy certain aspects of it. But I'm definitely not used to it."

"Do you all remember Harley, my girlfriend?" Cooper asked, loving the way that rolled off his tongue so easily.

"Hi, nice to see you again," Harley said. "I was at your wedding with Eve Monroe, her plus one since her husband had to work."

"Of course, it's nice to see you again," Imogen said with a smile.

But then Ty had to open his big mouth and say, "I thought you were Cooper's nanny."

"I am."

"Well, now that's convenient." He gave Cooper a nudge. "You get to live with her without actually living with her. Now that's a setup."

"Shut up," Cooper said. "You're making Harley uncomfortable."

"No, no, it's fine," Harley protested.

"I'm just giving you shit," Ty said. He looked at Harley. "I didn't mean anything by it. It's a guy thing, ribbing each other."

"I know. It's fine."

Imogen gave her husband a look before hooking her arm through Harley's and leading her out of Cooper's hold. "So please tell me how you manage children effectively as a nanny. I watch Tamara with her kids, and Suzanne with baby Track, and I'm just terrified about the possibility of procreation. I'm a bit of a control freak, I believe."

"You believe?" Ty gave her a look of amusement before putting his hand out to shake Cooper's. "No hard feelings, right?"

"No, of course not." Cooper shook it harder than was necessary. "You have the right to give me shit since I stood there at intro not two weeks ago and insisted she was just my nanny." He was a grown-ass man and he could admit it when he'd been wrong. Or flat-out lying to himself and everyone around him. "But I didn't think she was into me, bro. Turns out I was wrong."

"I wouldn't have thought she'd be into you either," Ty said with a grin.

"Suck it, McCordle." Cooper took a cocktail off a passing waiter's tray. "What is this?"

"I don't know. Just drink it."

"Let me get one for my lady, too," he told the waiter, grabbing another glass. "Harley, you want a drink?"

But she turned and shook her head at him. She still had a look of panic in her eyes. Maybe it was better if she didn't toss them back.

"Damn, now I have two."

"There are worse things in life." Ty gestured to the right. "Here comes Monroe."

"Which one?"

"Elec and Tammy. I'm ditching out of here. They'll corner me again with nine thousand pictures of their baby. I can't take all that cuteness, I'm going to wind up with diabetes."

"I would just like to point out that maybe you and Imogen don't need to be having kids any time soon."

"I agree," Ty stated emphatically. "I'm too busy enjoying my wife right now. Babies are for later."

Cooper had never given much thought to babies beyond the certainty that at some point he'd like to have some. But now . . . the thought of knocking up Harley in a couple of years did strange things to his insides. "I hear ya."

Ty gave him a long look. "I don't think you do. Damn. You fell hard and fast, my friend."

"Don't we all? I mean look at Evan over there. He's carrying Kendall's purse."

That made Ty laugh. "Never thought I'd see that. Shit, I'm outta here." He gave a wave as Elec and Tammy approached, then ditched out, even abandoning his wife.

"Where's he going?" Imogen asked, raising her head from her conversation with Harley.

"Call of nature." He greeted the Monroes and introduced them to Harley.

It wasn't two seconds later that Elec had his cell phone out and was showing Cooper pictures of the baby he and Tammy had adopted. "Did I show you our son?"

"No, you haven't. Congratulations again, my friend, that's awesome."

Elec was beaming as he swiped through his phone. "He's amazing, Brickman, I gotta tell you. And our older kids are doing fantastic with him. They're super protective."

A picture of a roly-poly baby sitting in the sink, sporting a drooling grin on his chubby face, was shoved at Cooper. "Wow, he is cute." Babies looked so freaking happy all the time. Then they grew into Mary Jane. Cooper found himself a little envious, he had to admit. "What's his name again?"

"Eliot. Named him after my father."

"Another generation of Monroe drivers, huh?" They were a driving dynasty at this point. Cooper wouldn't mind starting one of his own.

"Yeah, but before this little guy hits the track, it will be our daughter, Hunter. She's Briggs blood, Monroe training. The other drivers won't stand a chance."

The pride in his voice as he swiped through and found a picture of Hunter holding her baby brother, wearing a 56 shirt, was palpable.

Tammy leaned over and checked out the screen. "Is he boring you, Cooper? Just tell him enough's enough. Not everyone wants to stare at our kids for an hour."

Cooper laughed. "It's fine, Tammy. He's entitled to a few minutes of bragging."

Tuesday Jones and Diesel Lange joined them. "Brickman, your sister has Kendall cornered and is grilling her on her sponsorships and Evan's brush with daddyhood."

"Oh, Lord." Just when he was enjoying himself.

"I'll go get her," Harley volunteered.

Cooper eyed her. "You sure?" He didn't want her to feel like she was on nanny duty.

She nodded. She actually looked relieved to have something to do. "Absolutely."

"Alright then. Tell her I'll send her ass back to the hotel if she doesn't leave people alone."

But Harley raised her eyebrows at him in a way that indicated maybe that wasn't the right thing to say. He was about to ask her what she was thinking when she started off in the direction Tuesday pointed her in.

"So as part of this evening's entertainment, we're playing the infamous scuffle between Eliot Monroe and Johnny Briggs," Tuesday said, with a grin.

Diesel shook his head. "I can't believe my uncle agreed to that. He's spent years bargaining and blackmailing to never have that footage shown."

"They're in their sixties, for crying out loud. It's time to bury the hatchet and what better way to do it than in public, for charity?" Tuesday asked.

"I wouldn't be surprised if you see them shoving each other by the open bar before the night is out," Diesel commented dryly.

"Dad says he's all for it," Elec said. "Though I think he could do without seeing that video on the big screen."

Cooper wasn't known for being a hothead on the track, so he couldn't imagine spending thirty years at odds with another driver.

These guys and their wives were his friends, and he was damn pleased to be at the fund-raiser with Harley. He was frankly as happy as he'd ever been, and when he saw Harley returning with Mary Jane in tow, he knew he was grinning like an idiot.

This was his family. His two best girls and the racing world.

HARLEY was half listening to Mary Jane as she went on and on about someone's dress. "I'm so glad you don't have your boobs bouncing all over the place all the time," Mary Jane commented.

That got Harley's attention as they crossed the room. She looked down in amusement at Cooper's sister. "No. I like to keep the cookies in the jar, thank you very much."

"Why do men think that's sexy?"

"You got me. I guess they're just fascinated by what they don't have."

"Men are weird."

"I can't argue with you." Harley studied Mary Jane. "Now please don't grill the guests or Cooper is going to get upset. These are his co-workers, honey, and what you do reflects on him. You have to respect that your being here is a privilege."

"Fine." Mary Jane linked her arm through hers and tilted her head to smile up at her. "I was just curious. But if I go back to the hotel, you have to, too, and there is no way Cooper wants you to leave."

Harley knew Mary Jane had her there. Cooper wanted her at the party. She, on the other hand, would be perfectly content to go back and hang out with Mary Jane in their pajamas. "This isn't really my kind of thing," she admitted. "I don't know what to say to any of these people."

"They're not royalty. They're just people." Mary Jane made a funny face and used a low and goofy voice. "Be yourself. Keep it real, yo."

That made her laugh. But when she got back to Cooper there was an older gentleman in the group now and he gave her a wink. "Hear you're the nanny turned girlfriend, huh? I'm all about a good cliché."

She smiled weakly at him, not sure what to say.

Then suddenly Nikki Strickland was upon them, her beefy husband tagging along behind her. She was wearing hot pink and lots and lots of diamonds. She weighed approximately twelve pounds as far as Harley could tell.

"Hey, y'all!" she called out, waving and beaming. She homed in on Harley. "Who are you?"

"I'm Harley. Nice to meet you." Not.

"This is my girlfriend," Cooper said, slipping his hand into hers. He sounded confident and comfortable.

Harley felt anything but. She wasn't even sure how she felt about the label of "girlfriend." All of this was moving very fast and she was just a country girl with zero experience being at these types of social and corporate events.

"Nikki, meet Harley. Harley, Nikki, and her husband, Jonas, known on the circuit as Spark Plug."

The guys all laughed at the nickname. Jonas seemed to take it good-naturedly. But he clearly had to have a good nature to tolerate his wife.

Nikki looked confused. "Your girlfriend? Are you kidding me right now?"

"No, I'm not."

"But you're so plain!" Nikki said, taking Harley's free hand into her own. "Oh, sweetheart, you are my new pet. We're going to give you a glitz-over."

Fabulous. Harley waited for the earth to open up and swallow her. "Oh, um, thanks, but . . ."

"But hell no," Cooper said. "You touch a hair on her head and I will be one pissed-off driver. Harley is beautiful the way she is."

That was somewhat mollifying. But it was still damn embarrassing.

"If you want a pet, get a pug," Mary Jane told her.

"And who is this charming child?" Nikki asked with a frown.

"I'm Mary Jane Rawlings. My daddy was Bud Rawlings. Jeff Sterling is my stepbrother and Cooper is my half brother." Her chin was up and the implication was loud and clear. She was somebody and don't mess with her.

Harley thought it would be nice to have the force of a name behind her. As it was, she was just Harley McLain, Charity's quiet twin, and a nanny.

But she was also Cooper's girlfriend.

And most importantly, she was a good person. She was not going to stoop to petty games, name calling, or bragging. "I heard that you're expecting, Nikki. Congratulations." Though Harley couldn't see any evidence of a baby growing beneath the satin of Nikki's dress, she'd read about it on Mary Jane's blog, and for that reason, she would trust it as gospel.

"Why, thank you! Just seven months to go! I don't even have morning sickness. That's just for weak women and there is no way I'm going to put my head in a toilet. Hell to the no."

Suzanne Jefferson snorted. "Not without sticking your finger down your throat first," she said.

"What?" Nikki looked at her, puzzled.

Ryder coughed. "Babe, claws in."

"Just an observation." Suzanne winked at Harley. "I have a hard time keeping my thoughts to myself."

Harley had the opposite problem. "I kind of envy you. It takes a crowbar to get my thoughts out sometimes," she admitted. "But the upside is, if you have a secret I'll take it to the grave."

"Yeah, you do keep a pretty good secret," Cooper said, his eyebrows raised.

She knew he was thinking about the whole sex-as-Charity thing. Whoops.

He bent over and kissed the back of her head to take the sting out of his words, but she felt compelled to tease him back. She wasn't about to let him throw that whole business in her face every other day. "But just keep in mind secrets I know about you and might reveal if you don't stop teasing me in front of your friends."

The others all laughed. Cooper just grinned and shrugged. "What secrets do you have on me? That I can't figure out the coffeemaker? Honey, I'm an open book."

"Oh, I don't think they know *everything* about you." Like that sweet spot she had hit when she was giving him head. Or how generous he was with his tongue.

Wait. Actually, they probably did know that.

He seemed to get what she was hinting at, though, because his eyes widened and he coughed. "Point taken, sweetheart."

"It's okay, we all know you have a small dick," Ryder said. "That's no secret."

"Christ, Jefferson! My kid sister is standing here."

"Oh, right. Sorry." Ryder looked sheepish.

"Just watch your tongue." Cooper looked annoyed and embarrassed. "Look, the video's starting up. Y'all watch that and leave my girlfriend alone."

Harley definitely wanted the attention taken off of her. At the front of the room a man was giving an introduction and an explanation of how the money earned from the evening was going to fight children's cancers. It made Harley wonder how much it had cost per plate to attend. She had a feeling this was not a fifty-dollar ticket she was on. In fact, she was so curious that she leaned over to Mary Jane and whispered, "How much was each ticket for this?"

"Five hundred."

"Oh." So Cooper had paid fifteen hundred dollars just for the three of them to walk in the door. That made her cheeks feel hot and her stomach flip. This was not her world. It just wasn't.

A video started playing of a race from 1981. The announcers were talking about how the cars were running, and even though the footage was grainy Harley could tell it was Daytona. The track was unmistakable.

Suddenly there was a tap and a spinout and while the announcers exclaimed in shock, they all could see Eliot Monroe climb out of his car and instantly get punched by Johnny Briggs. They both had thrown down their helmets and were rolling around in the dirt in a full-on fistfight.

"Cracks me up every time I see it," Ryder said, chuckling.

Elec shook his head. "Evan and Eve inherited that disposition from my father. It skipped over me."

"What cracks me up is their hair. Damn, Farrah Fawcett had nothing on the two of them," Cooper said.

Harley had to admit, that was some glorious feathered hair on both men. She'd only seen Eliot Monroe on TV and he had a silver buzz cut now. It was a startling comparison. "In thirty years we'll be looking back on your hairdo and saying the same thing," she remarked.

"What?" Cooper looked at her, horrified. "Are you saying I need a haircut?"

"I said no such thing. I happen to like your hair." She did. But that didn't mean in the future it wouldn't look dated. But she was amused by his reaction.

"I think you need a haircut," Mary Jane said. "It's time to trim the hedge."

That made her laugh. But then her laughter died out when Cooper's expression fell and he swore under his breath. "What's wrong?"

He sighed. "MJ, it looks like Mom is back from France."

"What?" Mary Jane spun around and followed Cooper's gaze. The stricken look on her face made Harley's heart hurt. "She's here. What is she doing here? Why didn't she come home?"

Cooper's hands had risen to rest on his sister's shoulders from behind her, his gesture protective. Harley scanned the crowd and spotted the only woman who looked the right age and enough like she could be the mother of either of them. She was thin, blond, wearing a black cocktail dress, with a man in his twenties in a tux leaning over to whisper in her ear. She laughed and it was the kind of flirtatious but elegant laugh that Harley would never achieve on her best day.

"Come meet my mom," Mary Jane said, stepping forward and taking Harley by the hand. Her voice was cold, expression stony.

"Of course," she said lightly, but she glanced at Cooper over Mary Jane's head. He looked furious.

As they approached her, their mother finally seemed to realize they were in front of her. "Oh!" she said, hand coming up to her throat. "Darlings!" She moved to air-kiss Mary Jane, but the girl shifted out of the way.

"Mother," was her icy response. She sneered at the man with her mom. "Fallon. Nice to see you."

"Oh, sweet pea, this isn't Fallon. This is Sebastian."

"Oh, sorry," Mary Jane said with exaggerated sweetness. "I can't keep track of all your boyfriends."

"Cooper," his mother said, leaning over to offer her cheek for him to buss. "I see my daughter hasn't learned any manners while I've been gone."

Mary Jane's mouth opened and Harley hastily interrupted to avoid what could be shaping up to be an unpleasant confrontation. "I'm Harley," she said, sticking her hand out.

Perfectly groomed eyebrows rose. "Hello. I'm June." She briefly took Harley's hand before releasing it.

"She's my nanny," Mary Jane told her mother.

"Nanny? How positively British." She laughed. "Aren't you a little old for a nanny?"

"She needs someone to look after her," Cooper said pointedly. "While you're, you know, *busy*, with Sebastian."

These were family undercurrents Harley just did not understand. Her family was a typical two-parent family with just her and Charity. No one fought beyond the usual squabbling, and her parents still lived in the ranch house she'd grown up in. This tension, this passive-aggressive picking at each other, made her very uncomfortable.

"Then maybe have her take Mary Jane to the salon." June's finger reached out and smoothed her daughter's eyebrow. "Good Lord. Look at these caterpillars. She got these from her father. Bud was like a grizzly."

Considering Mary Jane was blond with wispy hair, her comment was ridiculous. But aside from that, Harley was utterly horrified that a mother would say something so critical to her own daughter. "There is absolutely nothing wrong with her eyebrows," she said, before she could stop herself. "I don't think you should be suggesting her appearance needs improvement."

It wasn't her right, but damn it, this mother had no freaking right either. Where the hell had she been? Off playing with her boy toy, that's where she'd been. Harley felt the flames of indignation flare on Mary Jane's behalf. This was bullshit, pure and simple.

"And did anyone ask your opinion?" June asked, voice dripping with disdain. "Just cash your paycheck and keep your mouth shut."

"Don't talk to her like that," Mary Jane said.

"Mom, Harley is my girlfriend," Cooper said. "You really don't want to go there with me."

"You're dating the nanny?" June rolled her eyes. "Good Lord, what is wrong with men? Why do you always feel the need to bed the help? It's such a pathetic need to feel powerful."

"Unlike dating a man thirty years younger than you who has no money of his own," Cooper said.

Ouch. Okay. This was firmly in ugly territory.

June reached out and slapped Cooper firmly across the face.

"Oh, my God," Harley blurted out, shocked to see Cooper's head snap to the right with the violent force of his mother's blow.

He didn't react at all, just accepted the slap. His hands remained in his pants pockets.

"Speak to me with respect. I'm your mother."

But then he just smiled and it was bone chilling. Harley knew how absolutely and utterly angry he was. He was controlling it only by pure willpower. "I'll see you in court, *Mother*. I'm filing papers for permanent custody of MJ."

June's jaw dropped. "You wouldn't dare."

"The hell I wouldn't."

Sebastian was glancing around, looking like he wanted to back away from the scene entirely. Harley understood where he was coming from. But she loved Cooper and Mary Jane and wasn't about to slink away. They needed her to have their back.

Harley put her hand on Cooper's arm. "Maybe we should discuss this privately."

Mary Jane put her hand in Cooper's. Then she reached out with her other hand and grabbed Harley's. She looked scared, like she was afraid her mother was going to snatch her and whisk her away. For the first time really since she'd met her, Harley was conscious of just how much a little girl Mary Jane still was.

"There's nothing left to say," Cooper said. "My lawyers will be contacting you, Mother. Until then, stay the hell away from us."

Cooper dragged Mary Jane away, and by default Harley.

The night was clearly ruined. He was keeping a tight lid on his anger and nothing more. Cooper chose a lounge chair in a dark corner and plunked down there, tugging at his tie. Mary Jane ran off to the dessert display, waving Harley off when she offered to go with her.

"Are you okay?" Harley asked Cooper, sitting down next to him and touching his knee. He looked so unapproachable, so ferocious. She didn't know this Cooper, had never met him.

"No. But I will be."

"I'm sorry."

"Don't be." His words were curt and he wasn't looking at her.

Harley sat there for a minute, then decided she needed to give him a minute alone. "I'm going to the restroom."

He nodded.

Harley crossed the room, glancing around to see if anyone had noticed their scuffle, but everyone's eyes were fixed on the front of the room, where Johnny Briggs and Eliot Monroe appeared to be hugging it out. She appreciated the distraction they created.

Unfortunately, when she entered the restroom, Cooper's mother was at the sink freshening up her lipstick. Damn. Harley tried to retreat, but she'd already been spotted.

"Don't run away. I want to have a word with you, Mary Poppins." June spoke to her in the mirror.

Part of her wanted to leave anyway, but then she thought that would just look wimpy. So she continued forward and said to June, into the mirror, if that's the way she wanted to play this, "Yes?"

"I'm sure you think you have a good thing going right now, and given that you're not exactly a supermodel, you clearly have managed to score big for yourself. But that good-girl act will only take you so far before Cooper gets bored with you."

It stung. It was offensive. But it was also just a mean-girl move, and Harley wasn't falling for it. "I don't think you really know anything about your son at all, so I feel confident that he appreciates my positive qualities."

"Keep telling yourself that. As for my daughter, I see what's going on here. You've got a little 'Hand That Rocks the Cradle' thing going on. Swoop in, save the day with baking bread and crafts or whatever the hell women like you do. But Mary Jane is my daughter and you are not going to replace me. Cooper has a lot of money, but so do I and I will fight him tooth and nail for custody. As for you, you don't want to mess with me, honey." June wiped the corner of her mouth where her cherry lipstick had strayed. Her blue eyes were hard, cold. "I'm mean when I don't get my way. I play dirty. And I never lose."

For most of her life Harley had avoided confrontation. She hated to think that anyone didn't like her. When she'd been bullied in school she had usually played the game to appease them until Charity caught wind of it and intervened with either fists, words, or underhanded methods of humiliation designed to shut the other person up. It had also worked, but it had always made Harley uncomfortable. It wasn't her style.

But June Rawlings was a fifty-five-year-old bully, and that might be something Harley could ignore if it weren't Mary Jane's future at stake. That she couldn't back down from. So for the first time maybe in her life, she found her backbone. "I'm not really sure what you're getting at, Mrs. Rawlings. If you're suggesting I quit, I can assure you I have no intention of doing that. I would also like to point out that you are free to waste your money if you like, but I don't think any judge in the world is going to award custody to a mother who abandoned her daughter so she could screw her way across Europe with a man half her age. I'm pretty sure there isn't so much as an e-mail or text or phone call from you asking about Mary Jane's well-being during that time. Do you know when her last checkup was? What foods she likes? How her grades in school are? Where she wants to go to college? No? Well, Cooper does, and I do. So we'll see you in court."

Her voice was trembling from anger a little at the end of her speech, but damn it, it felt good.

Cinderella never really got the opportunity to read the riot act to the stepmother, but Harley enjoyed putting June in her place.

Even when Cooper's mother said, "You'll regret that, you little cunt."

Harley was shocked by the language but just smiled at her in the mirror. "Not as much as you should regret that face lift. Very unnatural."

With that, she left the restroom, palms and pits sweating, hands trembling, heart racing. That last dig had been catty and more her sister than her, but nonetheless, it had felt good.

Cooper and Mary Jane were her little family, and this woman was not going to hurt them if she had any say in it.

CHAPTER
NINETEEN

"WELL, that was a freaking disaster," Cooper said, ripping his tie off and tossing it on the bed in their hotel suite. "I have a massive headache."

Here he had stupidly hoped for a relaxing weekend with Harley and MJ and so far, he'd had everyone he knew find one way or another to make his girlfriend uncomfortable. And that was before his mother had shown up. Like a Hermès hurricane, she had blown through the room and completely destroyed his cool. She'd ruined the night for all of them. Mary Jane was clingy and peevish, and Harley was pensive.

"I almost feel sorry for Serge," he told Harley as he peeled off his suit jacket.

"The llama?" she asked, taking her earrings out of her ears and tossing them on the bureau.

"Llama? No, my mom's boyfriend."

"His name is Sebastian."

"Oh. Right. Serge is the llama. Sebastian is the poor fool

stuck with my mother." He rubbed the back of his neck. "I want a hot shower and an ibuprofen."

"I have some in my bag. I'll get you some." She stepped out of her shoes and sighed. "I'm not used to wearing heels."

Cooper kissed the back of her head. "I'll rub your feet if you rub my shoulders."

"That's a deal. I'll go get some water so you can take the pain reliever."

"Thanks, baby. I'm going to talk to MJ for a minute." He wanted reassurance from his sister that what she wanted was to stay with him. Because he was about to have a low-down, dirty, nasty, and bloody fight on his hands. He wanted to go into this knowing that was what his sister wanted, without question.

"Hey, short stuff," he said, when he found her in the living room of the suite, watching TV, feet on the couch. She was still wearing her dress and her face looked pale, despite the glittery eye shadow she was sporting. "You okay?"

She shrugged, eyes still on the TV.

He sat down next to her. "So, uh, that was unexpected. I didn't know Mom was back in the country."

When she finally turned to him, there were tears in her eyes and it was like a hot poker shoved in his chest. Damn, he wished he could take away her hurt.

"Why didn't she ever check on me? She didn't know I was going to be there. That was just an accident that she saw me. Why doesn't she love me?"

Jesus. Cooper blinked hard to keep the tears stinging his own eyes from falling. "She does love you, sweetheart. But people like our mother are just selfish. She will always love herself more than she loves you or me, and that's just the way she's drawn. It doesn't have a damn thing to do with you."

"She left you, too, didn't she?"

He nodded. "Yep. Dumped me with our grandparents and took off for years." He put his arm around his sister and hauled her against his chest. "Some people aren't meant to be parents, only they don't figure that out until after the fact. So you know what? We need to be grateful to her for giving us life, but beyond that, we don't owe her a damn thing."

"I wish she had died instead of my dad. Is that bad?"

Sad thing was, it probably would have been better for his sister. But even though he was furious and disgusted, he couldn't wish his own mother dead. "I think that's a very normal feeling to have." He paused because he wanted to be honest, but he wasn't sure how to say it without making MJ feel like she was the pawn in the battle brewing. "I would like to file for full custody of you, but I need to know that's definitely what you want. Mom is going to fight me on this, so while I don't want to pressure you, I need to know that you want to stay with me. Because the courts will ask you questions and I want you to be sure of your answer."

But she was already nodding her head. "I want to stay with you. Please don't make me go back with her. I don't even want to see her and I don't get why she even cares. She wants custody so she can ignore me? It's stupid."

It was about power, but he wasn't going to tell his sister that. "Okay. Then I'll file the papers tomorrow." He had already filed for emergency custody months ago, figuring he needed to legally have the right to make decisions about his sister. He wasn't sure his mother even knew that because while she was supposed to be informed, he hadn't known where she was. The guardianship had been granted on the grounds that she had just taken off and left MJ. So Cooper thought it was damn stupid on her part to put up a fight. He was confident he could win.

"Get some sleep. You have Jeff's number, right? He's going to have you and Harley sit in his box for the race Sunday. Tomorrow you can hang out at the pool while I work."

"Cool." Then the tender bonding moment was over. She pulled away from him with a sniff. "You smell like sweat. Gross."

He laughed and stood up. "And you smell like brat."

She stuck her tongue out at him.

Harley was in the kitchenette and she called out, "Do you want water or juice?"

"Is there orange juice? I'll take that. Thanks, baby." He met her as she came out with two bottles in one hand, a bottle of pain reliever in the other. He gave her a soft kiss. "Thank you. You're amazing." He took the bottles from her and whispered in her ear. "Come take a shower with me."

The way she leaned into him was immensely satisfying. "I'd love to."

In the bedroom, door firmly shut behind them, Cooper kissed Harley slowly, loving the way she dug her nails into his shoulders and massaged at the knots of tension there, while their mouths met. He didn't deserve a woman this kind, this considerate. He hadn't done enough to be entitled to her, and he wanted to prove that he could care for her the way she innately cared for him.

Slowly taking down the zipper of her dress, he murmured, "You looked beautiful tonight. Thank you for being with me." He wasn't sure that she'd enjoyed herself, even before his mother had turned up like a bad penny. With a slight tug he pushed her dress over her shoulders and down over her body. It pooled at her feet and she was left in a nude bra and panties. He liked that they blended with her flesh and didn't give that eye-popping contrast of red or black lingerie. This allowed him to focus on her, the dip of her waist, the curve of her hip, the lush rise of her breast above her bra.

"Your friends are all very nice," she said softly, eyes on his chest as she worked to unbutton his dress shirt.

That was when he decided he didn't really want to talk. Yanking his shirt out of his pants, he stripped it off and took Harley by the hand and into the bathroom. The shower was huge, with multiple spouts, including several on the wall that were at the right height to hit strategic spots on a woman's body. Well, a man's, too, but he was more interested in her reaction than his. He knew he'd be turned on. He already was. While he turned the water on and tested the temperature, Harley ran her fingers over his bare back, then snaked around to undo the button on his pants. He never quite knew what to expect from her. Sometimes she was shy, sometimes bossy, always sexy, always perfect.

He helped her out by taking his pants off and gesturing to the luxurious shower. "Ladies first."

Harley undid her bra and took it off slowly, her eyes never leaving his. Then she bent over and divested herself of those little panties, giving him a showstopping view of her breasts and the curve of her ass. With a sassy little kick of the panties off her foot, she gave him a smile and stepped into the shower.

"Oh, Cooper," she groaned as the water hit her. "This feels so good." She rolled her head side to side. "I didn't realize how tense my muscles were."

His mother's legacy—shoulder knots. He got in and closed the glass door behind him. Reaching for the shower gel, he squeezed it into his hands and moved in behind Harley, starting a slow massage of her shoulders from inside to out. The sigh of pleasure she gave brought a strange sense of pride to him. He'd never really understood the satisfaction that could come from putting someone else first. Sure, he was well aware of his particular nickname because of his affinity for going down on a woman. But that was different. That was something he enjoyed because he liked driving women mad, making them completely insensible during sex, and shocking them at how far their eyes could roll back in their heads. That was pride, but a different sort of pride. It was pure ego.

But this . . . it was different. He just wanted to make sure that every day Harley was happy, comfortable. Was that what love was?

It felt like love, that was for damn sure.

Straying a bit from her shoulders, he moved lower and lower, massaging her back, before reaching around, hands slick and bubbly, to cup her breasts, squeeze her nipples. The steam rose between them and the gel smelled like coconuts. Harley tilted her head back toward him, the palms of her hands resting on his thighs. His cock was nudging between her cheeks and he felt relaxed, aroused. Rinsing his hand off first, he slipped his fingers between her thighs and stroked her clitoris. There was no rush, nowhere to be, just him and Harley in the warm heat of the water and their bodies.

So he stroked down, delving inside her slick heat, and nibbling her ear. But Harley had a different idea in mind. She spread her feet apart and leaned forward, putting her hands on the soap dish as she made soft sounds of pleasure. "Is that an invitation?" he asked.

"It's a request."

He smiled, urging her feet further apart with a nudge on her ankle. She obliged and he moved his hands to her hips. She was wet and slick everywhere and he took in the sight of her damp hair clinging to her shoulder, the droplets running down over her pink skin, the bumps of her spine leading right down to where he could sink inside her and lose himself in ecstasy. She turned her head so that the water wasn't hitting her directly in the face and he got to see her parted lips, her slumberous half-closed eyes, the tip of her pink tongue darting out to lick a stray drop.

Then Cooper shifted and took her with an easy thrust. He didn't want to pound her. He just wanted to go in, and out, and in, until she was panting and he had tight balls and no control.

But Harley said, "Harder. Please."

How was he going to argue with that? Gripping her more firmly, he thrust hard, yanking her hips back so that they collided violently, water kicking up, the sound of the hard slap making him groan. So maybe this wasn't such a bad idea after all.

Within seconds she shocked him by having an orgasm, the unmistakable sensation of her climax gripping his cock and plunging him over the edge. All the night's frustrations, anxieties, just ripped out of him as he gritted his teeth and embraced the feeling of coming inside Harley.

"Damn," he said, when he could finally breathe again. Harley was panting, too, and she shifted forward with a little laugh.

"My knees are knocking."

Cooper sighed when her movement broke their connection. He didn't want to let her go. But the water was getting cooler and he could see that Harley was ready to get out. So he didn't protest when she gave him a kiss and a smile and slipped out, immediately wrapping herself in a towel. Ducking his head under the water, he washed his hair and face quickly, rolling his neck to get the last remnants of tension out.

"My headache is gone," he told her as she dried herself off.

"Glad I could help."

If only she knew how much help she was to him. Maybe he should tell her. But he didn't have the words. Saying he appreciated her was too polite for what he felt. He would just have to show her. He turned off the water and took the towel she handed him, but he just stuck it around his waist and headed for bed.

"You're getting in bed wet? You'll dampen the sheets."

"They'll dry." He was tired, bone weary. He just wanted to lie down with Harley in his arms.

"It will make us both cold."

Before he could comprehend what she was about, Harley had laid into him with a towel from behind, rubbing his wet hair vigorously.

"What the hell are you doing?" he asked, amused, but perturbed by the sensation. No one had dried his hair since he was five.

"Drying you off."

Cooper reached back and yanked the towel out of her hands. "I don't think so." Instead he turned and hooked the towel behind her head, to draw her to him. Her warm chest pressed against his damp flesh. "Come here. And never leave."

That was the closest he could get to explain how he felt.

Her eyes softened and she cupped his cheeks. "I'm not going anywhere."

HARLEY hadn't been to a race yet as Cooper's guest. Or Jeff Sterling's guest. Or anyone's guest. She and Mary Jane had gone to the fateful beach trip in Daytona instead of the race, but in Phoenix she was sitting in a luxury box with a whole crowd of strangers. It was intimidating as hell. Mary Jane was of course perfectly comfortable with both the adults and the display of wealth. It was just another

Sunday to her. To Harley, who had only ever been to a race in person a handful of times, it was overwhelming. Despite being friends with Eve, she'd never expected any sort of perks, knowing that Eve couldn't get tickets for every friend she had.

Maybe if she had, the whole experience of being with the in crowd wouldn't have been so terrifying. But it was. Harley couldn't help it. She wasn't precisely shy, but she was no chatterbox either and she had no clue what to say to the assortment of drivers' wives, sponsor reps, media personnel, and Jeff himself. Mary Jane was running around the room making conversation, which was a clear ruse for ferreting out information from them. No one seemed wise to what she was doing, but Harley knew she was formulating a blog post.

Why couldn't Mary Jane be the typical kid who didn't want to say two words to anyone over the age of twenty? Then she would at least be someone Harley could huddle with. Instead, she was huddling with a plate of cheese. It was ridiculous.

Jeff came over and gave her a smile, right as she was popping a cracker with Brie into her mouth. "Are you enjoying yourself?" he asked.

She nodded. Then swallowed, determined not to let him walk away without her clearing her conscience. "Jeff, I've been meaning to tell you that I'm sorry for the night at the Buckle. That was just way out of line for me to accept your invitation and then to be, well, with Cooper." She would not blush. She would not.

But he put his hand up. "Hey, no apology necessary. I wasn't exactly being fair to you either. I was interested in your sister, but my ego was dented. Not cool at all of me."

Relieved, she shifted the cheese plate and held out her hand. "Even?"

"Even." He wore a suit like he'd been born in one, and he returned his hands idly to his pockets. "I hope your sister doesn't mind how much I'm on the road."

Considering every day Harley had gotten ooey-gooey texts from Charity about Jeff, she was pretty damn sure she was willing to overlook that. "She understands it's part of the business. I would say she's really looking forward to getting to know you better on a personal level."

His eyebrows rose and Harley realized that sounded a little sexual. "You know what I mean."

He laughed. "I hope I do. But I'm looking forward to getting to know Charity as well." Then he glanced behind her and frowned. "Damn."

"What's wrong?" Harley turned and before Jeff could reply, she saw Cooper's mother. "Damn" was right. Along with "shit" and "fuck."

"Excuse me for a minute," he said, and moved off in June's direction.

Harley took off for Mary Jane, wanting to warn her that her mother was there. She was at the window, looking down at the track. "You been watching, Harley?"

Yes, between cheese plates, she'd done nothing but stare at Cooper's car, with a mix of amazement, worry, and pride. "Cooper's driving well today. He's got a real shot at winning this thing if he holds on. But I need to let you know that your mom is here."

Mary Jane froze. "Ugh. Why?"

"I don't know. She's talking to Jeff."

"I'm going to the bathroom." Mary Jane spun on her heels and retreated into the bathroom, the sound of the lock audible through the door.

"Well, hello again."

Harley shared Mary Jane's sentiment of *ugh*. Suppressing

the urge to sigh, she turned and without bothering to smile said, "Hi, Mrs. Rawlings."

Partly she used the last name to make it clear they weren't friends. Partly to remind June that she was in her fifties and had run through three husbands.

"I have a proposition for you."

Oh, Lord. Harley just waited, sure she did not want to hear this. June was wearing a sleeveless, plunging stretchy top in an eye-popping lime, and skintight jeans with heels. Never mind that it was the third week in February and there was a cold snap in Arizona. Never mind that there were a bazillion stairs at the track.

She had an envelope in her hand. "I spoke with my lawyer yesterday. He said I have a strong case. But I'm willing to negotiate."

"Shouldn't you be discussing this with Cooper, not me?"

"No, because this concerns you. You see, the thing is, I don't want you replacing me." June's expression wasn't belligerent. It was simply matter-of-fact.

"Replacing you? How?" Though she knew the answer.

"As Mary Jane's mother. As the most important influence on Cooper. So I will allow Cooper full custody of Mary Jane if you agree to make yourself scarce."

For a second, Harley couldn't breathe. Give up Cooper and Mary Jane? The very thought was incomprehensible. But she also couldn't believe June would give in that easily. "Seriously? You must think I'm an idiot to fall for that. If I were to leave, you'd still pursue custody."

June smiled. "At least you do have brains, I'll give you that. It's in writing, honey." She tapped Harley's arm with the envelope. "All spelled out, right there. You quit the nanny gig, you move out of the house, you agree to never have contact with Cooper and Mary Jane, and I grant him full custody as long as he remains in Charlotte. Simple. Straightforward."

"You'd give up your daughter just to keep me away from her?" The whole thing was so beyond anything Harley could even comprehend. If she was ever blessed with children, nothing could keep her from them.

She couldn't leave Mary Jane either. Or Cooper. How the hell could she?

But June had given her an impossible choice. Did she break her own heart and walk away, knowing that Mary Jane and Cooper could build a life together? Or did she dig her heels in, fight for what was right, with Cooper's money, and hope like hell they didn't lose Mary Jane altogether? The thought of her living with June made Harley's stomach turn.

"I would," June said. "I want what's best for her, and with a nice grandmotherly sort of nanny, I'm confident she will be very happy living with Cooper."

"I don't understand what the objection is to me being her nanny."

"Because you'll poison her against me. You made your opinion of me quite clear and there is no way in hell I'm letting you have that much influence over my children."

June handed her the envelope and left, without even seeing Mary Jane as she came out of the bathroom.

Harley was stunned. So she had opened her mouth at the benefit two days earlier and stood up for what was right, and this was what happened? No wonder she'd always stayed away from confrontation. She had no skill in playing the game, in strategizing, calculating the other players' moves. Never in a million years would she have seen this coming as the result of her making a face lift crack, and now Mary Jane was going to pay the price one way or the other.

She felt absolutely sick to her stomach and wished more than anything her sister were there to reassure her.

But Charity was at home and Harley was alone with a heavy heart and anxious thoughts that went around and around like an emotional whirlpool.

So she stood at the window and watched Cooper go around and around on the track.

CHAPTER
TWENTY

HARLEY and Mary Jane had taken an earlier flight than Cooper's redeye after the race. So when he got home he wasn't exactly surprised to crawl into his empty bed at five a.m. for a few hours of sleep. Not surprised, but disappointed that Harley had chosen to sleep in her room. It didn't prevent him from crashing immediately, though. He'd come in second at the race. His best finish in eighteen months. Not that he was counting. But seriously. Best finish in eighteen months. Despite being super worried about what legal maneuvering his mother was already engaged in.

When he came downstairs at ten he knew instantly something was wrong. Harley was sitting at the kitchen table, biting her fingernail. She started when she saw him. His gut twisted. He had good instincts. It made him good at his job. And he knew that he was not going to like whatever was going to come out of her mouth in the next five minutes. "Morning," he said, testing the waters.

"Did you sleep okay?" she asked. "I can make you some coffee."

"I got it." He didn't particularly want her waiting on him. It smacked of guilt at the moment. "Where's my sister?"

"She's with her homeschool group at the library."

"She liking that okay?" Harley had suggested Mary Jane needed friends her own age and he had agreed. What surprised him was that MJ had agreed, but then again, after Daytona he figured she saw this not as an educational opportunity but a chance to meet teen boys. He supposed it was only natural even if it made him sick to his stomach.

"Yes, I think so. She hardly complains at all."

"That's saying something." Cooper bent over the coffeemaker, reading the little icons. He pressed open. "So, uh, everything okay? You look worried about something."

"Your mother approached me at the race."

Shit. Cooper rubbed his forehead. "Yeah? What bitchy thing did she say this time? Did she tell you I'm a lousy son?" He had to admit, no matter what he said to MJ, it did still hurt when his mother showed such callous disregard for both of them. He couldn't help it. He'd spent his whole life wanting her approval, and it was never going to be there. Not in any way that he could appreciate.

"She said she would let you have custody of Mary Jane, no contest, in exchange for one request."

Elation that she might slink away quietly was gone by the end of Harley's sentence. It wouldn't be that easy. It was never that easy with his mother. "What does she want? Money? Or a Tuscan villa?" He'd give her money or a house. It wouldn't be much more than legal fees would be when all was said and done and it would save him a shit-ton of worry and stress and ease MJ's mind. Cooper put a mug under the coffee spout and inserted his roast cup into the machine.

"No. She wants me to leave you both."

Cooper paused in the act of his finger reaching out to push the start button. "Come again?" That made no fucking sense. It was ludicrous.

"She wants me to quit my job here and leave."

Turning around slowly, Cooper resented the hell out of the fact that his kitchen was so goddamn big. He was fifteen feet away from Harley. But even at that distance he could see her pale face, the nervous shifting of her eyes. Oh, my fucking God. She was going to do it. She was going to leave him.

"Why?" he asked, carefully, holding on to his control. If he was rational and calm, all of this would go away. "Why would she want that?"

"She is essentially afraid that Mary Jane will love me more than her. She doesn't want to be replaced. Not by someone younger than her, anyway."

His anger exploded that his mother would have the goddamn nerve. "What does she care? My housekeeper has a more positive influence on MJ than she does. And sees her more. Of course Mary Jane is going to be close to you."

"It's selfish. I totally agree." Harley was speaking quietly, not expressing the outrage he personally felt. "That's not really the point."

"What is the point?"

"If I do what she wants, she will sign over all rights to Mary Jane indefinitely. And there is no chance that you'll lose custody in a heated court battle."

Hold the fucking phone. "Are you actually considering this?" he asked. Forget the coffee. He strode across the kitchen and got in her space. He leaned over and stared into her eyes, his palms on the table, wanting to read what was there. "You can't be."

"I've already decided that it's the right thing to do." She

pushed a pile of papers over to him. "Sign the papers, Cooper. I couldn't stand it if Mary Jane had to go back to your mom. It would break my heart."

He couldn't believe what she was saying. "So you're just willing to break MJ's heart instead? And mine?" It made no sense at all. "Fuck that, Harley. *Fuck. That.*"

There were suddenly tears in her eyes at his harsh words, but Cooper didn't care. No. This was unacceptable. But she looked away and leaned back in her chair to put more distance between them. He slammed the table with his hands and stepped away. "You have got to be kidding me. This isn't happening."

"I don't have a choice," she insisted, her voice thin and reedy.

"We always have a choice." He was just baffled that she thought this was the right thing to do. "You're going to sacrifice *us* because my mother is making threatening noises? She can't win this court case, you know."

"What if she does? Stranger things happen in court all the time. If Mary Jane has to go live with her, it will be my fault!"

"It won't happen." He didn't believe it for one minute. Sure, they would have to wade through a bunch of bullshit, but it wouldn't happen.

But Harley shook her head. "That's because you have had everything go your way. Life hasn't been as fair to me. I know the odds are fifty-fifty. And that makes the odds too high for me to risk it."

He was so angry and hurt he almost didn't trust himself to speak. "That's lame. Just lame. If you wanted an out to our relationship, you could have just told me."

"That's not what I want!"

She was crying now, tears streaming down her cheeks that she impatiently wiped at, but Cooper was unmoved.

She was breaking his goddamn heart. She should be crying. He felt a little like crying himself. "Then don't do this!"

"I have to!"

He just stared at her, still not entirely comprehending that she was serious. "So that's just it? For real? You're leaving me?"

She nodded, biting her lip.

Cooper needed to get out of there, away from her, away from the horrible wave of emotion that crashed over him. He wanted to kill his mother. He wanted to throttle Harley. He wanted to throw things.

So instead he would drive. It was what he could do. The one thing he was good at, the one place in the world where he felt in control. He grabbed his keys off the hook by the garage door and shoved his feet into the boots he kept in the closet. He was only wearing jeans and a T-shirt, but he didn't need a coat. He was flushed with anger.

"Where are you going?"

"Out. If you're really leaving me, then do it while I'm gone, or I'm going to say ugly and hurtful things." He paused at the door, looking back at her, giving her a chance to make this stupidity all go away. He waited. And waited. And she did nothing. She sat there, shoulders slumped. Crying.

Cooper swore. As he shoved the door open, it hit the wall of the garage so hard it broke the doorstop. Because it felt good, he slammed it two more times just to make a nice hole in the drywall. It appeased his frustration one thousandth of a percent. His garage had room for six cars. He usually drove the truck or the SUV, but he had several sports cars. He chose the Porsche, hitting the button to open the garage door. He wanted speed.

Harley appeared in the doorway, looking alarmed. "Be careful," she said. "Maybe you shouldn't—"

But Cooper cut her off. "You know what, Harley? I don't need a mother. I had a shitty mother but I had a good grandmother and she took care of me. I don't need you to take care of me. Mother me. Make decisions that are supposedly best for me. Okay?"

"That's not what—"

"Yes, it is." Knowing he was being a little childish on the heels of just declaring he didn't want her mothering him, he said, "I'm going to drive my Porsche too fast and there is nothing you can do about it. Just like I can't do anything about you walking out on me."

As an exclamation point, he got in his car and purposely made the tires screech as he backed out. Or tore out, if you wanted to be technical.

It wasn't until he was on the road, keeping it under sixty miles an hour, since he wasn't on the track, that he allowed himself to really comprehend what was happening. Fuck nuts. He was single again. Just like that.

He could argue with Harley until the cows came home, but if she was determined to be noble, then there wasn't a whole hell of a lot he could do about it. Which sucked. Hard. He couldn't imagine his house now without her in it. He couldn't imagine his life now without her in it. It was honestly far worse to have known what happiness could be like and have it yanked away than to never experience it at all. The cliché was true. He'd always thought it was melodramatic, but now he knew it wasn't.

The morning was crisp and clear, the sun shining and the sky blue. It was a beautiful day and as he turned out of his neighborhood and onto the rural road, the blacktop rose in front of him, mesmerizing him. For as long as he could remember, the roar of an engine, the feel of the stick shift beneath his fingers, the choreography of clutch, gas, brake had soothed him. On the road he could clear his thoughts and find serenity. He'd outdriven the demons his mother had left him with by the time he was in his early twenties. Life had been good for him since.

But this . . . this hurt. This was the first broken heart he'd had since he was fifteen and he had to say that even if he could completely open the engine up, he didn't think he could outdrive this pain.

HARLEY drove to Charity's, crying, worrying about Cooper off in that car. It had been six hours and he hadn't returned. She had picked up Mary Jane, had a heartwrenching conversation with her where Mary Jane had given her the most scathing look of disgust ever when she explained the situation and tentatively suggested maybe she should leave.

At that moment, knowing that Cooper was off half-cocked, and seeing his sister's face, Harley had changed her mind. She had decided that she couldn't hurt them, even if it was the best for them. She had backtracked with Mary Jane, but it was too late. The betrayal had been done, the hurt inflicted. Mary Jane had screamed at her to leave, shoving her out of her bedroom.

So she had.

And now she was sobbing on her way to her sister's, wondering how everything could have gone so horribly wrong. Despising June Rawlings. Despising herself.

"What the hell is wrong with you?" Charity asked as she let herself into the apartment with her key and careened into the living room. "My God, did someone die?"

"No. But I want to." Harley threw herself down onto the couch and swiped at her face, not even sure where to start. "Cooper's mom threatened to take Mary Jane and so Cooper freaked out and I freaked out and Mary Jane freaked out and I told her that her face lift was bad and so then she said she would give Cooper custody if I broke up with him and left so I did."

Charity's eyes widened, and she shoved at Harley's feet so she could sit down next to her. "What? You broke up with Cooper? Are you insane?"

Harley nodded. She couldn't repeat it again. She just couldn't.

"You broke up with Cooper or you're insane?"

"Both!" Harley felt like she had a fever. "Then I tried to undo it and I couldn't and I think Cooper is dead."

"What the fuck . . ." Charity stared at her. "I don't understand."

But she was crying too hard to explain it. She wasn't even sure what had happened. All she knew was June was evil and she herself had tried to be brave and do the right thing but in the end it felt totally like the wrong thing. Actually, there was no right thing. Because if she had blithely ignored June's threat and Mary Jane was taken away, she would have never forgiven herself. So either way she had been screwed, only this way the agony came sooner.

"I'm calling Jeff."

Harley wasn't sure why but she didn't care enough to protest. And now that she thought about it . . . "Ask him if he's heard from Cooper."

Charity was murmuring into her phone so that Harley couldn't hear. Her twin kept shooting her nervous looks, her hand over her mouth. Harley was pretty sure that she had never felt as awful as she did right then. Both Cooper and Mary Jane had looked at her like she had taken a knife and stabbed them in the heart. Which in a sense, she had. She'd said she would be there for them, and yet she'd been forced to leave them. It wasn't fair.

"I'm not brave like you," Harley told her sister when she hung up the phone. "I always act out of fear."

"I'm not brave. I'm just a big mouth." Charity sat next to her again and touched her leg. "Jeff said that Cooper is with his lawyer. Mary Jane is with Rosa. Everything is okay."

"Everything is not okay."

"So call Cooper."

"He's not answering me." A fresh torrent of tears started. "Neither is Mary Jane."

"I'm texting Jeff to text him to text you."

"What is this, six degrees of Kevin Bacon? Text him, too, while you're at it. Maybe he can fix the mess I made of my life." This was what happened when you let Cinderella out of the kitchen. She fell down the stairs at the ball. Lost her shoe. Went up against the evil stepmother and lost. Where the hell was her fairy godmother when she needed one?

"Maybe Cooper would agree to see me," Charity said. "And you can go instead."

"Now who is insane? I think we both learned the price of switching identities was a high one to pay." Harley got off the couch and went to the kitchen. "Please tell me you have ice cream in here or I am going to cry."

"You're already crying."

"Harder." She went rooting around in the refrigerator. "Do you think I mother the men I date?"

"Yes," Charity said without hesitation.

Great. "Cooper said he doesn't want me to do that."

"It's a fine line." Charity followed her. "There is nothing wrong with being nurturing. But you can't make decisions for people."

Harley wanted to groan. "That's not what I was doing. I was trying to avoid losing Mary Jane."

Her phone rang in her pocket. She pulled it out because it was Cooper's ring tone. "Oh, my God, he's calling me."

"Answer it."

Right. "Hello?"

"So you left."

It wasn't a question. "I talked to Mary Jane and then I wasn't going to leave but then she asked me to leave."

"So you just listened to the thirteen-year-old with the hurt feelings and left."

When he said it like that, it sounded awful. "I . . ."

"You what? Explain to me."

"I thought I was doing what she wanted. And I thought I was doing the right thing for both of you, to protect you."

"I think you were just afraid. I think you're afraid of being with me. You're afraid to be a driver's girlfriend. You're afraid to go a round or two with my mom. You're afraid to put yourself out there like your sister does."

What could she say to that? "You're right. I am. I changed my mind. I wasn't going to leave."

"It's too late, Harley. You did the one thing I asked you not to do—leave. All MJ and I both needed was someone to be there, who cared about us for us. Not for money or fame."

"Cooper . . ." She really was going to throw up. "But your mother . . ."

The argument was weak, even to her.

"Doesn't have a chance in hell of winning a court case. We could have faced this together."

She had nothing to say. Her sister would have turned it around, pointed out Cooper's flaws as well. She would have stood behind her decision and asked why he wasn't backing *her*. But Harley couldn't do that. When confronted, she retreated. She pulled inside herself and clammed up. Even wanting to, she couldn't force the words out.

What she wanted to tell him was what she had never said to him. That she was in love with him. That she loved him. More than any man she'd ever met. Not because he was famous or wealthy or did something cool for a living. But because he was still real. He wasn't arrogant or cocky or demanding. He was confident, sure of who he was. She envied that about him. But the best qualities about him were his kindness, his thoughtfulness, his desire to do the right thing. The way he teased and cared for his sister even though it wasn't easy and he didn't know what he was doing. The way he had forgiven her, even though she had lied, and set him up for unintentional humiliation.

He was a deep, deep well of loyalty and integrity.

She loved him.

But none of that came out of her mouth.

What did was simply, "I'm sorry."

It wasn't surprising to her when he made a sound of frustration and said, "Good-bye, Harley."

Still she said nothing, but her throat was closed and her pain was overwhelming.

The phone went dead.

All her dreams died along with it.

Unless she finally got brave and said what needed to be said.

CHAPTER
TWENTY-ONE

COOPER'S lawyer advised him not to speak to his mother directly. Cooper didn't listen. He had a key to the house she'd shared with Bud and he let himself in. He found her in the hot tub on the back patio with Sebastian. Fortunately, they were both wearing swimsuits.

"Cooper Brickman! What the hell do you think you're doing?" she shouted at him, looking every inch the outraged mother of a misbehaving teen.

He'd give it to her. She never backed down on being the one who had been mistreated. "Sorry to interrupt, but I am here to ask you to not interfere in my personal life. I don't want to argue with you. I don't want be one of those families who only see each other in court. But unless you see Harley and tell her she does not need to quit in order for you to relinquish custody, that's exactly where we're going to be. And I won't pull punches."

She took a sip of her wine and he knew it was a ploy to

gather her thoughts. It was cold outside, but his anger was keeping him warm.

"For heaven's sake," she said. "Don't get so worked up. Your little Mary Poppins was already here asking the same thing and I said yes, so maybe the two of you should discuss this and leave me to my relaxing."

That gave him pause. "Harley was here?" he asked in disbelief.

"Yes. And Jeff Sterling should mind his own goddamn business. Can you believe he brought her here? To my *home*? Zero respect for privacy."

"Why would she come here?" That made no sense at all. She had left him. Why would she confront his mother?

"Because apparently she is devastated at the idea of having to leave you and Mary Jane." His mother rolled her eyes. "It was all very dramatic. I swear she was vying for an Oscar. I had to give her points for acting like she was going to die a painful death if she didn't get to be with you."

Cooper wasn't sure what to say. If you had asked him the day before, he would have said that Harley absolutely wanted to be with him more than anything. But he was still reeling from the fact that she had left him. "So what did you tell her?"

"I thought about it, and honestly, I don't want to fight with you. It would be a brutal court battle. I would have to parade a bunch of your bed partners through court, and point out that you aren't any more fit to parent than me considering how much you're on the road. I figure we each have a fifty-fifty shot of winning and really, do we want to do that to each other?" She took another sip of her wine.

She was right. Cooper hadn't really thought about it from that perspective. While he hadn't abandoned Mary Jane, he was trusting her primary care to a nanny, and

really, he was only her half brother. There wasn't any guarantee that the court would rule in his favor. He understood
a little better where Harley had been coming from. He
didn't like that she hadn't allowed for the two of them to
discuss it, but the edge of his anger was shaved.

"I don't want to drag our family through court, no. But I
do think MJ is better off living with me for now. She's
happy and it's a stable environment, even though I travel.
And until this morning, she had a fantastic nanny." He was
trying really hard not to sound emotional, not to lose it, but
his voice cracked a little on that last part.

"Oh, relax. You still have your nanny extraordinaire. With
me dropping the contest of your custody, there's no reason
Harley can't continue working for you." She turned to her
boyfriend and presented him her back. "Sebastian, can you
rub my shoulders? All this drama is causing tension."

Sebastian dutifully obeyed. Cooper wanted to check the
bottom of the hot tub to see where the guy had dropped his
balls. He'd never even heard the guy speak. Apparently his
role was to see and be seen, not speak.

"Anyway, I thought she was going to your house to
plead forgiveness, which frankly, she doesn't even need to
ask for. She was trying to do the right thing, and if you can't
see that, then you're a fool. It's not every day you're going
to have a woman actually willing to sacrifice for you. God
knows I never will for any man."

Sebastian didn't even pause in the rubbing.

Cooper suddenly wanted to laugh. Well, at least his
mother was honest. Brutally so. But honest.

He was so relieved she was dropping pursuit of the custody, for a second he just paused to let go of the immense
burden of anxiety he'd been feeling since she had shown up
on Friday night at the event. "I'm glad we could work this

out ourselves," he told her sincerely. "Bottom line is we both want what's best for MJ." He wasn't entirely sure that was what motivated his mother, but it was a good parting line.

She nodded. "Now go away. You make me feel old."

Cooper grinned. "Sorry, Mom. I can't help the fact that I'm thirty-five now."

"Oh, my God, don't say it out loud!" She shuddered and reflexively touched her face, like his age was manifested on her face in wrinkle form.

"But I'm twenty-three," Sebastian said suddenly, sounding startled, like it had just occurred to him that his girlfriend was in fact more than thirty years older than him.

Before his mother threw the bottle of wine at him for speaking the unspeakable, Cooper gave her a wave and said, "I'll be in touch with papers to sign. Don't get pregnant. I hear that can happen in a hot tub."

The corner of her mouth turned up in a smile before she recovered and pasted a censorious frown on her face. "Very funny."

"It can?" Sebastian asked, his hands dropping.

Oh, Lord. On that note, Cooper was leaving. He thought about calling Harley but decided to just go home first and see if she was there.

He needed to see her eyes when they spoke.

He needed to tell her that he loved her. He'd never told her, and the day had shown him that there was no point in dancing around emotions. For all he knew, Harley had doubts about his intentions.

By the time they were done talking, no matter what the outcome, she would know he loved her more than any woman he'd ever met.

He'd put that on a piece of paper and sign it, damn it.

* * *

HARLEY looked at Mary Jane, sitting sullenly on her chaise in her room, and wished that she'd been given a better mother and that Harley had been given better words to take away hurt. "I know you don't entirely understand why I did what I did, but I did it to guarantee that you could stay with Cooper."

Mary Jane was picking at the knee of her jeans. "I know. But it still sucked. And why did you leave just to come right back again?"

"Because I convinced your mom to drop her petition for custody." Harley wasn't sure how exactly she had done that. Maybe it had been allowing herself to be pathetic and blubber in front of June. It made their mother feel like she had the upper hand and there was no reason to feel threatened by Harley. Or maybe she had just thought about how much easier life was if Cooper had Mary Jane. She didn't know. She just knew that June had been remarkably agreeable when all was said and done.

Hopefully it wasn't a ploy of some kind. But even if it was, Harley wasn't caving this time. It had been agonizing to see Cooper and Mary Jane hurt by her actions, no matter how noble in intent they had been. "The absolute last thing in the world I wanted to do was leave, but I wanted what was best for you. That's what adults who love kids do."

"What are you saying, that you love me?" Mary Jane made a face and rolled her eyes.

"I do. I love you a whole heck of a lot. I think you're funny and smart and sweet and I like hanging out with you. You're my favorite thirteen-year-old in the whole world and I am looking forward to watching you take over the fashion blog industry." She took a chance and planted herself on the chaise next to Mary Jane. "There is a lot I admire about you. I've been the kind of person who floats through life, you know. I'm a good person. I don't do anything that is rude or obnoxious or morally wrong. But I just . . . float. You and Cooper, you're doers. You get things done. And I wish I were more like that. Maybe if I were, I would open my mouth more and tell people how I feel about them."

"But you take care of other people," Mary Jane said. "That's not floating. You do an awesome job taking care of me and Cooper."

That made Harley's heart swell. She touched Mary Jane's knee, her throat tight. "Thanks. I hope I can take care of you both for a long time. And I'm going to be honest and tell you how much you mean to me."

"Are you going to tell Cooper, too?"

She nodded. "I love Cooper. A lot. Like the squishy kind of love you and I talked about."

"Good. I think you and Cooper should get married. If you have kids, I'll be an aunt and I will dress them in the cutest clothes ever."

"Let's not get ahead of ourselves here." Though nothing would make Harley happier. She'd been born to be a mother. It felt like her one true calling.

"He likes steak, you know. Maybe you can make him dinner," Mary Jane suggested.

Harley wondered if that was too grasping. Like she was trying to blackmail him with beef into taking her back. "He does like Tex-Mex. Lots of salsa."

"I do like salsa, that's true."

She snapped her head up and saw that Cooper was standing in the doorway. "Cooper!" How long had he been standing there? Normally Mary Jane's door was closed, but she'd opened it to Harley and turned to walk away and

Harley hadn't bothered to shut it. "I hope you don't mind I'm here without permission."

"Of course he doesn't mind!" Mary Jane said.

Harley stood up, thoughts jumbled. She wasn't sure what to say first or how to say it.

"I don't mind. Can I speak to you privately?" He looked serious, intense. Nary a smile in sight, but he seemed calm. It was a big improvement from when he had left that morning, anger etched across his face.

"I was just leaving," Mary Jane said, leaping off the chaise and pushing past her brother.

Cooper raised his eyebrows at her retreating form. "Wow. I've never seen her move that fast."

Harley was used to waiting. Just waiting for someone else to direct the conversation. Her relationship with them. But she couldn't do that now, not after what had happened. She stepped forward, not sure what his reaction was going to be. "I'm sorry for this morning. I should have discussed it with you. I should have explained better that the last thing in the world I wanted to do was hurt either of you, that I did it for both of you. Cooper, I *love* you." Her voice cracked. "I am absolutely and completely in love with you."

"I heard your whole conversation with MJ." He reached out and took her hand loosely, absently rubbing his thumb over her skin.

Harley took it as a good sign. "Everything I said was true. I'm no Charity. I've spent my life letting her speak for me. I wait for her to touch something to find out if it's hot or not. I don't take risks."

"There is nothing wrong with caution. I know why you did what you did. But sometimes it's better to go for it and lose it all than to just hand it over without even trying."

Tears filled her eyes. "I think I realized that about five seconds after you left the house."

"I talked to my mom. She said you were there."

Harley nodded. "She may be planning a full-scale secret attack, or she was sincere about dropping the case."

"I think she is actually sincere." He touched her cheek with his free hand. "I love you, too, you know. You're the first woman to genuinely capture my heart." Dropping her hand, he thumped his chest with his fist. "Like, this, right here? It's all yours if you want it."

The tears came openly now. "I want that more than anything. I didn't realize how insecure I was feeling about that until I left. It means a lot to me to hear you say that. I don't want to be here just because Mary Jane needs a mother."

He winced. "I'm sorry I said that earlier. I just meant that you have to take your worth at face value. You don't need to do stuff for me to have value in my life. If you want to mother, let's make a baby. But I'm good, baby. I want you as a best friend, not here to take care of me."

"I want you as a best friend, too." Harley felt so immensely emotional, so overwhelmed by the way Cooper looked at her, that she leaned into his chest, needing, wanting to touch him. "I've never been best friends with a guy before," she whispered.

He laughed. "And I've never lived with a woman before, but I'm about to start. Because I think we should just accept Rosa's evil eye and move you into my room."

"I think that's the best idea you've ever had."

"The best?" Cooper gave her a dirty grin. "I can think of another one."

Yes, please. "So you forgive me?"

"If you forgive me for throwing a temper tantrum. And if you can forgive me in advance for how often I'll be on the road and how many important occasions I will probably miss because of my job. And you should probably forgive me for my inability to control myself when you're in a bikini. And for bugging you to make coffee for me every morning."

It wasn't every girl who got so lucky, and Harley kissed him with everything she had inside her. "Done."

And so Cinderella and Prince Charming lived happily ever after.

Or something like that.

FINAL LAP
by Tuesday Talladega

It's the end of an era, racing fans. Cooper Brickman, driving in the cup series for oh, like, *half his life*, has announced his retirement at the end of the current season. It would seem that the perpetual bachelor has been hooked by his nanny, one Harley McLain, and an engagement is imminent as the ring has already been purchased from a local jeweler. Lest y'all think I'm spoiling a special moment in a woman's life, Harley knows, folks, so don't get your panties in a wad. I will not, however, reveal the when and where, but I think it's safe to say her answer will be yes. Watch for an intimate ceremony sometime this fall, with the groom's sister, Mary Jane Rawlings, daughter of Bud Rawlings, as junior maid of honor, and the bride's sister, Charity McLain, as maid of honor.

Also of note, the Brickman manse has a For Sale sign in the yard, so if you have a couple or five mil to spare, go buy yourself a house. It seems Cooper is set on downsizing (who does that?!) to a more manageable five thousand square feet. Harley, honey, just make sure he doesn't stiff you on the closet space.

Look for the racing legend to be calling races on Sundays as he has just inked a deal to go from the driver's seat to the network announcer's chair next season, so if you've spent two decades loving the "Brick" like I have, no worries, we'll still see his cute face at the track every week.

Until next time . . .

McLAIN-STERLING WEDDING
(aka the Royals)
by Mary Jane Rawlings

Last Saturday at the Ritz-Carlton Charlotte my stepbrother married my sister-in-law's identical twin sister in the biggest event like *ever*. Jeff Sterling, owner of Sterling Motors, and so old that everyone thought he would never get married, accepted his fate and got hitched to Charity McLain, former Little Miss Southern Grace and a driver handler. The bride wore Oscar de la Renta (for a complete breakdown of her gown, <u>click here</u>) and the groom wore Armani in a beautiful and over-the-top New Year's Eve celebration.

Five hundred guests were in attendance, including every driver in the cup series, media moguls (I've always wanted to use that word), sponsors, and family and friends. Matron of honor was the bride's twin sister, Harley McLain-Brickman, and the best man was Cooper Brickman. I was, of course, a bridesmaid and wore Vera Wang in a glorious shade of almost-but-not-quite-navy that brought out the blue in my eyes, blink, blink, blink.

Moments of note: When NikJo (Nikki and Jonas Strickland) got caught knocking boots in the coatroom, and when Eliot Monroe and Johnny Briggs got drunk and reenacted their infamous "Armageddon '83" fistfight.

The reception was followed by a Southern brunch on Sunday for close family and friends (which means me, yo) before the happy couple jetted off to the Seychelles for a BABYMOON. That's right, the bride is pregnant, as is my sister-in-law, Harley, so it looks like a diaper invasion is on the horizon for our neck of the woods.

Tomorrow I'm leaving for Vegas for my mother's wedding to her boyfriend, Sebastian, who could easily pass for my homecoming date. My llama, Serge, will be my escort. Mom won't mind, I'm totes sure of it.

So I will report from Sin City and until then . . . Peace Out.